EVERYTHING BURNS

Also by Christopher Klim

Jesus Lives in Trenton, **the first Boot Means novel**

"Understated humor and lack of pretension lend this wry urban fable undeniable charm. ... Klim's lighthearted entertainment possesses genuine heart."
   —*Booklist*

"Klim has a colorful past, and it comes to life in *Jesus Lives in Trenton*, which has an ear for realistic dialogue and an eye for city grit that would make Dashiell Hammett Proud ..."
   —*Philadelphia Weekly*

"It all comes together in a compelling and funny new novel called *Jesus Lives in Trenton*."
   —*KYW News Radio Philadelphia*

"Christopher Klim is that rare talent who brings characters and stories that resonate with the working class and excite the sensibilities of literary connoisseurs. Maybe he's the New Jersey reincarnation of John Steinbeck. More likely he's destined to become someone quite unique in the pantheon of American novelists."
   —*Robert Gover*, author *Hundred Dollar Misunderstanding*

"Boot Means is no ordinary man. ... Klim drew upon his personal experiences to bring Boot Means to life."
   —*The Home News Tribune*

"The book is indeed a riotously funny, quick read. It also works on a deeper level, serving as an allegory about man's thirst for grace in a chaotic world."
   —*Time Off*

"[Klim] has managed to stake his claim amid a welter of clever plot twists, machine-gun dialog, and generally amusing scenarios. ... this book was such a damn good read."
—The Circle Magazine

"Laced with the first hints of satiric leanings from its opening volley, *Jesus Lives in Trenton* is clear about its intentions from the start: its first and foremost goal is to entertain ... Jesus Lives in Trenton is laden with laughs, insight and an overflowing abundance of literary skill. Amen."
—The Boox Review

"With the edgy wit of Carl Hiaasen, and the detailed, clear description of Raymond Chandler, Christopher Klim takes us on an accurate, fun, and sometimes scary look inside the newsroom of a small city daily newspaper."
—Bradley Grois of **The Times**

"The interesting characters, hilarious plot, and believable but humorous dialogue keep the readers turning the pages. ... *Jesus Lives in Trenton* is delightful."
—Writers World

"Christopher Klim gives us a slice of life, complete with funny characters, amusing situations, yet with an underlying theme of melancholy that makes us want to hug this poor little orphan kid who just can't seem to grow up and get it together."
—Book Crazy Radio

Books by Christopher Klim

FICTION
Jesus Lives in Trenton
Everything Burns

NONFICTION
Write to Publish

Get the latest information about
the author and learning programs at:

www.ChristopherKlim.com
www.Write-to-Publish.com
www.WritersNotes.com

7/7/09

EVERYTHING BURNS

Christopher Klim

Hopewell Publications

Eva: Oscar Van Hise is my personal Hannibal Lecter. I got the most mail from his dark brag. He's coming back eventually to a town near you!

Oh, this novel is optioned by Satan Films.

Published by Hopewell Publications, LLC
PO Box 11, Titusville, NJ 08560-0011 (609) 818-1049

info@HopePubs.com
www.HopePubs.com

Library of Congress Cataloging of Publishing Data
Klim, Christopher, 1962-
    Everything burns / Christopher Klim.
       p. cm.
   ISBN 0-9726906-5-4 (pbk. : alk. paper)
   I. Title.
PS3611.L555E94 2004
 813'.6--dc22

                        2003017608

First Edition

Printed in the United States of America

For Karin always.

For firemen who defend our lives and sacrifice their own.

*Special thanks to Robert, Margaret, and Karin
for painstaking edits.*

*Additional thanks to Ann and Matt
for encouragement.*

O scar Van Hise sat in his Chevy, watching a building on Harp Street burn to conclusion. The ground level shop was destroyed, and perhaps the second floor as well. He wasn't exactly sure. That was the nature of fire. It appeared to rip through ceilings and walls at random, incinerating even bricks and mortar. Fire had a mind of its own, keeping its path secret until Oscar unleashed it.

The firemen cut the water to their hoses. Smoke and chaos marred the clear desert evening. Oscar noted the onlookers beyond the flashing lights. People always came to watch and wonder. Some huddled and gasped. Others seemed to drink it in like the climax of a movie. The worse the fire looked, the more they loved it. One day, they would understand his handiwork and honor him.

The sound of an approaching motorcycle rattled Oscar from his thoughts. He saw the speeding cycle skid to a halt. The rider didn't wear a helmet, and he leapt to the sidewalk, slinging a camera over his shoulder. He was dark-haired and lean, and his eyes were set like a prowler, like he was missing something and aimed to take it back.

The dismounted rider spun his sights through his surroundings before slipping into the crowd.

CHAPTER 1
THE MEMORY OF FIRE

Boot Means stopped his motorcycle at the curb and jumped off. Ladder trucks hummed outside a line of shops in Concho's commercial district. A hardware store on Harp Street stood gutted, and wisps of gray smoke crept from the second floor apartment windows. He was late. The flames were already knocked down. That's how the firemen put it—'knocked down'— as if they had toppled a big bully and left him for dead.

With his camera loaded and ready, he panned the street and then wedged through the assembling throng. A hot wind swept out of the West Texas plains, and even without the jostling crowd, Boot felt overheated. His T-shirt stuck to his neck and chest, damp with perspiration.

He nudged into an opening near the police barrier. A yellow strand of tape barred onlookers from the meat of the fire scene. He wondered how far he'd get. The department never let reporters inside. Concho groomed itself for the newspapers and the commerce brochures that headed out of town—smiling faces and spotless streets. They'd whitewash a train wreck and sell it as a tourist attraction.

Rubbing the grit from the back of his neck, Boot stared at the sky. The broiling sun returned his glare.

"The weather's not so bad." Fire Marshal Ryan Galloway emerged from a red Caprice with a gold department emblem on the door. Gally's thick hair seemed pasted to his scalp. He grabbed his toolbox and cut a path toward Boot. He didn't appear to be sweating at all. "Wait a couple of months. In August, you'll want to turn your skin inside out."

Boot wondered if Gally really meant this. Boot had lived in a number of places, but adjusting to desert life was like being in an episode of *National Geographic*. Extreme climates were better left to experience on television.

"Did you finish that job?" Gally asked.

"Almost."

"Is there a problem?"

"I'll have the proof sheets in a day or two." Boot had taken pictures of the marshal's grandchildren as a special favor. He tried to avoid working with kids. He had hated being one and was pretty sure he'd never want to father one. Kids often showed the bad sense of grownups but lacked the foresight to cover it up. They were hopelessly vulnerable to whimsy and malice.

"I hope you're as good as you say you are."

"You were right about those triplets." Boot recalled the pre-school boys attempting to topple his camera stand. Boys liked games and competition. Once the first one started, the other two joined the assault and worked the tripod legs like a giant wishbone.

"I warned you about those rascals."

"I have some nice shots of them playing before I tried sitting them down."

"You got them to sit down?"

"I said I tried."

Gally bent beneath the police tape and glanced back. "Are you coming?"

"Where?"

"Where do you think? You've been bugging me for months to get a closer look."

Boot patted his pocket for spare film and darted beneath the tape. Interior photos might gain space in the newspaper. An exclusive might resurrect his career. "Are you going to let me shoot or just watch?"

"We'll see."

"I'll make good use of the pictures."

"Don't get obnoxious."

Boot let that comment drop. Gally wrote the book on obnoxious. People cut a wide path around the marshal, but Boot absorbed Gally's sharp remarks without flinching. For weeks, he'd stayed close, angling for a break. He'd even accepted the thankless photo session with Gally's grandmonsters, all in the hope of creating a chance like this.

He followed the marshal into the alley between the buildings. He felt relief when the sun disappeared over the cornice. "Why don't you take me through the steps of the investigation?"

"Is that what you have in mind?"

"I can turn it into an interview."

"What the hell for?"

"People are interested in your line of work."

"People?" Gally rolled his eyes. "Sure, I'll be the next Governor of Texas."

A fireman dragged a deflated hose past Boot. The man's breathing apparatus hung from his neck, and with his mask pulled down, a ring of soot outlined his nose and mouth.

Gally spoke over his shoulder. "Find that trinket?"

Boot thought Gally was talking to the fireman.

"For your pop's birthday," Gally said, "that trinket?"

The question surprised Boot. He didn't think the marshal paid any attention to small talk.

"Did you buy him something?" Gally asked. "It's your pop, for shit's sake."

"Not yet," Boot replied.

"Don't fret. Men always want one toy or another."

"I don't know his hobbies that well." Boot shielded the truth. He'd only met his father last summer and hadn't seen much of him since. Charles Goodner owned a ranch outside San Angelo, while Boot scratched out a living one hundred miles away. Boot preferred the distance. "He has everything already."

"How about a saddle?"

"I don't think so."

"You said he has horses."

"A saddle's beyond my budget."

"Linda suggested it."

"Who?"

"My wife. She's got a million ideas."

A metal door swung open in the back. Benjamin Sheerssen, the Second Union Captain, stepped outside and slid his helmet from his head. Muddy trails dripped along his temples. "Who's tagging along?"

"A photographer," Gally said.

"When did we hire a photographer?"

"His name is Boot Means. He's a reporter."

"You sure about this?"

"I'll keep tabs on him."

Sheerssen scanned Boot, as if viewing a code violation, deciding whether or not to write him up on the spot. "Have I seen you around?"

"Maybe."

"Who you with?"

"The paper." Boot was fast-talking. Down south, this only got people's eyeballs spinning. There was no need to break a sweat over simple conversation. He metered his words to mimic the captain's laconic style, an act that contradicted his better instincts. When you talked slowly back east, people took you for a politician or a liar.

"You with the *Democrat*?" Sheerssen asked.

Boot slid a piece of gum into his mouth. "Not exactly."

"Where then, *San Angelo Times*? They send you out this far?"

Boot worked on a freelance assignment for *The Concho Democrat*. He'd applied for a fulltime position, but the decision appeared indefinitely delayed. Whenever the editors questioned him about his previous experience, Boot produced the wrong answers. "I'm an independent."

"Oh, a freelancer?"

"I pick up work where I can."

"Does it pay anything?"

"Not really."

"Who am I to question it?" Sheerssen fanned the flap to his fireproof jacket. "I'm not one to talk about career choices."

Two fighter planes from Fort Stead raced overhead. Afterburners streamed through the sky. Boot flinched from the sonic boom.

Sheerssen spit ash into a puddle of water by his feet. "Gentleman, shall we tour the damage?"

Gally turned his patent stare on Boot. "Here are the rules. Don't touch anything. Don't step anywhere I don't step. Got it?"

"Got it."

They entered a storage area at the rear of the hardware store. The gushing fire hose had brushed charred items aside. Collapsed metal cans were piled on a twisted steel shelf against the wall. Water dripped everywhere. That was all Boot recognized, beyond the basic forms of architecture. The rest was burnt to cinders and blobs. The acrid residue stung his eyes.

Gally aimed a halogen lamp on the doorjamb and chipped away a section with his screwdriver. "Lacquer, paint—typical chemical cocktail. Hot and fast."

Sheerssen spit again. "I'm still tasting it."

"There's plenty of fuel in here, but it doesn't start burning by itself."

"Nope."

Boot listened to the banter. They probably had this conversation countless times.

The heat of the fire lingered in the spent rafters and walls. He raised his Nikon, pausing to see if he'd get away with it. He squeezed the shutter release, and the hotshoe flash bathed the room in white light.

"The smoke was nice and dark," Sheerssen said. "You can imagine the rest."

"Lucky it didn't blow," Gally said.

"Amen. We cooled it off in time."

"Like I said, lucky it didn't blow."

"Lucky, my ass. I hate these places."

Gally ran his light over the floor for Boot's benefit. "See the V-shape? It leads toward the origin."

Boot stepped deeper into the room, careful not to touch anything, just as Gally ordered. Pools of black water splashed beneath his feet. He noticed the fractured grain in the burnt wood. "What are those crackly marks?"

"You're paying attention."

"What do they mean?"

"They point the way." Gally stopped the light at a pile of warped metal on the floor. He bent over it, pinching a spiky scrap between his fingers.

"It looks like a fried computer chip."

"It's not that complicated." The marshal flipped it over beneath the light. "It might be an electric starter from a hot plate or coffee-maker."

"That heap on the floor is a coffeemaker?"

"What's left of it."

"That started the fire?"

Gally dropped the piece in a plastic bag. "We have to see about that." He took a small spade from his tool kit and scooped the plastic clump and fragments into the bag.

"I'm impressed."

"Don't be. There are all kinds of bad leads at a fire scene."

"What else might do this kind of damage?"

Gally ignored the question and knelt down. He studied the floor and walls, eyes shifting as if reading a map of the fire. "This is definitely the origin."

"That's my guess," Sheerssen said. "But the middle of the room is a weird place for a fire like this to start."

Boot tried to follow the path of the blaze. It all looked the same—charbroiled and incinerated.

"I don't like it," Gally said.

"What's to like?" Sheerssen wiped the wet soot from his eyes. He seemed like the type of captain who'd always handle the fire hose, instead of letting the others get close. Guys like Sheerssen spent so much time beside fires that they smelled arson from miles away.

Gally suddenly seemed careful with his words. "What do you know about the guy who owns this place?"

"I've been coming here for years. It's usually crowded in the afternoon."

"This fire doesn't look accidental."

"You know how it goes. It might not add up to anything. I'll put you in touch with the storeowner."

Gally sealed the evidence bag and wrote on the label. He eyed Boot. "I want you to take pictures."

Boot lifted his camera, not really knowing where to focus.

"Every angle," Gally said. "Can you do that?"

"Yes."

"Right from this spot here. Don't leave anything out."

Boot turned in a circle, shooting overlapping perspectives of the room. He'd read about investigators who pieced together panoramic views of fire scenes. They stared at them for hours, visualizing the course of the blaze.

Gally poked Boot's back. "Shoot over there too."

Boot loaded another roll of film. He operated by the favor principle. That was one area where the southwest didn't differ from the east. Business churned on debts and favors. He suspected the whole world operated that way.

"Where does this terminate?" Gally asked.

"Second floor," Sheerssen replied. "Not too bad. It burned through the kitchen floor, but it's stable."

"Is the fire completely down?"

"Oh, yeah. I've got my men up there now."

"Boot, you want to see some more?"

"Definitely," Boot said.

"If it's alright with Ben."

The captain crowned himself with his helmet. "Doesn't matter to me. He's seen the worst of it."

They took the rear fire escape to the second floor. Boot followed the last man on the metal stairs, which rang from their ascent. The lingering smoke caught in his throat. He fought back a cough.

The men disappeared through an open window. Boot straddled the sill and peered into the apartment. A fine layer of ash coated the bedroom furniture. It looked as if the place hadn't been dusted in years.

"You wanted inside one of these so bad," Gally said. "Well, it's a filthy business."

Boot touched his shoe to the floor, and the baked linoleum crackled where it rose from the base. He tried to imagine the room being hot enough to do this without catching fire. He stamped down a few times.

"It's not going to collapse," Gally said.

Boot diverted his thoughts to his camera. He snapped a picture of the marshal donning a smirk and another of Sheerssen with his arms folded over his barrel chest. The floor appeared to be holding the men up. Boot threw his other foot over the sill and came onboard.

"Although everyone has to fall through at least once," Gally said. "Isn't that right?"

The men laughed and then filed into the hallway. Two company men and a rookie named Diaz were already there. Boot recognized Diaz from another fire. 'Probie,' they called him. Every new fireman received that name during their probation period, which lasted a year or longer. They wore bright orange stripes on their fireproof jackets. It was easier to single them out in the thick of firefighting.

Today, Boot was the rookie. He greeted Diaz, and the probie merely nodded. He looked young, perhaps twenty-one or twenty-two.

Boot walked the main corridor that divided the upstairs apartment. The firemen continued checking rooms, pushing aside furniture, testing the walls and floors. The place reeked of smoke and ash, but no embers remained. It was a clean job, no injuries. No smoldering pockets hid inside couches or walls. They'd axed through enough plaster and found nothing. The burn hole in the kitchen floor wasn't a worry either. Melted vinyl tiles curled from the edges of the jagged floor opening, and someone had slid a table over the two-foot void. Boot made certain not to walk within twenty feet of it.

Diaz checked the hall closets. His thick boots clapped the floor.

By now, everyone's jacket was open, and the metal buckles jangled and swayed. The men joked about the smell.

"I'll have that smoked bacon for breakfast," a company man said. "And throw in some smoked eggs and smoked toast too."

Another man kicked up a blue gown and hung it from the tip of his boot. "Hey, honey, put on that smoking hot dress of yours."

As the comments flew, Boot snapped shots of the men finishing their work. These created great stock photos. He might apply them to any fire story in the news, especially to fires with restricted access. This was a run-of-the-mill blaze, the kind you spotted on a slow day for the metro page—a big picture and a couple of paragraphs. The average person never realized how often news photos didn't emanate from the same story.

Someone gasped, actually inhaled, like the sound of a fireman breathing through his Scot pack. Boot saw Diaz standing rigid before the last open closet. He locked onto the probie's drawn expression. He saw a look that any field journalist recognized. No one ever expected trouble, even cops and firefighters who chased it down for a living.

"Captain." Diaz shuddered. "Cap?"

Sheerssen quit jawing with Gally and went to the young fireman. Pretty soon, every company man surrounded the closet and stared down.

Boot came also. He expected the worst but needed to see it. Once, he'd photographed a car accident on the interstate. The people were mashed up pretty badly, yet still alive. But the scene unfolding in the hallway was creepier. No one said anything or tried to help.

On the closet floor, a Chicano boy lay curled into a ball. He clutched a red blanket. A gentle smile graced his mouth. Not a hair was out of place, as if he'd just fallen asleep.

Boot paced closer. It wasn't a blanket in the boy's arms but another boy, a toddler curled up the same way. One cupped the other. Boot counted two dead boys—brothers maybe. It was worse than twice as bad. They were dressed in pajamas, permanently asleep. A veil of dust coated their faces. There wasn't a single burn on them. Not a splinter of wood was charred. Everything resembled life, except for the stillness and dust.

Boot wanted to stamp the floor to see if they'd move. He wanted to shout and break the trance but kept silent. The image of those dead boys burned into his memory, a promise of sleepless nights ahead.

"Smothered," Gally said.

Boot's mouth fell open. He was conscious of his own chest rising and falling.

All eyes held to the inside of the closet.

Sheerssen snorted the ash from his nostrils. "Diaz, did you touch anything?"

"No, sir," the probie said. "They were beneath their mama's raincoat."

A lavender raincoat lay bunched to the side.

"For shit's sake," Gally said. "They're so damned good at hiding."

"They thought they were safe in here." Sheerssen knelt down. He blessed himself and then the boys.

"We missed 'em, Captain." Diaz verged on tears. Boot heard it in the probie's voice.

"You did what you could."

The other firemen stood hunched over, turning away from the view.

"We missed 'em." Diaz kicked his foot, striking the air. "We plain missed 'em."

"You did no such thing," Sheerssen barked. "The place was fully involved with smoke when we arrived."

"Yes, sir." Diaz's voice cracked.

"They were probably good as dead when the alarm sounded."

One of the firemen prayed. Boot watched him make the sign of the cross over his chest.

"That goes for all of you." Sheerssen looked around, catching the faces that peered his way. "You did what you could."

"Thank you, Captain." Diaz spoke like he didn't mean it.

Boot's gum had rolled from his mouth. He noticed a beige lump—wet and clean upon the ashen floor.

He raised his camera by instinct, framing the children in his lens. A strobe of white light shot forward, capturing those sweet, embracing boys on film.

"Where are their parents?" Sheerssen draped the raincoat over the boys' faces. "Are they on the street?"

"No," one fireman mumbled.

"Damn it!" Sheerssen rose to his feet. "Are they in the apartment? Do we have more bodies to find?"

"No sir," the other fireman replied. "We've searched the complete structure."

The men stirred. Boot snapped pictures of Diaz, Sheerssen, and even Gally scanning the hall for clues. Their eyes reflected his camera flash. They looked like coalminers; only they were mining for dead people.

Boot tried not to think or feel, just react to the unfolding drama. This was it. This was where he needed to be. He squeezed the shutter release a few more times, stealing the moment, sealing it away on film.

"That's enough of that." Sheerssen waved a hand in front of Boot's lens.

Boot let his Nikon fall. It hung heavily by his side. Horrible images lurked inside his camera, each one a deadly frame. It was the same camera that captured Gally's grandsons. They'd been knocking around on the lawn, trying to tear out each other's hair, unknowing but alive.

Adrenaline jump-started Boot's heart. 'What's done is done,' an old newspaper mentor used to say. 'Don't get a frigging conscience. Get the story.'

Sheerssen addressed the probie. "You ever see anything like this?"

"No, sir."

"Take the freelancer outside."

"Right away."

Boot let Diaz do the leading. He was willing to go. He wanted to run. Arson or not, he had the front-page photos. *Don't get a frigging conscience.* He conjured the opening words to his article—the sentences that caused people's morning coffee to grow cold.

"Hold up," Gally said.

Boot clutched his camera.

Gally grabbed the flap of Diaz's fire jacket. "One more thing."

"Sir?"

"Get on the horn to Homicide. Tell them we've got a deuce up here."

CHAPTER 2
CRYSTAL STAG

Around 10:00 P.M., Boot tracked down Shep Newell at the Ink Blotter Cafe. He rushed to the editor's table and slapped down his article and photos of the fire. "Looking for news?"

The bistro presented a sunken dining room with skylights, hanging begonias, and tiled tabletops. A handful of diners glanced up from their meals to eye Boot. None was more disturbed than Shep Newell. He backed his wheelchair away from a plate of grilled chicken and fresh fruit. He touched his mouth with a crisp linen napkin, but it didn't wipe away his frown. "I might have expected you."

"Did I make the deadline?" Boot already knew the answer. *The Concho Democrat* went to press near midnight, and Newell held the power to bless this story on the spot. There was plenty of time.

"You know, I have an office down the street."

"I was told to quit showing up unannounced." Boot bit the inside of his cheek. Concho was no bigger than Trenton. He'd steal the headlines in this city too, out-hustle everyone. "Take a look at my work."

Newell slid the file atop his atrophied legs and sifted through the photos and article.

Boot leaned over, proofing his words. He'd hammered out 1000 words faster than a cop writing a ticket. "Have a better lead for tomorrow?"

"No."

"What about my story? I was inside the apartment on Harp Street."

"You weren't the only one."

"Who else?" He wasn't letting a staff reporter beat him out. He was there when it happened.

Newell grabbed the wheels on his chair and pivoted toward Boot. The long tendons flexed on his lower arms. He was training for the marathon. Boot once spotted Newell wheeling as fast as a bicycle outside the civic center.

"I'll end this debate," Newell said. "If you supply me with proper job references, no more test assignments."

"I'm working on it."

"Supplying references is usually a cursory event."

"I guess that means you like my work. Are you talking about a staff position?"

"I've seen your articles from your last job. It's not a question of skill." Newell folded his right arm across his chest, stretching the rotator cuff muscles. From the waist up, he looked solid. "Why can't you supply references?"

"My work speaks for itself."

"No one's work speaks for itself."

"You haven't even read my fire story yet."

"Where's your photo portfolio?"

"We've been over this. I lost it in a flood." Boot knew how stupid that sounded, even if it was true. He promised himself to devise a better story. Perhaps he'd say it was stolen.

"Can you appreciate my position? The job you want requires experience."

"You've seen everything I've done in the last eight months."

"It's the last two years that worries me. It's like you didn't exist."

"Look at this story." Boot heard his pleading tone. It echoed across the room. "You won't be disappointed."

Newell jockeyed his chair back and forth, keeping his eyes locked on Boot. This continued until the hostess approached the table.

The woman was very thin, with pants cut below her navel. She regarded Boot with practiced aplomb. "Can I be of assistance, Mr. Newell?"

"He was just leaving," Newell said.

Boot leaned toward Newell. "Are you printing my story or not?"

"Let me think about it."

"It'll be stale tomorrow."

"I want to eat first."

"I'll wait."

"Get yourself a drink. Go for a walk. Give me a minute of peace."

Boot hit the street. The stifling heat matched his temper. Across the way, he spotted the sheer stone facade of Neiman Marcus. A blue and white plastic banner proclaimed that it stayed open later on Fridays.

He pushed inside to soak up the air conditioning and waste time. He felt edgy from the long evening. Images of the boys on Harp Street worked the back of his mind, like a photo with no good place to file. He should've taken Newell's advice and stopped at the bar.

In the men's department, Boot wandered through the clothing racks. A woman worked behind a glass counter, sifting through the stock. He felt grateful that she didn't approach and start a sales pitch.

He flipped through the XXL vests with Navaho embroidery. He held one up to the light, trying to picture it on his father. He didn't really know what he was doing. He saw other people do this, talking to friends or relatives, holding up a garment in faux dress, but it seemed bizarre when he did it. What was he doing in Texas? He didn't fully understand his reasons for staying. By his own design, he never embraced Concho but rather tried to dissect it. He didn't love barbecue, football, 4-H Club—the stuff that lit the fire of local residents. God knew he was in a foreign land. He'd arrived broke and jobless, and almost a year later, he was still broke, and his career languished in the hands of a mistrusting editor, and that was his fault too. At least, he was alive. He took solace in that simple fact, like a man did when his pockets and belly were empty, when every desire felt like a bad idea. Sometimes treading water was progress.

"That doesn't work for you," the woman at the counter remarked.

Boot glanced at the tag: $60. He stabbed it back on the rack. "No, it doesn't work for me."

He eyed the woman now. Her face caught his fancy. She possessed the kind of features he liked to photograph beneath natural light. She had soft brown hair and a pleasing shape to her mouth. Her lower lip swept down, full and round.

"I'm sorry," she said. "It was only my opinion."

"You're entitled."

"I should keep quiet." She wore an expensive blazer with embossed gold buttons. She shifted ornate glass bottles inside a display case, creating a visual hierarchy with the shapes and colors, but she noticed Boot watching and stopped. "The girl will be back in a moment."

"That's alright. I don't know what I want anyway." He knew what he needed: cheap, yet somehow expensive-looking.

"I'm sure the girl can help you."

"I don't need help."

"Good, because I can't do it." She looked toward the women's department for assistance, revealing a slight downturn of the eyes.

He strolled to the counter. Several perfume bottles sat open on the glass top. She handled a crystal decanter in the shape of a horse's head. At close range, her mouth looked much sexier. The distraction drew him from his troubles. Sometimes, he'd stew for hours, and tonight, he had plenty to throw in the pot.

"Are you looking for a vest?" she asked.

Boot noticed the Navaho vest lumped on the floor. The hanger spiked from the rack. "Sorry about that."

"I don't care. Are you in the market for one?"

"Sort of."

"That style doesn't work for you. I think leather or plain suede suits you better."

"It's for someone else."

She leaned forward with a bottle. "Try this."

He sniffed the wide opening. The pungent concoction made him sneeze.

"Don't dip your nose in it," she said.

"I wasn't trying to."

"What do you think?"

"I can't tell one from the next."

"It's Crystal Stag. It's marketed all wrong. The pricing says upper class, but the commercials say cowboy cologne."

"You're making a great sale."

"I hope you don't buy it. I hope no one does."

"Why not?"

"It's not one of ours."

"You don't work here, do you?"

"I'm Jacki Rush." She plunked down the horse's head and shook Boot's hand. A jeweled watch draped from her wrist, raw opals in sterling silver. "I develop scents for LeMaxxe."

"I've seen their tower downtown."

"The lipstick building? It's a monstrosity."

"It makes someone feel important."

She laughed big but not too loud. The uninviting look disappeared from her face, replaced by an open smile. A few people on the floor glanced over. "I guess you're wondering what I'm doing."

"If you're shoplifting, you're not hiding it very well."

"I know the store manager. He lets me fiddle back here. It pays to see the competition at the point of sale."

He noticed that every forward bottle in the case was a LeMaxxe product. "I don't know a thing about perfume."

"This is men's cologne. You wouldn't believe the work that goes into each product." She cocked her chin. "What scent are you wearing?"

"I'm not wearing one."

"You smell like ... like a fireplace."

Boot sniffed his shirt cuff for proof. The fire on Harp Street lingered with him, clinging to his hair and hands as well. He immediately thought of the two dead boys curled up in the closet. An involuntary shiver gripped his spine.

"What?" Jacki asked.

"Nothing."

"What is it?"

"I covered a fire for the *Democrat* tonight." He followed her glance to his camera. He carried it everywhere, still following his mentor's advice. "The smoke gets on you."

"I thought you were wearing a really bad musk."

"Well, it is." Boot recalled the firemen joking right before they discovered the boys. He glanced at his watch. "I've got to meet someone across the way."

"The Ink Blotter?"

"That's it."

"I love it there, the smell of the flowers on the terrace."

He wanted to chat. It was easier than engaging Newell again, but Newell represented a ripe payday, and that came before everything, including cute perfume ladies in ritzy department stores. "Good luck with the cologne."

"I was hoping you'd sample a few more." She jiggled two bottles in the air, flirting.

He'd encountered similar women at banquets for the foster homes in which he was raised. The orphans lined up on one side of the table, put on display like the buffet and flower arrangements. All that was behind him now. This classy specimen was closer to his age. She didn't seem to read any of the past in his eyes.

"I've got to go," he said, although he really wanted to invite her for a drink.

"It was nice meeting you." She shook his hand again, her long fingers squeezing his lower knuckle.

Boot walked away, turning back to spy Jacki once more. She swirled a silver decanter in the air and put it to her nose like a glass of wine. Then that look returned to her face, the one she held when she thought he wasn't watching. She appeared a little sad.

On Mission Avenue, Boot weaved through the lazy parade of weekenders after dark. Shep Newell waited outside the Ink Blotter, where the enclosed terrace met the brick sidewalk. The fastidious man bent over his chair, adjusting the resistance in his wheel springs.

Boot stopped several feet shy of Newell's position. He didn't like hovering over him. He never knew whether or not to crouch down and meet him eye to eye. "Did you read my article?"

"It's good," Newell said. "It's at least as good as what I have."

"What do you have?"

"Bob McGrath's story."

The stranglehold of the past embraced Boot, a collar forged by his poor decisions in Trenton. He felt it every time Newell tugged the leash. What was the statute of limitations for one mistake? Did he have to start his own newspaper to clear his name?

"Bob," Newell continued, "doesn't have photos. Yours are superb. In fact, they're so vivid; I can't use many of them. I'm surprised the fire department let you walk away with them."

"I can be persuasive, at least to some people."

"Don't take this the wrong way. I need your photos."

"They go with my article."

"They don't have to."

"You gave me that piece." Boot felt a flush of heat rising to his ears.

"Slow down, Means. I gave you an R&D piece."

"I was doing the lousy R&D, when I ran into this story. That's journalism."

"Like it or not, I gave you an R&D. You were supposed to be researching whether the fire department is underfunded."

"Sure, they need money. I can add a sentence to my article."

"Not this one."

"Terrific."

"But you can still do the R&D piece."

"And every time I come across real news, I hand it over to Bob McGrath?"

"Bob's worked the city desk for five years. You know what you need to do."

"References?" Boot nearly spit out the word. "My story is all the background you need."

"I want to believe you." Newell extended the file folder in his hand. "If you don't want to give me the photos ..."

"That's my article." Boot watched his window closing. He'd have to hand over his photos to salvage the evening. Another compromise.

"Bob knows how to handle the story."

"Not like me."

"I'm not relinquishing the front page to an unknown."

"The front page? I've written features before."

Newell dropped the file in his lap. He put his hands on his wheels and pointed his chair down the sidewalk. "You know what you have to do. I play by the book."

CHAPTER 3
RED

O scar Van Hise entered the YMCA and slipped past the front office. The woman at the desk looked up, disinterested. He didn't expect her to recognize him. His face struck a chord with no one. Like Van Gogh and Faulkner laboring in obscurity, his best work stood on the horizon, waiting to burst into view.

In the halls, Oscar passed a pair of women in sweat suits. He avoided eye contact, as one gestured to say hello. He liked to plan ahead, devise a safe route, and get in and out unnoticed, but when he stumbled across a gem like this, he leapt at the chance. In an old building, there'd be nothing but options in his favor.

This one was going to be different than Harp Street, but there'd be a connection that only he'd know. His tool kit rattled with the common screws and wires used to spawn his creations. The fool that owned the hardware store on Harp had unknowingly helped replenish his supplies. People were that willing to destroy their lives.

Oscar wandered through the complex, turning corners, changing directions at random. Open doorways rolled through his vision. Women bobbed in aerobics class. Two men debated a baseball game by a water cooler. Children splashed and screamed in the swimming pool. Every nuance of sound and light channeled through his veins like electricity. He forgot the awful feeling—the fist that hammered inside his skull. He fast-forwarded to the future when everyone understood his burden, even admired it. Beauty emanated from a million terrifying sources. History proved that.

The kitchen waited for Oscar, silent and empty. He pushed through the swinging door, conscious of his footfalls upon the noisy tiles. The isolation made him vulnerable. He'd have no excuse for being this deep inside the building. He measured his heartbeats. The thrill formed an added bonus.

He turned in a circle. He saw everything in the room, not just the dented metal pots and scratched wooden countertops but a schematic of switches, wires, and tiny transformers strung together in a circuit. He eyed the refrigerator, imagining frayed cables and faulty designs. Why didn't people take pride in their work? He spotted the wall sockets; perhaps wire connections were barely wrapped around the screws. He'd rehearsed so many combinations in his mind that he fumbled over the choices.

A simple solution served him well. He reached for the toaster and removed the four screws that fastened the housing. He mulled over the sparse layout: springs, coils, several inches of wire. He retrieved a nail from his tool kit and jammed it into the release spring lever.

A man strolled past the bay door to the kitchen. Oscar ducked below the counter, listening to the man pass. Oscar's mouth went dry. His lips quivered. He understood the finer points of fear. It tasted like aluminum. It smelled like smoldering wire.

He slid the toaster beneath the cabinet and plugged it into the socket. The heating coils swelled from dull gray to brilliant glowing red.

Blood rushed to his groin. *At two hundred degrees, the plastic laminate on the cabinet doors will peel, exposing the particleboard interior to ignition. At five or six hundred degrees, the senseless machine will self-destruct.* It was more than enough to set this old building aflame.

His pulse soared as he paced the halls. His feet felt numb with the charge of exhilaration. He crossed a line of children leaving the pool, coming close to knocking one down, but they never suspected. He kept moving, passing the water cooler, piecing together his retreat. He often forgot how he entered a place or where he parked his car. It was what he did inside that required genius.

As he penetrated the doors, he regretted not seeing his fire come to life. Just once, he wanted to stay and absorb the incredible warmth, to watch the slow dance of the flame from birth. He paused on the sidewalk and projected the fire's path. It might creep through the air vents or up the inner walls. They wrote textbooks on the subject, but no one knew for certain. Each fire revealed its own personality. It only needed to be awakened.

He found his Chevy down the block and shut himself inside. Smoke seeped from the rear of the YMCA, threatening the clear blue sky with a haze of gray. He dug into his pocket and massaged himself. He created this moment. He unleashed it. He whispered to the people inside. "Your day is different. Your life has changed in an incredible way."

Professionals walked the streets, as yet unconcerned. Oscar checked their faces, waiting for the change. A woman licked an Italian ice, giving a double take toward the YMCA. She stopped her female companion and pointed.

Flames tickled the steel mushroom vent in the roof. Oscar turned his eyes upon the building exits. There was no sprinkler system and probably no escape plan either. People trickled from the building, gazing upward. A handful merged on the walkway, until the bodies streamed outside the vestibule, massing and pushing like wild animals. Raw panic painted their expressions.

They stumbled, wide-eyed, gasping for fresh air and answers. Oscar leaned his head against the seat and stroked his cock.

A fire alarm sounded somewhere in the city of Concho. He loved that sound—the oscillating drone of madness. A woman screamed on the sidewalk. That was even better. His chest expanded. Up in the Texas panhandle, he'd wandered between towns and jobs, picturing this moment. His brilliance, his sheer inspiration composed his burden.

He unzipped his pants and made himself fully erect. He glimpsed the flames that mounted the roof. He conjured the scent of smoke—the byproduct of manmade objects transforming into vapor. His hopes rose with it. The ugliness inside his head began to dissipate, and all that noise fell silent.

CHAPTER 4
UNION STATION

Boot stood in Ryan Galloway's office above Union Station No. 2. The converted attic space overlooked the meat-packing district, and across the street, cattle marched into a processing warehouse. The smell of freshly eviscerated beef wafted through the window.

"We've got another one." Gally paced behind his desk. A collection of sprinkler heads lined the shelves, and about the room laid charred pieces of evidence in various states of disassembly.

"Another what?" Boot pulled away from the sill.

"Another suspicious electrical fire."

"You're not talking about the fire on Harp Street again? What's it been? Two weeks?"

"I've asked Homicide to reopen the case."

"I thought that was a coffee pot failure."

"That's how it looks, and if it's left alone, that's how it will stand."

"Why shouldn't it?"

"The owner claims he didn't own a coffee pot."

"You're saying somebody planted a coffee pot to start a fire?"

"Yes."

"No wonder the department squashed the investigation."

"It wasn't just a coffee pot." Gally tossed a schematic on the desk in front of Boot. "It was a JavaMaster 200."

Boot scanned the lines and numbers on the page. For all he understood, it might be a breakdown of his clock radio. "This is supposed to prove something?"

"The JavaMaster was recalled last spring for faulty wiring. Didn't you see it in the news?"

"I don't read the same journals you do."

"I'll make it simple. The owner says he didn't have one in the shop. He used to get coffee across the street, and I believe him."

"He killed two boys by accident. What do you expect him to say?"

"You're looking at this all wrong."

Boot felt the same as Gally. He wanted to make someone pay for the boys' deaths, but horrible accidents happened every day. "Explain it to me. Why is this someone's fault?"

"I started poking around the evidence at the YMCA. The kitchen toaster started it."

"What's that have to do with Harp Street?"

"Don't you see the pattern? Both fires were started by electrical devices."

"But no one was killed at the YMCA."

"That has more to do with luck, although the cause was no accident. Someone jammed the toaster spring with a nail."

"Can you prove that?"

"It's right in front of you."

Boot looked at the corroded lever on the desk. It was blackened and warped from the extreme heat. If the marshal claimed it was a cooked up piece of car engine, Boot would never spot the difference. "What did the Fire Chief say?"

"There's no gold in burning down the YMCA."

"I happen to agree. What about the hardware store?"

"There's not much of a payoff there either."

"Don't arsonists get hired for a reason?"

"This isn't about money. It's worse."

Boot folded a fresh stick of gum in his mouth. He'd tailed Gally all summer and seen how excited he got by the slightest scrap in the ashes. "You need that vacation you've been talking about. Didn't Linda want to go to Spain?"

Gally dropped in his chair and massaged his temples. "My wife would have me touring Europe, dry as a whistle too."

"How about I buy you a drink?" Boot checked his watch. In four hours, he was meeting an excited new mother about shooting a baptism. How many times could he say, 'ma'am, it's going to be perfect.' A few beers ahead of time sounded like a good idea. "It's almost happy hour."

"Listen to me. You write for the paper."

"Sort of."

"You can get the word out."

"You're serious, aren't you?" Boot had never seen him this worked up. "What am I going to say?"

"Consider this: a typical structure is filled with tons of electronics that can set it on fire. It was only a matter of time before some clever torch figured that out."

"Do you know what you're saying?"

"There was a guy in Dallas who planted small devices beside light bulbs. Flick a switch, and poof, your place went up like a candle."

"What's that got to do with our fires?"

"Everything. This guy doesn't even need devices. He's figured how to torch a place and make it seem like an accident." He picked up the burnt evidence from his desk. "But nails don't slide inside toaster ovens on their own."

"You can't be serious."

"I am."

"I don't know, Gally. It's not a lot to go on."

"You sound like Homicide. Nobody's got their eyes open."

"I guess they want to see something first."

"Like what? Two more dead kids?"

"That's not fair."

"Just wait." He stood up and came around the desk. "Do you know why arson is down in this town? We're too short-handed to tag every suspicious fire for investigation. Guess what. If you don't call it suspicious, it ain't arson."

Boot recalled his original freelance assignment for the *Democrat*. Gally created a tough fit. If the police department wasn't buying it, the paper wouldn't.

"I get your point," Boot said. "But a kitchen fire? And a coffeemaker? Those seem pretty common."

"I saw your face after Homicide swept through Harp Street. You know what this is about. They were two Chicano kids. If they'd been regular white boys ..."

Boot clamped down on his gum. He recalled the first detectives on the scene. They shrugged it off like 'there's another one.' It wasn't that different than the way the cops treated him as a kid.

"Here's the ironic part," Gally said. "I owe it all to those boys. If their mother was home, if she didn't work nights—God, if she just had someone look after them, they might still be alive, but because they died, I looked even closer. That's when I noticed the coincidence between both fires. Otherwise I would've written them off like everyone else."

"Nobody could help what happened. You can't change that."

"I'm talking about the next fire. Who's that going to harm? There's a guy out there. He can burn the whole city down right under our noses."

"There might be a guy out there."

"I'm saying there is."

"You swear?"

"On my mother's grave. On those kids' graves."

Boot liked nothing better than to blame someone for the kids' deaths. He felt bad enough just mulling around their apartment, taking in the jokes of the fire department, laughing along a few times, and all the while, those dead boys were hiding in the closet. "I'll see what I can do."

"You have to do it. I'm in a difficult position. I've been told not to talk about this."

"Why not?"

"Because of the same doubts you have, but I think you're changing your mind."

"I'll take it to the paper. Don't hope for much."

Boot rode his motorcycle to the Concho Civic center at the edge of town. The huge, oblong structure affronted the wavering mountain ridges to the west. Redbuds and catclaws flowered in the sandy dividers within the parking lot.

He pulled up to the blacktop path surrounding the arena and dropped the kickstand. He checked his watch. He remembered Newell's schedule better than his own. Newell trained before the afternoon editorial meetings.

Newell led a wheelchair trio around the back edge of the arena. He huffed and dug into the turn, but when he noticed Boot, his exerted grin lost its grit.

Boot stepped onto the path, ignoring Newell's displeasure with the impromptu visit. He waved his arms in the air. "Hello!"

Newell palmed his wheels to a stop. His skinny legs were strapped to the stirrups with bright red velcro tape. The two other racers whirled past, a flurry of elbows and spinning wheels.

The editor unsnapped his helmet strap, letting it fall to his sweat-soaked shirt. "I hope this isn't going to become a regular interruption."

Boot let the comment pass. He presented Galloway's theory as succinctly as possible, playing up the deaths on Harp Street. "What do you think?"

Newell scooped a twenty-pound hand weight from beside his hip and curled it to his shoulder. He pumped the dumbbell with precise rhythm. He looked Boot over, exhaling with the exercise. "No."

"You don't like it? Or you won't run the piece?"

Newell switched hands with the dumbbell. "I mean 'no' as in never."

"But."

"No way."

"You won't even consider it?"

Newell rested the weight in his tiny lap. "We don't make the news. We report it."

"I have a city fire marshal who swears an arsonist is loose in Concho. He's got evidence."

"Is it an official investigation?"

"Not yet."

"Listen to yourself. Is this what sunk you in hot water before?"

Boot bit his cheek. "What makes you say that?"

"I made a few phone calls to your old job. I like your work, Means. I want to find out why you keep sabotaging your chances at the *Democrat*."

"Did you get the references you wanted?" Boot braced himself for the worst of it: the rookie oversights in reporting, the embarrassing terms of his resignation.

"No one said much, other than you fell into a disagreement and quit."

"I was just starting out."

"I'm waiting for a return call from your former editor."

"Art Fontek?" Boot cringed. Art was straightforward and blunt in his delivery. His irascible old boss would tell all.

"I've seen reporters adopt a certain view about a story, never admitting he or she was wrong. Was that the case?"

Boot wished that version were true. He'd been dead wrong in Trenton, duped actually. No apology seemed good enough to cancel his mistakes. "I look at things differently now."

"You're not helping me here." Newell clutched his wheelchair rims. "I have to admit. This has been a frustrating experience for me too."

"Then I guess you've drawn your own conclusions." Boot was tired of bosses. *No more bosses.* He wanted to control his own fate.

"Here's what I'm going to do. I'll let you write a community piece on fire safety. You shouldn't get into trouble with that."

"Can I mention the two fires?"

"I'm offering you a spot in the paper. Isn't that what you want?"

He recalled his stock photos of Concho's bravest. "How about pictures? Can I use photos?"

"Only in the context of the story."

"Right."

"Keep the article to the point. No conjecture about your arsonist. I'll strike it out."

"Have it your way."

"I will. Don't forget that."

The racers turned the corner. Newell aimed his wheels to rejoin the drill. He pushed the chair up to speed, head down, engaging the others.

"I hope you're not sorry later." Boot yelled loud enough, so that anyone in front of the arena might hear.

Newell slowed, losing the rhythm of the pack. "That makes two of us."

CHAPTER 5
BLOOD MOON

The article ran in Tuesday's *Democrat*, page D-7, at the rear of the Community section, not quite the headlines. Boot had no trouble rounding up Gally's fire safety tips. The marshal went crazy over smoke detectors with dead batteries and businesses without fire extinguishers. Gally complained for hours about inefficient sprinkler systems too, but the best stories came from firemen who knew the marshal. Once at a stoplight, Gally spotted a man flicking a cigarette butt through his car window. The marshal politely approached, waited for the man to roll down his window, and tossed the smoldering butt on the driver's lap. Boot loved that bit of fire prevention. He wasn't sure if it was a victory for Smokey the Bear or Green Peace, perhaps both, but he knew enough to omit that anecdote from the article. Sometimes the best parts never see print.

On the evening of the morning paper, Boot rushed into the Ink Blotter Café, hungry for more work. If Shep Newell wanted it, Boot was Concho's new fire expert. He sketched more articles on fire prevention, another on the social effects of fire, and even one on the commerce of fire.

Boot penetrated the restaurant foyer and scanned the checkered tables, ready to serve up his best ideas. He expected to find Newell hovering over a plate of healthy greens and low fat meat. Guys like Newell were content with their place in the world. They had families and solid nights of sleep. They wanted fast answers to keep the momentum going, but Boot understood the waiting game that fast answers required. The solution involved arriving on time, all of the time. He recalled a hooker that he knew in Trenton. She worked the streets on rainy days, just in case.

The skinny hostess intercepted Boot at the door. She didn't bother with the menus. "Do you have a reservation?"

"I'll go straight in."

She immediately dropped her gracious smile, which Boot never believed in the first place. "He's already gone."

"Gone where?"

"Mr. Newell had an early dinner."

"Really." Boot twisted his neck to see if Newell sat at his usual table. An unfamiliar couple studied the wine list.

"He left this for you." The hostess swiped an envelope off the desk at her station. "He said you might be stopping by."

The envelope was addressed to Boot in odd block letters. A post-it note hung from the front. The handwriting didn't match.

```
Boot:
        This arrived at the paper today.
Are you telling people that you're on
staff at the Democrat?
                          - S. Newell.
```

Boot carried the envelope onto the terrace bar. What the hell was Newell's game? At least, Newell couldn't fire him. He'd have to hire him first.

The suspended begonias on the terrace draped over the baskets like pregnant spiders descending from the ceiling. Boot noticed a familiar woman at the bar.

Jacki Rush sat in profile, her gorgeous lips complimenting her angular cheeks. His eyes immediately locked onto her, no different than when he spotted her sniffing perfume behind the counter in Neiman Marcus. He stuffed the envelope into his camera bag and grabbed the stool beside her.

"Boot Means." Jacki swirled a near empty glass of white wine. "I'd never forget a name like that."

"You'd be surprised how many people do."

"I doubt it." She caught the bartender's eye. "I'm bored. Let me buy you a drink."

"Just don't ask me how it smells."

She ordered a round of drinks. "You're in a better mood tonight."

"You didn't catch me on my best day."

"I don't mind the sarcasm."

"I'd just left a bad fire scene."

"I saw it in the paper. You took those pictures?"

"That's me."

"How can you do that?"

"It comes with the territory. Besides, they could have used stronger pictures." Boot recalled the rejected photos. He wanted to go with the firemen huddled by the closet, but Newell selected the covered stretchers exiting the building instead. Editors typically chose the wrong photo to match the article. It took a photographer to recognize a picture in words. That was how Boot knew he was a photographer above being a writer.

"Is it always like that?" she asked.

"You try to put it out of your mind. It's just a photo."

"No, it isn't."

"I know, but that's what you tell yourself."

"It's like that then."

"Yes."

"I know a thing or two about that." She raised her glass. "Here's to never thinking about it."

Boot clinked her glass with his beer mug. The envelope from Newell was at the back of his mind. Who knew what was in there? Maybe it wasn't so good. On the other hand, a beautiful woman was paying him attention. It'd been a while.

"So you're a news photographer," Jacki said.

"Some days."

"Do you like the work?"

"That's my preference, but it doesn't pay the bills."

"What does?"

"Every other kind."

She laughed, loud and unpretentious. The bartender glanced in their direction. Jacki made Boot feel like the only interesting person in the room. She'd done the same thing inside the department store.

"Then you're open to side work?" she asked.

"It depends." He sipped his beer. *No more kiddy birthday parties please.* He scanned her finger, relieved not to find a wedding ring.

"I'm an artist. I'm putting together a portfolio, and I need to make slides."

"So take some photos and send them off to be developed."

"That's what I want you to do, silly."

"I usually don't shoot paintings." In fact, he'd never done it.

"I'm worried about the lighting. I'm good for the money."

"Keep talking." He figured she was good for it. She looked like it, and it was none too soon. A stack of bills screamed for his attention.

"Of course, I'll pay. My day job is worth something."

"Here I mistook you for the quintessential business woman."

"It's an elaborate facade."

"I see."

"Sometimes I even fool myself." She reached down to grab the purse by her feet. "Want to take a look at my work?"

"Sure." He caught a glimpse of her legs. He liked what he saw already. Everything from her clothes to her shoes defined top quality. Obviously, perfume work paid handsomely.

"Let's get it in gear." Jacki drained her glass. "My studio's across town."

She drove a red Lexus with soft gray leather seats. Boot jumped into the passenger's seat, taking a ride into the gentile section of Concho. The fancy row homes along Lee River Park rolled past his window.

"Do you get to the park?" she asked.

"It's not my section of town." He wished he hadn't said that. He looked down at his camera bag, remembering the recent envelope from Newell. He resisted the temptation to open it in front of her.

They stopped outside a doctor's office. Boot followed Jacki through a narrow set of stairs leading to the second floor. He watched her feel along the wall for the light switch.

"I rent the apartment as a studio," she said.

He let his eyes adjust to the light. Stretched canvases scattered about the room, and pencil sketches hung from the walls with pushpins. Cups with soaking brushes lined the windowsill. He smelled turpentine and acrylic paints.

Jacki dropped her purse next to the door. "This is it."

"Are any of your paintings finished?"

"In the bedroom."

They looked over her paintings for almost an hour. Boot commented on an abstract piece. A furious blend of color intertwined as if it were the artist's palette. He kept his remarks brief. He knew little about the medium and even less about her intentions. A photograph was honest, and the subject matter was evident.

"I went to Texas State," Jacki said. "I began in the art program."

"What happened?"

"Life got in the way."

"I see."

"An economics minor became my major, and the rest is history."

Boot knew about getting derailed en route to somewhere else. By the thinnest thread, he clung to his dreams. If he bottled his ambition, he'd be an instant success. "I'll do it. I'll shoot your artwork."

"I want to enter my best work in the city art show; then maybe submit the slides to the galleries."

"That's not my department. You pick the paintings."

"I need four dozen slides. What's that going to run me?"

"500, plus expenses." He'd already devised a price on the trip over, including a dozen ways to spend the cash.

"I don't know if that's fair."

"It's fair, and I'm warning you, slide film is expensive."

"I know."

"You'll get to review the proofs. Don't drive me nuts with the redos."

"It's a deal." She shook his hand, quick and firm like a man. "Want to drink on it?"

"Why not."

A half empty bottle of scotch stood beside two bottles of wine by the kitchen sink. Jacki poured scotch into tumblers and led him to the front window. They didn't speak for a while. Boot gazed down the sleepy street. An old man watered geraniums in a half whisky barrel by the curb. Dusk approached, and shade and shadows blended into one.

"I love this place," she said. "No one can reach me here. I leave the phone unplugged. I don't even know why I have one."

"You must be under a lot of pressure."

She pulled away from the window as if in a fog. "Huh?"

"Your job?"

"It's a job. I'm good at it."

"That helps." He watched her drink, studying her hand and mouth on the glass. Vermilion rays of light washed over her face. He suddenly placed the colors in her paintings. They stemmed from the sunset over the badlands.

"You're staring at me," she said.

"I know."

She reached behind his head and pressed the icy glass at the base of his skull. It raised the hair on the back of his neck.

When he flinched, she kissed him. It was long and open-mouthed, not a friendly peck or even a first date kiss. What did a woman of her caliber want with him? Since the start, he felt the attraction. He let her finish the kiss as she pleased, riding the moment as he did most, waiting to see where it led.

Jacki sipped her drink, pulling away as if she closed every deal with a kiss. "The smell of scotch is fantastic."

"Yes." Boot thought of the taste of it on her tongue. She was a game player. He'd play for a while.

"You better go."

He didn't feel like leaving, but he walked to the door. "I'm still getting paid." He hadn't let a woman literally screw him out of money, not yet at least.

She rolled her lower lip. "I can never tell if you're serious."

"I am."

"I can't wait to work with you."

He hit the street, before remembering his motorcycle parked across town. He often left the cycle in strange places, because it wasn't exactly his. The original owner bellied up on the payments, and the cycle passed into Boot's hands as a return favor. It was a Springfield Chief with a jet-black frame and stitched leather seat. Boot considered hocking it for cash, but after a few rides, he fell in love with it, like a kid with a favorite toy. He savored the feel of the powerful machine tearing up the street—a luxury he might never afford on his own.

Boot glanced at the window to Jacki's apartment. Her shadow shifted in the light. He considered returning and asking for a ride, but he didn't want to ruin the evening, so he walked away.

Several blocks later, he recalled the letter from Newell. Life has a tendency to bubble up when you're alone. He stood beneath a streetlight on the edge of Lee River Park and tore into the envelope. He found a brief note written in the same block letters as on the package.

DEAR STUPID:

MOST PEOPLE HAVE THEIR HEADS UP THEIR ASSES. TRY SMELLING FRESH AIR, AND YOU WILL NOTICE SOMETHING DIFFERENT.
THOSE FIRES BELONG TO ME. I CREATED THEM. SO YOU KNOW, SO THERE WILL BE NO MISTAKE, EXPECT MORE. I WANT YOU TO WRITE THAT.

EARTH RANGER

Boot recalled Gally's rants about an arsonist loose in the city. A torch like this begged for attention. For certain, there'd be more fires to come.

He stuffed the note into his bag, as if someone was watching, but no one was around. He shivered and faced the sky. The relentless heat painted the moon orange, almost red. People called it a blood moon. It looked heavy enough to crush the Concho skyline.

CHAPTER 6
MR. FIX IT

"**H**ow about the red head?" Boot stood in the Concho YMCA, outside the swimming pool. Construction crews labored to restore the burnt-out kitchen, and the noise of saws and hammers echoed down the hall. "What'd you think of her story?"

Gally rose from the water fountain and wiped his mouth on his sleeve. "What red head?"

"The one who lived behind the hardware store on Harp Street."

"The chick with the bulging eyes?"

"They weren't that bad."

"I thought they were gonna pop out of her head."

"Did you believe her story?"

"I believed it, but so what?"

"She saw a preppy looking guy behind the building before it burned."

"Big deal."

"It might be our man."

"She didn't see him doing anything specific. She saw him from three floors up and can't give much of a description."

"We know it's a young white male."

"I knew that before we started this morning, before we interviewed—for shit's sake, how many—three dozen people. It fits the profile of an arsonist."

"I thought it was something."

"I'll tell you when we strike gold. Right now, we've got scratch."

Boot smelled last night's whiskey on Gally's breath. Gally reminded him of a drunk he knew in foster care. At night, he'd soak himself blind, but in the morning, he stood upright like a storefront mannequin—hair perfectly combed, clothes crisp and pressed. Gally was like that too. Boot once came across Gally slumped over on a barstool after midnight, and the marshal didn't even recognize him, but Gally's transition to sunrise coherency never failed to impress.

"You don't waste any time with leads," Boot said.

"Today was nothing but a waste. It's making me nuts."

"We'll find what we need."

"That letter's driving me nuts too."

"I've stopped thinking about it," Boot said, although he wondered why the arsonist chose him and not Bob McGrath. It had to be his photos. Once again, he made friends in the wrong quarters.

"Earth Ranger." Gally flipped the pages in his notebook. "Crazy name. I've been trying to put my finger on it for days."

"What did Homicide say?"

"Forget about them." Gally twisted his mouth, like a dog about to chomp a bare ankle, not unlike his grandkids tooling around in their playroom.

Boot was used to Gally's gruff nature, but the stubborn Concho police detectives defied reason. "Why aren't the cops here?"

"Forget them. I own the case."

"They still aren't concerned?"

"Not like you think."

"How is it then?

"The PD has issues."

"What kind of issues?"

"Problems with the people involved in the investigation."

"I understand," Boot said. If there existed infinite ways to phrase a sentence, Gally picked one that pissed off most people.

"No, you don't," Gally said. "It's not me that bothers them."

"Well, who then?"

The marshal turned to Boot. "What happened in Trenton?"

Boot tried to hide his surprise, knowing he did a lousy job.

"I didn't expect you'd have an answer for that," Gally said.

"I don't need an excuse for what happened."

"The PD wants to hear your version."

"Let them ask."

"They know you implicated the Trenton Police in a smuggling ring."

Boot felt as if his entire history was tattooed on his forehead. He resented the marshal's tone. "I had the facts right, if that's your worry."

"Did you honestly think the PD wouldn't check you out?"

"Why would they?"

"Think about it. You walk through their front door and present an alleged letter from an arsonist. Even the *National Inquirer* would check the source."

"It doesn't matter, because it's true."

"You're the only one who knows whether the letter is real or not."

"You believe me?"

"I might be the only one who does."

"So the police don't."

"They won't be joining your fan club."

"You keep tell me that."

"You should've told me about your past before I decided to back you."

"If you don't want my help ..."

"You screwed me up a little. I don't like surprises."

"It's only one incident."

"One big incident. It puts you on the wrong side. You crossed the blue line. Do you understand me? It's tough enough having you riding shotgun with me."

"What does that mean?"

Gally didn't reply, but Boot knew the answer. He wasn't part of the system. He wasn't part of the city in any respect. He cruised from street to street, thinking he'd finally found a home, and then guys like the detectives at Homicide pulled him aside just to show him his place. "If there's something specific you want to ask me ..."

"I wish I'd known ahead of time. That's all. Now, never mind it." Gally tugged his shirt cuff away from his watch. "It's time for the kids."

Seven sopping wet children climbed from the pool. Boot watched them huddle into towels in front of their teacher. He kept thinking about his trouble with the local police. Old prejudices hounded him. One day, he'd have to leave Concho, just like Trenton. He hoped to resurrect his career first.

Gally walked onto the cement floor of the pool area. Boot followed the marshal, loading a fresh roll of film into his camera. The heavy chlorine smell jogged his senses, wrenching him from his thoughts.

"It's exactly one week since the fire," Gally said. "These kids were here when it happened."

"Do you think they saw our arsonist?"

"What else do we have? No one has seen much of anything."

"That's true."

"Kids are honest at least."

The swimming instructor donned a rubber bathing cap. Her one-piece suit pinched her chubby thighs. "Class, this is Fire Marshal

Ryan Galloway from the city fire department. He wants to ask you a few questions about last week's fire."

Gally moved to the edge of the pool. "Good afternoon, kids. I was going to bring my fire hose, but it looks like you're wet already."

Boot watched from the bleachers, shooting random portraits of the children. They ranged from five to six years old, eating up Gally's silly jokes. The marshal held a surprising ease with kids. Boot would've bet his camera that Gally frightened children and small animals.

"In a fire," Gally prompted, "who knows what to do?"

A boy in Batman swim trunks shot up his hand. "Stay low and look for the fire exit."

"Very good. And did everyone remember to stay calm?"

The children agreed. A few remarked on how cool it was to see the firemen and the big red trucks.

Gally leaned over, propping himself on his knees. "What else do you remember about that day?"

"I saw three fire trucks," yelled a boy.

"My mommy was crying," said a girl.

"The fix-it man bumped into me," said another girl. "He almost knocked me down."

"You must be confused, Cherise," the instructor said. "He didn't work last Tuesday."

"I saw the fix-it man," Cherise insisted. "He had tools. He bumped me."

Galloway straightened up. "Do you mean a fireman with a helmet and an ax?"

Cherise had dark skin and braided pigtails, which whipped from side to side as she shook her head. "No, a toolbox like Daddy's."

The instructor shrugged. "Maybe Mr. Crocket came in last Tuesday." She pointed to a heavyset black man working on the ladder across the pool.

"That's not the fix-it man." Cherise poked Gally's leg. "He looked like you."

"Like me?"

Boot yelled from the bleachers. "She's trying to say he had white skin."

Gally faced her again. "A white man with a toolbox bumped into you?"

She scrunched her mouth to the side and nodded.

"Where?" Gally's voice deepened, adopting the tone he used with probies and sloppy company men at fire scenes. Gally didn't scold so much as disapprove. "Where was he going?"

Cherise backed up. "Out the door."

"Was it before or after the fire alarm?"

"Ummm, I don't know."

Boot left the bleachers and came alongside the marshal. If he'd learned anything from shooting child portraits, it was never to rush a young subject, otherwise they shut up tighter than a bank vault, and every picture came out with the relaxation of a police mug shot.

"Let me." Boot knelt down, making himself less intimidating. "Was this before the fire?"

"I think so."

"What happened after the man left?"

"We walked to the locker, but we didn't finish."

The instructor tapped the girl's arm. "We were getting changed when the alarmed sounded. We left the building half dressed."

Boot glanced at Gally. "What do you think?"

"There were no outside workers here that Tuesday." Gally double-checked his notebook. "No, no one."

"Did you see him again," Boot asked the girl.

She shook her head.

"Did anyone else see the fix-it man?" Gally asked.

Boot scanned the class. No one responded. A few children weren't paying attention, pushing and shoving each other in line.

"Great." Gally muttered. "Our only witness is a six year old."

"I saw 'em. He bumped me." Cherise grabbed her waist with impertinence, certain she knew something.

"I think ..." Boot stood next to Gally, formulating a plan on the spot. "I know a person who can help us."

CHAPTER 7
CAMP WARS

A t noon the next day, Boot rode with Jacki in her Lexus. She sported a powder blue linen pants suit with a striped shirt. Her hair was pulled back with silver combs, and pink lipstick adorned her mouth.

"I can't believe you came to my office," she said.

"It's sure snazzy in there." Boot poked fun at the LeMaxxe building lobby. It had polished stone, exotic sculptures, and ornamental trees. He'd seen at least a dozen like it in Manhattan. What a waste for a room that people breezed through in seconds.

"I'm serious," Jacki continued. "I was set for a conference call at lunch."

"I wonder what they paid for the marble. Do you think they might turn that into a mausoleum one day?"

"Stop it. I had a meeting with the European office."

"Don't they allow time for lunch?"

"Am I getting lunch out of this? I mean, why am I doing this?"

"Because you're the only person I know who can sketch."

"That's it?! Don't the police have people for that?"

"This isn't exactly a police case yet."

"Am I about to do something illegal?"

"I'd never ask you to do that."

"Why don't I believe you?"

"Trust me."

"I've heard that before."

Boot liked tweaking her. He thought she was sexy when she got worked up. Her neck arched, and the words flew out of her mouth.

"You owe me big time," she said.

"I figured."

"And I won't have trouble guessing how you'll pay me back."

"I wasn't worried." Boot imagined the extra slides he'd have to take of her artwork. He wasn't letting that get out of hand. "We'll talk about it later."

She shot him a look. "Oh, we'll talk alright."

Miles outside of town, they reached a spot where the trees tamed the jagged escarpments. Boot pointed out the sign for Bradley Day Camp, where several mature mesquites flanked the entrance.

They parked the car on the lawn and walked toward the main office. Two kids in goggles emerged from the shrubs. Boot and Jacki found themselves staring down a pair of fat rifle barrels with neon yellow tubes mounted on top.

"Halt!" A man stomped from the office in army fatigues with yellow blotches. He waved a white flag in the air. "I told you not to point your paint guns at civilians. Get back undercover."

The children lowered their rifles and disbursed into the bushes.

"General Trotti, Camp Bradley director. Wednesday is skirmish day."

Boot threw a mock salute. "Pleased to meet you, General. We're reporting to see Cherise Jackson."

"You must be the reporter and the sketch artist."

Jacki held a dumbfounded expression, until Boot nudged her with his elbow. "That's us."

"I'll go find Cherise," Trotti said.

Boot and Jacki waited in the cafeteria for Trotti to return. They sat on smallish plastic chairs at the end of a column of tables. A map of the campgrounds showed blue and red flags spread out along opposing lines.

"I don't like this place," Jacki announced.

"It's just kids having fun."

"I don't like it."

"We'll be out of here in a few minutes."

"We better."

General Trotti escorted Cherise into the cafeteria. The petite black girl rested her paint rifle against the table and sat down. A blue armband strapped her right elbow.

"Hi, Cherise," Boot said. "Remember me from the YMCA?"

"I know why you're here. You want me to draw a picture of the fix it man."

"Jacki's going to draw the picture. She works with me."

Jacki opened her sketchbook. She unzipped a leather satchel and removed several graphite pencils.

"I want you to think about that day," Boot said. "Is there anything you remember about the fix it man?"

Cherise scrunched her mouth to the side. "He was white."

"Is there anything else? What shape was his head?"

"The shape?"

"Was it oval-shaped like General Trotti? Or was it triangular like Jacki's?"

Jacki and the General gave Boot wide-eyed glances. Boot supposed that people didn't like having their heads sized up like that. He did it in silence every time he aimed his camera for a portrait. Different shapes required unique lighting.

"Ummm. It was like Tony." Cherise decided.

"Tony's a pudgy kid," Trotti said. "His face is round."

Jacki drew a circular outline on the paper.

"Great," Boot said. "Was he fat?"

"I don't think so." Cherise glanced at Jacki's paper. "That's too round."

Jacki tore out the page and started over with a full U-shape.

"That's better," the girl said.

"Let's think about his eyes," Boot continued. "I'm sure he looked at you."

"Yes."

Boot worked with Cherise for forty-five minutes, interpreting her remarks until she grew impatient. He must have viewed thousands of people through his Nikon. He understood the nuances of the human face.

Jacki had sketched a youngish man with fine hair and thin lips and eyebrows. Boot stared at the paper. The arsonist looked ordinary, someone that he might pass in the street and put out of mind. The possibility chilled him. How close did the imagination of a child intersect with reality? Even the pros missed the mark.

"Incredible," Jacki said. "You did it."

"I did something."

"You made a face. I didn't think you'd get that much detail from her."

"You helped." Boot realized he'd impressed her. He cast it off as if he performed small miracles every day.

Cherise left her seat and came around to view Jacki's pad. "That's him. Can I go now?"

"Thanks, Cherise." Boot presented her with a photograph of her swimming at the pool.

"You're welcome, Mr." She picked up her rifle and scampered outside.

Boot and Jacki finished up with Trotti and left him behind in the cafeteria. They crossed the lawn to find her Lexus. Five children marched to their left where the woods met the grass. They wore red armbands. Boot watched Jacki sneer at the orderly formation.

"Don't look now." Boot noticed a handful of children from the blue team assembling on the right. He heard a thump before the first paint pellet whooshed past.

"Tell them to stop." Jacki turned toward the bushes, ducking her head. "Hey! Stop!"

Boot glanced at the office. The general was nowhere in sight. As far as he knew, they were in the firing line of paintball guerilla warfare.

Another pellet replied from the left. Jacki huddled next to Boot. "What do we do?"

"I don't know." He spotted the custom mag rims of her car tires on the lawn. "Run."

They sprinted as the battle heated up. Boot took the first hit. A pellet struck his arm, exploding like a giant neon yellow bird dropping. He'd laugh if it didn't sting. "Shit!"

Jacki caught one in the side and another on her leg. She stumbled and cursed beneath her breath. The bright colors on her linen suit did nothing to enhance her looks.

"Brats!" Her temper materialized with the change in fashion.

Boot tugged her arm, spurring her onward. They reached the car, out of breath and disheveled, but more importantly, they were clear of the war zone.

Jacki dug a towel from her trunk and wiped the paint from her lapel and sleeve. "If they hit my car, I swear I'll run them over."

"Calm down."

The towel only smeared the paint. She threw it on the grass. "Don't ask for any more favors."

"Okay."

"Don't call me at the office ever again."

"I get it." Boot felt his advantage with her draining away. He hated the kids too but for different reasons.

Jacki dropped into the passenger's seat and slammed the door shut. "Drive."

Boot directed the Lexus to Jacki's studio. She bristled in the plush leather seat. The notion of her returning to work seemed out of the question. He clutched the steering wheel, waiting for an opening to apologize. He lacked the cash to buy her a new suit.

When they went upstairs, Jacki dashed into the bedroom to change. She called to Boot through the slit in the door. "Pour us a scotch."

"Coming right up." Boot dug up ice cubes from the kitchen freezer and spilled three fingers of single malt into the tumblers. *A quick drink, a quicker apology, and I'm out of here.*

He heard her rummaging in the bedroom. She popped a CD by The Doors in the stereo. It was one of the few rock'n'roll groups that he tolerated. Blues and jazz sounded closer to the core of music.

"Where's that drink?" Jacki walked from the bedroom in cut-off jeans and a white shirt stained with oil paint. The shirttails hung loosely around her waist. She plucked the silver combs from her hair and let it fall.

Boot balanced the tumblers in one hand. He had nothing to lose. "You look good in paint."

"Don't joke."

"I was hit too." His hair was wet on the side where he washed out the neon yellow spatter. He was sure there were still traces in his hair and on his shirt. "Look at my clothes."

"You can replace your wardrobe at the Salvation Army."

He laughed at her spicy mood. Any minute, he expected her to toss him outside. He avoided talk of the photo job. He needed to keep that payday marching toward the bank, if at all possible.

"That place was ridiculous," Jacki said.

"I suppose."

"Who sends their kids to war camp?"

"I got the impression it was a once a week thing."

"It's asinine. You can't raise children like that." She took a hit of scotch.

Boot let the drink sit in his hand. "It sounds like you have experience."

"Experience?"

"With children."

"Ahh." She waived him off. "That didn't get you mad?"

"It took me by surprise."

"It got me mad."

"I noticed."

She doubled-back, starting to play. "I think you planned it."

"Random paint ball ambushes are my specialty." He made her laugh, and it pleased him.

"I think you liked it too."

"You guessed it. I'm the thrill-seeking type." He liked excitement now and then, but he liked her more, especially in bare feet and shorts, with the painting smock unbuttoned halfway down her chest. She definitely appeared more obtainable in rags, as opposed to Anne Klein.

The song 'Light My Fire' played in the bedroom. Boot thought of the arsonist and his pledge to Gally. Boot had promised to produce a sketch as soon as possible, but the mystery standing in front of him was much more palatable than trying to uncover a hellbent torch. For a moment, he wiped that dirty business from his mind.

"Do you know what would turn this afternoon around?" she asked.

"I don't know." He found her on the backside of her temper and cooling down. He didn't mind her heated opinions. It was better than her not caring about things. "You want another scotch?"

As he turned to retrieve the scotch bottle, she latched onto his belt. Her fingers yanked the waist of his pants. She pushed her lower lip forward and squinted her eyes.

"You still angry with me?" he asked.

"Are you going to keep cracking jokes?"

"What then?" Boot found himself exactly where he wanted to be. Set against the dicey circumstances of his life and career, a pretty woman coming onto him seemed like the sweetest mercy in the world. He kept silent, so not to veer his good fortune in the wrong direction.

Jacki pulled his waist harder. "Aren't you going to make another guess as to what I want?"

"What I want, or what you want?"

"Is there a difference?"

"You're right. I'm not going to crack any more jokes."

She caught his eyes. "I'm counting on your discretion."

He thought it was an odd thing to say, but he didn't dwell on it. He concentrated on her body instead. He viewed a lilac camisole peeking through her shirt. He wanted to see the rest. "What did you have in mind?"

"You know why you came back to my apartment."

"I think I did the first night." He eased a hand around her waist.

"I don't have to spell it out for you."

He brought her close and touched his lips to hers. He felt her tugging at him, and he smelled the anger on her. It aroused every bit of his desire.

She scooped her tongue below his and worked it off the corner of his mouth, until she found his ear. "Do you want this?"

"Yes." He picked up the flavor of scotch on her, like something burning. He could have her any way he wanted, and this might be his only chance.

He forced her against the wall by the couch. She dragged her nails through his scalp and down the back of his head. The sharp points scraped the nape of his neck, as he nipped her earlobe.

Their shirts came off. Their pants and underwear slipped from their limbs. They didn't struggle with their clothes. That was a kids' game of snaps, hooks, and unrelenting elastic bands. They pulled themselves free, able to smell each other and the changing chemistry between them.

They fell on the couch. He found her already wet and ready to accept him. It seemed he'd known that about her from the very start, and that moment at the perfume counter rushed back to him. How do these things happen? They held nothing in common.

He thrust deep inside her, feeling her push back. He fought to keep himself from going over the edge too soon.

"Let me." Jacki wriggled on top and mounted him. She smiled and stroked his penis, before inserting it between her legs. She eased into it, jutting her jaw. "You want to make this good, don't you?"

He watched her lean forward and begin to rock her hips. She breathed with the motion. Her breasts touched his chest. He bent to take one in his mouth.

She laughed and then moaned as he caressed her. She moved faster, more deliberate, talking her way through her pleasure. His urgency passed, fascinated with the woman above. He wanted to make it perfect. He needed to be shown how.

Her legs began to shake. She arched her neck toward the ceiling. "Just fuck me, Boot Means."

He'd never heard his name called like that. A woman's orgasm was a secret, revealed at the final minute, a flurry of adrenaline and surprise. Now he watched it build up from a seed.

"You must," she called.

Working, sweating, he let her rise and finish. She sunk her nails into his shoulder and dropped her head. Her hair brushed his face.

Boot kissed her forehead and put himself on top. She followed his cue, letting him assume the dominant position. It energized him to take control of her. She hooked her legs around his hips. His pride expanded with his liberty.

When he finished what they started, she swept her hand along his spine. He stared down at her. She played both parts—

aggressive and passive. He could take a long time exploring this territory.

"That's a good boy." She was laughing again. "I wondered when you were going to give up."

CHAPTER 8
SHAME

Before Oscar arrived in Concho, he worked up in North Gate, moving lumber and bricks, eating hot dust. He understood the triteness of his job and the stupidity of the people. He was killing time. His hands were not cut out for hard labor, but he learned to blend in with the crowd, hiding his education to appear unskilled. He discovered how easy it was to walk away from the lecture halls and study groups. Yes, a man could disappear—live from the trunk of a Chevy, change his name at will, pay for things with only cash. Graveyards brimmed with dead men who'd never complain when he borrowed their credentials. These weren't new tricks, but no one ever seemed prepared to see through them. People were always ready for a sucker play. He liked to think that they just needed an education. One day, those who'd encountered him would speak of their association and pretend they knew him. He made certain to offer only a passing favor, like a celebrity during a chance encounter.

At night, he laid in a motel room overlooking the interstate. Cars raced past his window, off to unknown locations. The previous border left magazines in the nightstand, and Oscar leafed through a real estate booklet, searching for his next destination.

The question challenged him for months, years even, before he fully knew it was a question. He needed the right place to implement his masterpiece. A sculptor never chose materials at random. A true master took time to uncover the right stone and drew from it what it had to offer.

Oscar flipped through the glossy booklet pages, eyeing the color photos of parks, schools, and spotless homes nestled in the grassy hills. He discovered Concho, like a sudden flush of inspiration. He ran his fingers over the homes and shops for sale. The booklet held a profile of the city proper. It was one of the finest places in the state, and its residents posed for the camera, smiling, proud of their sunny oasis, each one more ignorant than the next. They believed they were immune to misfortune.

Standing by the window, Oscar watched the cars speeding down the interstate. He felt restless. An urge to pack his bags and assume a lane on the highway consumed him. He tucked the booklet beneath his arm and closed his eyes. He saw his path, mile by mile, fire by fire, a collection of seemingly unrelated black stains, until someone recognized their beauty and said, 'Now we see.' The trail descended from the high plains and into the heart of Concho.

Off a quiet residential street, Oscar approached an apartment building within the Concho city limits. The basement steps were hidden from the street, and he snapped the padlock with a pair of bolt cutters. Since the first blaze, he felt his greatest work assembling. He remembered the story of Van Gogh discovering color as if no man had seen it before. It was a lot like that for Oscar. Soon, he'd clearly envision his masterpiece. It'd fall together by second nature.

The fluorescent security light cast an artificial sheen over his arms and legs. Oscar stared at the glowing tubes. Tiny electrodes excited the gas, until white light exuded from inside. He knew every part of an electrical device. He heard the electrons passing from wire to switch to gas. It sounded like flowing water.

He descended to the basement floor and switched on his flashlight. Steel cages ran to his left, stuffed with the possessions of the tenants above. He made out a folded beach umbrella, a nylon net bulging with soccer balls, a worn folding table, cardboard boxes with labels, and a child's bicycle.

Oscar stopped at the bike. His flashlight roamed over the flashy orange paint, a tear in the seat, and splatters of road tar near the pedals. He thought of the kids popping wheelies in the park. It reminded him of a time before any of this. His sister Heather used to tail him on her tricycle. She wanted to be close—so close. In a way, she still tailed him, surfacing in his thoughts. Oscar recalled her favorite things: the doll with the red velvet dress, her toy zebra, a pink hat that glittered rainbow colors in the sunlight.

But Heather was dead. She'd be twenty years old soon, if she was still alive, but she was dead. She was never nineteen years old or fifteen or even ten. Five years was all she got.

Oscar flicked his middle finger several times against his thumb. The noise between his ears mocked him, a recoil of sound from history, beating a constant theme. For all of his genius, he possessed the power to change everything but the past. Like Einstein, he expected his altered future to bend in on the past, until it formed a perfect circle and eradicated plausible distinction.

Near the stairs, Oscar located the electrical panel. If electrical wiring formed the bloodlines of a building, then this rectangular metal box was its heart. He opened the panel, revealing a bank of glass fuses inside. He examined the round stubs no bigger than a half dollar. The decades old engineering made his future entirely too easy.

The main conduit for several light bulbs ran along the ceiling. Oscar traced the wires and pulled the fifth fuse. He gripped a copper penny with a pair of insulated pliers and bridged the open circuit. His pulse gathered energy as the current prepared to reach infinity. Where will the flames roam tonight? Goose bumps rose on his arms. His fingers tingled.

He turned his attention to the first light bulb, removing the ceramic fixture. He exposed the hot lead and grounded it to the junction box. He stepped off the folding chair he'd used as a stool. The short circuit flowed with the life he'd given it.

Sometimes he thought electricity had a consciousness of its own. It resented men binding it within circuits and twisting it through transformers. The freedom and randomness of lightning strikes suited its style, and when Oscar set it free, it somehow knew this and rewarded him.

Amid his fantasies, thoughts of Heather resurfaced. He blamed those damned kids on their bikes. They jerked around the streets, not knowing the time of day, ignorant of the static circumstances that governed their lives. They counted on it. They plied it to their advantage. Oscar needed to control it, teaching them once and for all a primary lesson. It was as simple as following them home.

He flipped the light switch and sat on the basement steps. After midnight, he might remain unnoticed for hours, but he didn't have that much time. He put his face in his hands. His wristwatch ticked in his ear. The light bulbs popped one by one in the ceiling. There was a woman out there, probably several, who'd recognize his genius. They'd drop to their knees and suck his cock for what he'd done.

The fire gave birth overhead. As a boy, the doctors made him feel guilty for his talent. They discussed the facts. They posed simple questions. They tried to force an admission of things that they already knew, but he understood their jealousy. They wanted to make him like everyone else. He always knew this was impossible.

The heat rose in the basement room. Oscar didn't feel it, but he knew it was there. Magic occurred when electricity turned into flame. It arrived as if from nowhere, taking hold like a cancer, burning, devouring everything adjacent. It changed people. They'd be sleeping, dreaming, planning a different circumstance. Then they'd be awake, deciding what's important, choosing life or death in an instant. It came that quickly for many.

When Oscar smelled the first cinder, he pulled himself from a haze of cursed memories. Smoke kissed the ceiling, testing the floorboards for the slightest elevation. He longed for this transformation—the passing of calm into chaos. It made his cock hard.

He yearned to experience the flames up close. He owed Heather at least that much, but this was his punishment, the part he'd never get. Smoke curled between the rafters. Someone might smell it soon.

Oscar pushed himself up from the basement floor and took the steps. It was getting late, and a great deal of work still lay ahead.

CHAPTER 9
ARMADA ROAD

Boot bent over the developing trays in his kitchen. The shallow room offered a sink, running water, and no windows—perfect for developing film. He swiped a proof sheet from the enlarger and sunk it in the tray. Portraits from a wedding job rose in the solution. He knew the saturation times by heart and switched the sheet to the finishing tray without consulting a timer.

The phone rang, and the answering machine spun its creaky wheels. Everything was digital now: phones, answering machines, photography. Boot created the exception, a holdout due to a lack of funds and an overabundance of fundamentals. He convinced himself of maintaining purity within the trade, but he knew that if a modicum of success embraced him, he'd assume the current technology, casting aside the cumbersome mixing of chemicals and lengthy test runs with proof sheets and enlargements.

The voice on the machine sounded effeminate, laced with the pitiless tones of a man. "I have a gift for you. 274 Armada Road. Don't be stupid."

Boot sunk the next proof sheet, watching the bride emerge like a ghost in the chemical wash. He considered the payoff: a month's rent, a new clutch for his motorcycle, or a decent present for his father's birthday. He freelanced at baptisms and birthdays too—anytime people wanted two-dimensional memories. If he landed a position with the *Democrat*, he'd break from this tireless chain of assignments.

The phone message worked through the back of his mind. He tried to place the voice, until the caller's words sunk in. The image of the arsonist shot to the forefront of Boot's thinking. He dropped the tongs in the tray, leaving the bride to drown in the acid bath.

"Who?" Gally barked over the phone. He sounded a whiskey or two shy of useless, muting a belch in the receiver.

"The torch." Boot pinned the cordless phone between his ear and shoulder, darting about his apartment. He grabbed his camera from the end table and stuffed it into a nylon bag. "It's the arsonist."

"Him?"

"He's left us a tip." The word 'gift' stuck in his mind.

"I see." Gally groaned as if sitting up in bed. "I'll get the boys together."

Boot rushed like a fireman at the first alarm. He ran downstairs and pointed his cycle toward Armada Road. His camera bag hung by his side, banging his hip with every bump in the road. He throttled the bike over seventy, bearing down on his destination as if in one fluid motion.

The streets at 2:00 A.M. looked deserted, but even at top speed, he was too far away. He ducked into a shortcut between the Concho Savings Bank and a Chinese restaurant.

A pair of truck taillights met him in the alley. He squeezed the brake in time, locking his wheels behind a garbage truck.

The truck kicked up exhaust and the foul odor of festering garbage. Boot straddled his bike, watching a trash man plod toward a mound of plastic bags. The husky man leaned over the pile and flung two bags into the payload.

"Hey buddy." Boot revved his motor. "Can you pull aside?"

The trash man scowled. "Go to hell."

Boot banged the clutch in neutral and walked the bike back onto the street. He cursed over his shoulder, before throttling up to speed again.

The intersection for Armada lay ahead. He took the turn hard, burning rubber on the still warm asphalt. He threw out his foot to guard against wiping out. His knee kissed the road. His heart beat faster.

An orange glow lit up the night sky. The hum of his engine filled his ears, but an eerie feeling gripped him—a vacuum of worry and anticipation. He'd heard firemen mumble about this. 'The jump,' they called it. Nervous energy pumped in their veins when they approached a fire. They may have been in the stationhouse, laughing, playing cards, or sleeping, and suddenly the alarm hits, and the adrenaline flows topnotch. They fall into the back of the fire truck, double-checking clips and straps, listening to the calls over the dispatch. No words run between them, as they imagine the worst.

Boot saw people in the street outside a four-story apartment building. Eager flames engulfed the first floor, threatening the adjacent row homes. The fire department and police were nowhere in sight.

He stopped and dropped his cycle against a parking sign. People shouted at the building. A longhaired man in pajamas carried a two-by-four length of wood. Two small dogs cowered beneath a van, shaking.

"Did someone call this in?" Boot called to a couple on the sidewalk.

"I think so." The woman said, as if answering a different question. She huddled beside her mate. She was frightened and shaking, flushed from her secure pocket yet unable to wander too far, not all that different than the dogs under the van.

"Is there anyone inside?"

"I don't know." The man drew her tight to his side. "We were sleeping."

Boot heard a shattering sound. The man with the two-by-four rolled away from a basement window. Heavy smoke gushed from a spiky portal of glass.

"Is there someone down there?" Boot called.

The man fell back on the sidewalk, coughing. Strands of hair snaked past his reddened cheeks. Flames reflected off the glass mosaic on the sidewalk. "My surfboard. It's custom."

Boot scanned the horizon, begging for a glimpse of lights or sirens approaching. It was only a few seconds since his arrival, but it seemed longer with mayhem controlling the scene. The woman started sobbing. A teenager gathered CD's into a torn box by the curb. Boot prayed Gally hadn't gone back to sleep or passed out. He trusted the marshal was more of a fireman than a drunk.

The empty road offered no relief. Boot recalled Gally's comments about critical times and fire progression: fire burns up and out; smoke kills you first; the people in the back get out last.

He cut through the alley between the buildings. People descended the rear fire escape. Panicked steps pattered the metal stairs.

On the third floor, the decorative cut stone gave way to a sheer rise of bricks. A woman stood on the landing, screaming into an open window, fighting to get inside.

Boot watched for a moment. People went nuts over property. He put his foot on the first step and called up. "Forget about it."

She glanced down, looking genuinely crazed. "It's Ethan."

Boot dropped his camera bag and climbed up.

He squeezed past a family of three on the second floor. The father clutched his daughter in one arm and a strongbox beneath the other. "Her little boy's in there."

The incredible heat singed the hair on Boot's face and arms. "Where is he?"

"In the bedroom. I tried to get him out."

On the third floor landing, the woman jammed a shovel into the window. Boot saw vertical bars covering the window from the inside. She took the shovel and smashed it into the metal risers. The tie in her hair was half undone, and her bathrobe hung loosely, exposing her nightgown.

She thumped the bars again. "It's locked. God, I locked them."

"Locked?"

"I locked them." She wore pink fuzzy slippers and braced the thin rubber sole against the bars. She grunted, trying to force the bars open. "I locked them."

Wisps of smoke seeped from the top of the open sash. A boy, no older than three years, reached through the bars and grabbed her slipper. "Mommy, don't shovel the window."

Boot yelled to her. "What's locked?"

"The bars are padlocked."

"Does he have the key?"

"He can't open it." She knelt down. "Ethan honey, put the key in the lock. You've got to try."

"It doesn't fit, Mommy."

"God." She fisted the rails. "Where's the key?"

"I dropped it."

She shook the bars. "Find it, honey."

"It's dark."

"Find it!"

"I'll turn on a light."

"No!" Boot yanked the woman aside. "Ethan!?"

Ethan disappeared from sight. More smoke rolled over the top of the sash.

"Ethan!" Boot reached between the bars. He felt the padlock. The hot metal almost burned his arms. "Ethan."

"Hello?" Ethan returned to the bars, rubbing his eyes. When he lowered his hands, two pale blue gems stared back at Boot. A curl of hair twisted over the boy's forehead.

"Stay by the window." Boot turned to the boy's mother. "Go find someone with a crowbar."

"What?"

"I'll stay with him."

"I can't leave."

"I'll get him out." He saw faint yellow light inside. Flames flashed on and off at irregular intervals, teasing entry into the room. He tried to draw the mother's attention away from it.

The woman knelt down and grabbed Ethan's hand. "Mommy's getting help. We'll get you out."

Ethan started to cry. "Don't leave me."

"Mommy will be right back."

Boot rattled her shoulders. "There isn't much time."

"I love you, honey. I–I'll be back." She ran down the fire escape, stumbling on the first set of steps.

"Mommy!"

Boot yelled from the landing. "Hurry!"

He shook the grate. It was a metal frame mounted at all corners inside the room. It was designed to keep people out. It did its job well.

Boot picked up the shovel and wedged it behind the lower left bolt in the wall. He pried with all of his strength until the frame snapped loose.

"Hang on, Ethan." He sat on the landing and punched the bars with his boots until the first bolt popped free. If he busted two bolts, it'd be enough to free the boy.

"Mommy?" Ethan stuck his plump hands through the bars. "It's hot in here."

Boot enclosed the tiny fist in his own. It felt like a warm stone. "Stay close."

A window shattered below them. Thick smoke rose up, followed by a wave of heat. Boot felt the hot stench of it in his lungs, knowing he'd have to escape to the roof. He hoped to find a clear path with the boy.

He drove the shovel behind the second bolt and dropped his weight onto the handle. Men on the ground yelled for his retreat, but he ignored them, forcing his weight downward. He coughed, eating the smoke in gulps.

The shovel snapped, and he fell on the landing, knocking his head against the railing. He stared at the splintered chunk of wood in his hands. It was too short to gain leverage. His lifeline to the boy was severed.

"Mommy!" The pitch in Ethan's voice raised.

Boot knelt before the window. Ethan pulled back. The iron bars felt searing hot. A trail of flames zipped across the carpet.

"Stay close as you can." Boot brought his face near the opening.

"My tummy hurts."

The fire attacked without conscience. A shelf with stuffed animals burst into flames. A picture frame cracked and fell to the floor.

"Mommy! Mommy!" The boy yelled.

"Keep low."

The flames shot below the boy's feet, and he released a piercing scream. It shocked Boot, and he threw his shoulder against the bars.

The boy cried, moving past hysteria. He choked on smoke, heat, and his own tears. Boot fought all of it, gripping the rails, shaking the wretched immovable iron, until his arms nearly pulled from the sockets.

As flames took the sill, Boot thrust his hands between the bars, resisting the natural urge to withdraw. His eyes burned. The skin on his face scorched. The boy fell back, but Boot thought he grabbed hold of him. Then his hands ached with excruciating pain, and he let go.

Boot wavered on the landing, watching the smoke and flame envelop the window. A suffocating cloud closed around him.

He considered another charge at the boy, but he was being pulled backward. The air cleared around his head, and his throat burned. He gasped for air, fighting the nausea that churned his gut. The ground drew closer. He saw the length of a ladder and men reaching up to pass him along.

A familiar voice spoke to Boot, soothing and confident. Captain Sheerssen wrapped his big arms around Boot's waist. He draped Boot over his shoulders like a limp bag of sand—the deadman's carry, something all firemen knew and hoped never to use.

"I've got you, sonny," Sheerssen said.

Boot listened. His mind went blank, no words, just a sound of that boy screaming.

"You're gonna be alright," the captain said.

CHAPTER 10
THE MIDDLE OF THINGS

Boot stared at the floor in the Concho Medical Center emergency room. He stopped looking at the swollen pink and black slashes across his palms. The pain throbbed with the beats of his heart. He felt woozy. The stench of burning flesh lingered, teasing every sense, but it wasn't his hands that stunk. They didn't have an odor. Nothing in the sterile room seemed to possess a scent. It was that kid on Armada Road, burning alive. He caught the smell from miles away—skin, bones, everything cooking. It was part of his brain now. Memory played no favorites.

"It's going to sting." The surgeon swabbed silver cream along the slashes. She worked with deliberate strokes to mask the open wounds.

He flinched, his hands shaking. He wondered if had the will to steady them at all.

"Please, hold still." She adjusted her glasses on the bridge of her nose. "I don't know about these."

"What is it?"

"The burns are so close to the nerve groups."

"I can feel everything." He closed his fingers gingerly, balking at the pain that surged through his wrists and elbows. Pain was a good sign. Pain meant that the skin still held a chance of living. "It hurts like hell. That's all."

"That's all?" She checked his face.

He'd heard the staff discussing his condition in the hallway. They knew about the fire and the dead boy—what happened up there on the landing. The staff held him to scrutiny, waiting for shock to set in. The surgeon kept asking the same questions, but it only forced him to maintain his wits.

"You should stay overnight," she said.

"Forget it."

Charles Goodner barged into the ER. He looked stiff-legged and tired. A suede vest strapped his big chest and belly. "Is he alright?"

The surgeon looked at Boot. "Who is this?"

"Charles," Boot said. "My father."

"This is how a journalist earns a living?" Charles asked.

Boot ignored the question. Charles didn't understand anything about his job, and if he did, he wasn't going to ask the right questions.

"You didn't have to come all the way out here," Boot said.

"I left as soon as I heard."

"You could've settled things over the phone."

"Those hands look pretty bad."

Boot had little choice but to give Charles's name at the desk. Boot lacked the money or insurance to pay the hospital. He wanted to get out of the ER before the bills piled any higher. "Put it on my tab."

"I want you to get the best care, you understand."

The surgeon cut a length of gauze and began wrapping Boot's hands. She seemed relieved by the gravity of Charles' stature and started soliciting his help. "I recommend overnight observation."

"Don't worry about the cost," Charles said.

"I'm worried about it," Boot interjected.

"I settled it up front already."

The conversation reminded him of foster care, where he didn't get to choose his next move. "Well, thanks anyway."

"It's my pleasure."

"I owe you too much already." Boot had borrowed a grand when he first came to town. He still owed Charles most of it.

"It's a pittance." Charles placed his hands behind his back. His silver and turquoise belt buckle flashed in the surgeon's bright light. The brads on his boot tips were sterling silver too.

Boot wondered if Charles polished his boots to make them shine like that or slipped on a new pair every day. "The money's not a pittance to me."

"Look," Charles said, "you've got two hands that look like medium rare steak. While that's pretty good for steak, I think you need the full treatment."

"I think his hands will be alright." The surgeon's eye's shifted to Charles. "But I'm worried about ... the patient."

Boot figured that Charles had heard the stories too. "I'm not knocking around a hospital room all night, just to prove I'm sane."

"I can't persuade him to stay," she said.

Boot didn't want to pursue this line of talk. He always made the wrong decision in Charles' eyes. It wasn't so much that Boot cared. It was more that he'd never be his equal, not in money or thought or anything that mattered. He wasn't even sure he wanted that, but he needed the chance. He needed the resources to decide on his own and not be second-guessed. That was freedom. "I'm not going to discuss it anymore. I'm leaving."

Charles looked like he wanted to say more. He pulled a handkerchief from his pocket and dabbed the sweat from his brow. "If you find yourself a little tight ..."

"You don't need to keep bailing me out." Boot turned to the surgeon. "Are you finished yet?"

"Almost." She cut the last wrap and taped it down. She called to the nurse at the station. "Is Dr. Melbourne coming?"

A nurse looked up from a stack of paperwork. "I called him twice, doctor."

"Call him again."

"I don't need a chat with your shrink," Boot said.

"Dr. Melbourne just wants to talk," the surgeon said.

"Dr. Melbourne wants to talk because you asked him too. Geez, I've covered bad stories in the news like this before. I know the routine."

"Yes," Charles said, "but have you ever been the story before?"

"That's almost funny enough to make me laugh, but I don't feel much like it tonight. If I was crazy, I guess I'd laugh." Boot tested his hands, bending his fingers. He took a breath and slipped off the table.

The surgeon sighed. "I'll prescribe some pain killers, and I want you to change those wraps at least once per day."

"Yes."

"More often if they get dirty."

Boot noticed his father's pasty complexion. The big man scanned the drawn curtains and stainless steel fixtures. A smattering of gauze lay upon the floor. Dried blood and bits of dead flesh stuck to the discarded cotton balls and swabs.

"This making you uncomfortable?" Boot asked.

Charles tucked the handkerchief away. "I suppose you've seen a great deal for a young man. I suppose you're used to all this."

"I suppose."

"That fire sounded pretty bad."

"Don't you start with the forty questions. I'm going to be alright."

The surgeon took off her gloves and dropped them on the floor. She stood up. "I've done all I can."

"There you go," Boot said. "That's as good as a release form."

"Everyone's worried about you," Charles said.

"Everyone?"

"Jake, Sandy. Lord, you never come by the house, and now this."

"I didn't plan this."

"I know but ...."

"I'll manage." He sensed his feet firmly planted on the hard hospital floor, yet he caught a whiff of that burnt odor again. Geez, it wasn't even real, but he kept smelling it. Images from Armada Road flashed through his mind. The pain in his hands felt elementary, penance for not saving a life. He'd nurse it, carry it for a while.

Boot left the ER, feeling Charles track him into the lobby. Part of him wanted to see Charles close behind, but he never wanted the big man to know that. That's why he had the hospital call Charles. He wanted to see Charles's reaction, and now he had it.

"You didn't have to come," Boot said. "I wasn't sure if I needed to pay."

"Sometimes," Charles said, "you're the spitting image of your mother."

"I don't look anything like her."

"I'm not referring to her looks."

"Oh, I get it."

"You act like her. It breaks my heart."

"I'm sorry she left you."

"It's because I know how she ended up."

"You think I'm like her. You think I'll do something crazy." He held up his hands. "You think I did this on purpose?"

"I think your heart is bigger than you need."

"Was that a compliment?"

"You're like me too. You're a risky combination of both of us."

"Thanks for the insight. Looks like I'm seeing the shrink anyway."

The ER automatic door slid open as they stepped toward it. Boot was moving so fast that he almost walked into the glass.

Nervous energy propelled him. He slipped outside. An orange sun rode the morning haze, ready to shower the city with its relentless heat. What was it about the south and the Sun? Technically, they weren't that many latitudes closer to it than Minnesota.

Charles accompanied Boot to the curb. "I didn't mean to bring up your mother like that."

"Forget it. That's partly the reason why I came west."

"You don't ask a lot questions about her."

"I'm not sure you're the one to answer them."

"Everyone's going to put their own slant on things."

"I know how stories go. I write them for a living."

"I won't speak of her if you'd like."

"I don't know about that either." Boot scanned the street, wondering where to turn next. He might wander the city for a while, but his camera bag felt too heavy to lug. It all seemed like too much to handle. He couldn't grip his Nikon, and fingering a typewriter was out of the question. Besides, did he have the words that he needed? He wasn't ready to dredge up the details of last night, even though they insisted on pressing to the forefront of his thoughts.

Charles tugged a pocket watch from his vest. "I should be heading home. It's a couple hours ride."

"Thanks for helping me out," Boot said.

"I guess I could cut the ride short and go straight to the office."

"That sounds good." Boot watched Charles fiddle with his hands behind his back. Their goodbyes were awkward at best.

"You might consider coming by the house, next month."

"Maybe."

"Sandy's throwing a party for my birthday."

"I'm sure your wife will do a great job."

"She asked me to invite you."

"Oh?"

"It's only family and friends. You won't have to feel put out."

"Maybe you should stick with immediate family."

"That includes you."

"I keep forgetting."

"I know. It's gonna take some time."

Boot saw the look on his father's face. The comments that others made about their families made sense. Certain connections were hard to avoid, and tonight, undeniable connections appeared everywhere: the kid on Armada Road, the kid's mother on the stair landing, Boot's father and dead mother too. Boot strung them together. He realized that his presence was all that his father really wanted, although he longed to be more amazing to Charles than that.

"Should I bring someone?" Boot asked, almost joking.

Charles smiled for the first time since he strolled into the ER. "Yes, if you want."

"Okay."

A red Caprice pulled up to the curb. Gally leaned across the front seat and rolled down the window. Boot was never so relieved to see the marshal. "Need a ride?"

Boot eased into the car. He wanted to leave Charles on good terms and appreciated the timely exit. "I'll see you in August."

Charles agreed.

Gally's uniform looked soiled. Black stains marked his elbows and cuffs. He pulled away from the curb. "Sorry I took so long to get here."

"Did you get my bike?"

"It's at the stationhouse. The boys at Second Union tossed it on the truck."

"They're allowed to do that?"

"No, I asked them to."

"Thanks."

Gally turned the corner. "Who was that with you?"

Boot saw Charles in the window. Charles was watching the Caprice drive off.

"My father," Boot said.

"That's him? And you didn't introduce me?"

Boot considered waving or turning his head but didn't. "So where were you?"

"Digging in the ashes on Armada." Gally offered Boot a sideways glance. He seemed curious about Charles, but Boot wanted no part of that discussion. He wasn't in the mood for confessions, real or imagined.

"You arrived not a minute too soon," Boot said.

"You know how I get lost in a job." Gally scooped his helmet off the seat and tossed it in the back. "I don't know about you, but I need a drink."

"You read my mind."

They reached M Bar—a dilapidated joint, not far from Boot's apartment. The exterior was painted red cinderblock, occasionally broken up by foggy glass block windows. Inside, old wood and outdated beer posters decorated the walls. Scribbled notes of love, debt, and promise were tucked into the cracks in the paneling. Boot guessed that those messages had been waiting a long time.

"This place is a firetrap," Gally said.

"Yeah, I know."

The men sat at the bar and ordered beer and whiskey. Hank Williams crooned from the jukebox. The lights were so dim that the handful of patrons remained insular. Boot liked it that way, and he suspected Gally did too.

Gally put down two rounds, before he got into it. "It was our torch on Armada Road."

"You don't have to tell me."

"He's not hiding his work anymore."

"What do you mean?"

"He created a ground fault in the basement. Simple stuff. Pretty but obvious. It causes uncontrolled current across the line. The fire can begin almost anywhere."

"Speak in English, please."

"It didn't matter to him where the fire started. In the previous two cases, the evidence was trace, because the fires started in the spot where he set them. Nearly every clue was destroyed. Last night, the fire started far enough away to preserve his methods. He had to know that might happen."

"What are you saying?"

"He wanted us to find it."

"Our torch wins again."

"The bastard's proud of what he did."

"I wish I knew nothing about him."

"It's too late for that. He wants you to make him a star."

"What does Homicide say?"

"They're listening to me now."

Boot counted the bodies since the start. He shuddered to think how many more lay undiscovered or, worse yet, ahead. "Three dead boys, Gally."

"I know."

"Did they find the body, you know, the last one?"

"Don't concern yourself with that."

"Then I guess he's dead."

"What'd you think?" Gally cracked, but he seemed to hope for the same miracle, even though he knew the facts. "Hell."

"I had him in my hands." An involuntary shiver took hold of Boot. He saw himself in the mirror. He was turning to stone.

"You need another drink."

Boot wondered if there were enough drinks to quiet his thoughts and squelch that awful smell. Whenever he imagined himself moving past the evening, he started to slip backward, replaying it. It returned in pieces, the decisions that he already regretted.

Gally whispered to the bartender, and in a few seconds, the entire bottle of whiskey stood on the counter in front of them.

The marshal filled their glasses. "Forget the beer."

"Good idea."

"Did I ever tell you why I moved up to investigations?"

"No."

"You never heard the story?"

"You don't have to tell me if you don't want." Boot drained the whiskey from his glass. The booze went down easier with each mouthful. He relied on that.

"I had to," Gally said. "They forced me out."

"Did you get hurt?"

Gally poured another round. "The wife wanted me to quit. After the Massey Dock fire, I wasn't much fun anymore."

"Massey Dock?"

"It was a warehouse along the river. It doesn't exist anymore. I think they turned it into a boat slip or damned tennis club."

"How long ago was this?"

"Ten years, now that I think about it." Gally found the bottom of another whiskey. He wiped his mouth with his sleeve. "It was a hot summer like this. Lots of brushfires on the edge of town. We never expected Massey to be a problem."

"What caused it?"

"I don't remember. Some kind of shit they weren't supposed to have in there to start with. Second Union—that was my company—showed up to the docks first. For shit's sake, we should've never gone in there like that. Nobody was thinking. On a pier, you have only one way in. The rest hangs over the water."

Boot sipped his shot glass.

"I lost two men," Gally said.

"Sorry."

"I won't tell you their names."

"I wouldn't recognize them anyway."

"I sure as hell remember them. We were on the lifeline together. The fire cut us off, and I couldn't get the last two out."

"Geez, Gally. Were you alright?"

"It was simple to avoid. Today, they write about it in the manuals. All that water around us, and we burned up like we were in the middle of the badlands. It'd be stupid if it wasn't so tragic."

Gally stared off for a while. Boot figured he'd lost him, but the marshal shook his head and regrouped.

"Hey," Boot said. "It's a rough line of work."

Gally dug into his shirt pocket and produced a piece of paper. He unfolded it on the bar between them. It was the sketch of the arsonist, a copy of the one Boot made with Jacki. Boot realized he badly needed Jacki's company, but he was sitting at a bar with a drunk, getting drunk himself.

"This is the creep that lit up Armada," Gally said. "He looks like a kid."

"You guessed he'd be young."

"They're always young, this type. It fits the profile: young and angry."

"You guessed everything right so far."

"I don't know anything but two dead boys."

"Three."

"Shit, three."

Boot found himself falling back into the Armada Road fire. He lifted his glass with his fingertips. His hands throbbed, but as long as he didn't squeeze or stretch them, he didn't feel too much pain. He fought to balance himself on the barstool. It was good to be alive in any condition. He'd been way too close to the other side once already. It was better to be alive and in pain, than dead. The rest served as mere degrees of misery.

"You can't do that to people," Boot muttered.

"What you talking about?"

"You can't burn people up. It's not right."

Gally examined his empty whiskey glass. "No, you can't."

"You can't burn people, people you don't even know."

"No."

"I want to watch the fucker burn like that kid."

"You don't want that."

"I do."

"Burning's bad, the worst way to go. Get burned bad enough, and you wish were dead."

"I wish he was dead, Gally. I want it evened up."

"You'll get your chance to even up."

"I don't see how."

"You know what he looks like."

"That's all I know."

"He talks to you. Like it or not, you're the front man on this one. You'll get your chance."

Gally made sense, although Boot failed to see a clear solution. He sloshed down his last shot of whiskey. He'd lost count of his drinks. He figured it was too late to avoid getting sick.

"Something will break," Gally said. "Keep doing what you do."

Boot only knew how to shake up a situation until something fell out. It was the bread and butter work of a journalist: ask questions, probe, show up where you didn't belong. It took people out of character and made them operate without a façade. It made people real— real enough to see through. "I'll get in the middle of things."

"What's that?"

Boot needed to find a soft spot and irritate the arsonist, perhaps force the torch to make a dumb move. Sitting and waiting for the next fire was a terrifying idea. "I'll poke around and shake things up."

"That's the right idea."

"The last thing anyone wants is me in the middle asking questions."

"I noticed that about you."

"It's not all my fault. I know I don't belong here. Maybe that's an advantage."

"What are you talking about?"

"Don't bullshit me."

Gally let the remark pass.

"I'll find a way," Boot said, "and I'll try not to screw up too much while I'm getting there."

CHAPTER 11
INSIDE CONCHO

By 3:00 P.M. the next day, they were waiting for Boot at the *Democrat* main office. Two Homicide cops and two editorial heads flanked an oval conference table. Boot was stepping into the worst part of his hangover. He felt angry and bilious, and several anti-acid tablets kept down the contents of his stomach. He resembled Gally, minus the crisp uniform. He hadn't even showered.

Boot assumed the chair at the head of the table. It was the closest position to the men's room down the hall. He saw Ryan Galloway, and then Shep Newell wheeling beside the editorial tandem. Boot tasted whiskey on his breath, but people only noticed his hands. Everyone knew the story. They weren't about to push too hard.

"Three bodies." Boot uttered. He wondered what everyone was doing here. He eyed Gally sipping coffee from a styrofoam cup. The marshal was unusually quiet.

"Three dead boys," Boot said. "That's what it takes to draw your attention."

"Good morning, Mr. Means." Homicide Detective Manuel Ojeda acted as if he hadn't heard Boot's remark. He was overdressed like most city employees. Concho was a city on the rise, charging into the new millennium with white-collar industries and super clean streets. It fought to erase its history as a honky-tonk stop beyond the gates of Fort Stead.

Ojeda donned a double-breasted suit with a slick blue tie and tasseled loafers. He looked like the mayor with a handgun. "You haven't been living here long."

"No."

"Are you planning to stay on?"

"What business is it of yours?" Boot gave Ojeda a hard look—part hangover, part disgust. He was familiar with the 'you don't fit in' speech in a variety of flavors and locales.

"I'll excuse your unfamiliarity with procedures."

"I wish I knew what they were." Boot looked at Newell.

"Be that as it may," Ojeda continued, "we have a serious situation blooming, and you sit at the crux of it."

Boot rested his bandaged hands upon the conference room table. "Yeah, I have a habit of showing up at the wrong place at the wrong time."

"Gentlemen," the marshal said. "I think we're getting off on the wrong foot. Boot's not from Concho, but he's good people."

"If you say so," Ojeda replied, "I'm willing to accept it."

"If you want to question me," Boot said, "take me down to the station, but not in front of the newspaper staff."

"I assure you, Mr. Means. It's not like that."

"I had a long day yesterday, so unless someone can tell me why I'm here ..."

"Let me." Detective Wendy Ancrum opened a case file on the table. She had medium dark skin with a cute freckled nose and long frizzy hair. Like Ojeda, she appeared dressed for court, in a light gray suit and black shoes with low flat heels. A chrome-plated pin of a lizard coiled on her lapel.

She laid a copy of the arsonist's letter on the table along with the sketch. "He wants a dialog with you."

"I'm guessing that he's contacted no one else," Boot said.

Ancrum glanced at Ojeda, before answering. "Only you."

"I assumed as much."

"Why?"

"I promoted his work. I mean, I shot the pictures at Harp Street and the YMCA. A picture's more powerful than words, and this guy seems a little full of himself."

"He does."

"He wants the credit. Crazy or not, most people want credit for their work."

"How do you know he's responsible?"

"That's a good question."

"He could be a glory seeker?"

"Then he has incredible timing. He phoned me last night, just before the Armada blaze."

"By our records, the conversation lasted less than a minute."

"Did you track the number?"

"It originated from a pay phone around the corner from the blaze."

"That makes sense." Boot imagined passing the arsonist as he raced to the fire. He searched his memory and came up empty. "I didn't see him. Have you checked for fingerprints?"

"We're looking into those now."

"Did you take pictures outside the fire, especially of the spectators? I wish I had. Arsonists can't help but watch what they've started."

"We don't have a decent record of that."

"I figured that." The detectives studied Boot's face. Boot tried not to flinch. He'd been through this process before. They let him pace the conversation, searching for a flaw in his story, but he related merely the facts. He dug in for the long haul, a mind-bending dialogue with Concho's finest. "You have everything I have."

"Have we?" Ojeda asked.

"One letter, one phone call, one witness, and her description of the arsonist. I've been open since the start."

"Are you certain?"

"Definitely. Lying gets too complicated. I don't have time for that."

"You appear very busy." Ojeda wore his disfavor for outsiders like the bright red scarf poking above his breast pocket.

"Do you think I wanted to get wrapped up in this? I could use a paying job. Know what I mean?"

"That's it? That's what you want to say?"

"I have my own questions. For example, do you have anything on the torch, other than what I've given you?"

"It's an ongoing investigation."

"I'd like to stop him too, you know. I've seen what he does up close."

"We regret what happened last night."

"I know you don't trust me. Gally told me." Boot watched Ojeda fidget in his chair. Boot didn't mind calling people out. He was entirely unsuited for politics. In public dealings, people rarely said what they meant. They'd rather preserve the peace than expose the truth.

"I need to ..."

"Excuse me." Boot was tired of playing games. Cops and reporters weren't supposed to agree. They stole information from each other. "I can live with your suspicions. It's better that I know where I stand."

"I want to know if we're getting information in a timely fashion."

"Can I ask another question?"

Ojeda peered down his nose.

"What are we waiting for?" Boot asked.

No one answered.

"Let's make a move on the stinking torch," Boot said

"We're interviewing people in and around the scene," Ojeda said.

"Gally's already done that."

"We're canvassing the fire scene areas with his picture."

"That's good, but how about a larger zone? How about all of Concho? Does anyone know why you're asking about this guy?"

No one replied. Gally massaged his temples. Boot knew he'd said too much already.

"How about we print his sketch in the paper?" He waited for a reaction, but the Conchonians banded together in silence. The detectives folded their hands. Newell bit the eraser tip of a pencil. Even Gally held his tongue. Boot wondered what they'd think if they knew his father owned a million dollar trucking company in San Angelo. Would that bring him into the fold? He refused to throw that card on the table, not with this crowd, not yet.

"What are you aiming for?" Ojeda smoothed the front of his suit jacket.

"Let's bring our man out of the closet. People deserve to know."

"And spawn widespread panic? We can keep control of the investigation ..."

"You don't have control. He kills when he wants."

Gally grinned. Those were his words exactly.

"We can't be certain if he's still in the city," Ancrum said.

"You'd like that to be true. Hell, I would. I'd like him to be five hundred miles from here, but he'd still be burning kids."

"We can't be certain."

"You'll be certain before long. You think he's just going to stop?"

"I don't know."

Boot's courage merged with his hangover. He felt nastier than he'd felt in months. "You've never encountered anything like this before, have you?"

He waited for a sign from the assembled team. Ojeda looked insulted, drumming his fingers on the table. The editors didn't budge. They knew even less about the lunatic who burned their city.

"He's not motivated by greed or jealousy," Boot said. "It's rage. This guy wants to burn, and he'll keep on burning."

Ancrum closed her file. "There's no guarantee he'll strike again."

"Excuse me, ma'am. I'm as certain of that as anything."

"No one is certain."

"Ask Marshal Galloway. He's sitting right over there, not saying a word."

"I think he's right," Gally said. "The torch has promised as much to Boot. Besides, there are case histories. It's a compulsion. He can't stop. He'll just get more brazen."

Boot felt the chill cast about the room, as they each connected on that thought.

"Find him before he chooses his next target," Boot said. "Publish his picture. Someone will spot him buying a soda or walking the dog. Someone has already seen him."

"I don't think so," Ojeda said.

"Don't you understand what I'm saying? It's not about sweeping up the ashes anymore."

"I couldn't have said it better myself," Gally chimed in.

"Well," Ojeda said, "you've certainly spent a great deal of time thinking about this."

When the meeting broke up, Gally followed Ojeda and Ancrum out the door. Boot stayed in his seat, listening to the marshal combing over details of a serial arsonist. Bits and pieces of the conversation drifted from the lobby near the elevators. Gally's knowledge sounded bookish, stemming from his experience with juvenile delinquents, but the longer Gally spoke, the more Boot knew they had a deadlier, grownup version on their hands. He was glad to hear the conversation close behind the elevator doors.

He went to the water cooler and filled a paper cup. How was Homicide going to react to all the bad news? They'd never tell him. He put his wrist against his forehead. He felt lightheaded and feverish, and his hands throbbed. He heard two of the editors leave without saying goodbye. He'd gotten a strong vibe they disliked him too. *Screw them both.*

Newell remained at the opposite end of the oval table—the spot reserved for his wheelchair. His complexion looked superb, tan and healthy. His upper body seemed as fit as ever, and his biceps tugged at his shirt. He looked capable of whipping Boot's ass, working legs or not. "I might have guessed you were going to irritate everyone."

Boot downed the water, swallowing hard. He needed another drink and a handful of aspirin. "You put me in this position."

"So it's my fault?"

"I don't know why the torch picked me. Why didn't he contact Bob McGrath? You gave Bob the story."

"Bob didn't have the passion you did. It must have shown in your photographs."

Boot looked at him. A backhanded compliment from Newell?

"It did show," Newell said.

"At least I was able to sway someone."

Newell pivoted his chair in line with Boot's position by the wall. "What are you doing in Concho?"

"You sound like—what's his name—Detective Ojeda."

"I'm not asking the same questions."

"What are you asking?"

"You're obviously talented and sharp. What brought you here?"

The question stopped Boot cold. It was what Newell really wanted to know. Not where were his references, or what was his previous job experience? After all, Newell was a journalist, fighting to get to the core of the story. He wondered what thrust Boot from the limelight and sent him running from the east coast?

Boot drew another cup of water. It didn't matter why he was in Concho. He was here and intended to revive his career, and now he needed to help find an arsonist. The rest was none of Newell's business.

The phone rang on the conference table, and Newell picked it up. "Yes. ... This is Newell ... Good."

Boot walked to the window. The buildings in Concho followed the river. Terra cotta roofs reflected the sun, but the stunted skyline rarely challenged the sky. It reminded Boot that he better reach for what was close at hand. He needed to deal with the situation as it stood, instead of how he wanted it to be.

"He's still here," Newell said. "I'll tell him. ... Can I call you later?"

When Newell hung up, he eyed Boot for a while without speaking. "That was Manuel Ojeda."

Boot dropped his cup in the garbage and sat down. "What did he want?"

"He thinks that printing the arsonist's sketch might be a good idea."

"Hooray," Boot said flatly. He suspected Ojeda's intentions. "I guess he came to his senses."

"You certainly voiced your opinion on the matter."

"I had to say something."

Newell jockeyed his chair wheels back and forth on the carpet. "You usually do have something to say."

Boot shrugged.

"I accept your input," Newell said. "It's forthright, but when you write an article for this paper, the editor gets the final say."

"It's no different anywhere else."

"Keep it in mind."

"Are you trying to tell me something?"

"I'm leery of having you write for me, but as I see it, there's no one else to follow this story."

"Are you offering me a job?" Boot felt tired and impatient—the essentials of a rotten mood. In his current state, the offer seemed comical.

"Let's call it a trial basis."

"Hold on. I've been on trial all summer."

"This is a job. I'm offering you a job. Your primary responsibility, your only responsibility, is this story."

"You're kidding me?" Boot braced himself for the punch line. There had to be some unacceptable condition attached.

"This story is right up your alley. I've seen your work."

Amen, Boot thought. This was real. Newell was actually opening the door.

"You've got more guts than most of my staff," Newell said. "Either that or you're off your rocker."

"You won't be sorry. I'll ..."

"Do me a favor. If you really are nuts, don't tell me."

Boot let Newell ramble. A minute earlier, Boot wanted to vomit on the conference room table, but now his headache lifted.

Newell backed away from the table. "I hope I can survive ... No, I hope the city can survive Boot Means in print."

CHAPTER 12
SOLD OUT

By the weekend, the August heat subsided to a low sizzle. Boot toted his camera into Lee River Park. He spotted two men standing in front of a box for *The Concho Democrat*. The SOLD OUT sign hovered in the glass window, and one of the men was reciting lines from the front page. Boot had seized the headlines for three days straight. He paused to eavesdrop on the conversation.

A black man opened the paper and shook the pages flat. "It says they're combing through older fires. He might have started them too."

The second man wore a cowboy hat with a broach of feathers. "Yup, somebody's setting the buildings on fire."

"He looks like a regular dude to me."

"I heard they don't even know his name."

"I've got one—sick bastard?"

"That's about right. Did you see that brush fire yesterday?"

"Outside town?"

"You think it was him?"

"I'm sleeping with my bat. If he tries it with me, I'll smash his head like a watermelon."

Boot pulled away, savoring the raw power of newsprint. The arsonist may have lit the fires, but Boot's words aroused the commotion. He noticed the news box across the street. It was empty like the others. Shep Newell probably regretted not hiring him sooner.

With a fresh roll of film, Boot walked into the shady trees along the river. Thick bandages bound his hands like mummy paws. He expected to merely point and shoot. He wasn't looking for prizewinners, just wasting time before seeing Jacki. They'd planned to meet at the park and go to her studio for another round of slides and whatever else she suggested. He didn't need to guess. They'd already made love several times there. Her passion ran deep, almost too much to handle, but he found a way. He began entertaining those crazy thoughts a man got when he found a woman who pushed his buttons the right way.

Boot walked along the edge of the park. The oaks and a smattering of mesquite trees gave way to lush rolling lawns. He climbed a grassy hill and viewed the footpath that wove through the park. The crushed red stone trail overflowed with contestants for the Annual Goat Cook-Off, and brightly colored stands and smoking barbecues lined the path.

From up high, Boot smelled the hickory choked grills and strange sweat meats. His brain finally settled with the idea of cooking goat. When he'd first heard of the festival, he believed it was a trick played on greenhorns, like a snipe hunt or a prank phone call. He quietly balked at the stories, until he noticed the billboards arriving in early summer. People traveled from across Texas to flaunt their skill at spicing, frying, and grilling the hairy horned critters to perfection. Every town had its quirks, and right then, he started to believe in Concho as a place all its own.

He descended into the throng, aiming his Nikon at a woman preparing goat kebobs. She waved a skewer of dripping meat. Boot snapped a picture and nodded. The meat seared to the grill. The pungent odor of cooking goat spit into the air.

"A dollar for a sample," she called.

"No, thanks." Boot passed by her. He scanned the next set of booths. He craved a larger animal, searching for his first glimpse of Jacki Rush.

The stones on the path crunched beneath his feet. He spied on the celebration in his old way. He stalked the crowd, stealing portraits at random. He held to the fringes, careful to not draw attention. He wanted to keep the poses natural.

In the next clearing, he spotted his main subject of the afternoon. Jacki weaved through the crowd. She wore jeans and a shiny olive shirt with a wide collar. A judge's ribbon hung from her chest. Her appeal was even stronger in person: smart, sexy.

He raised his camera. She held a plate of ribs, fanning the steam toward her nose. He imagined her without clothes. She clung to him after sex, as if time ran short and little else mattered. Undressed, some women became less of themselves, hiding from their lover's gaze, embarrassed, but Jacki's spirit soared in bed, more and more each time. He'd discovered this trait and encouraged it. He believed he owned that change in her.

Stepping off the path, Boot walked behind a row of booths for the rib competition. He remained out of sight. Jacki sniffed the meat with her fantastic nose and scribbled on a clipboard. She dipped the rib into a cup of sauce. He aimed his camera between two stalls, catching her biting the rib to the bone. He pressed the shutter release. Perfect.

He noticed the sun in her hair. She'd dyed it blonde, at least a much lighter shade of brown. It made her brown eyes look darker. Her lower lip became more pronounced with the aid of deep red lipstick. A surge of desire swelled inside him. They were going to make love as soon as they reached her studio. He already planned his first move. He'd whisper something outrageous in her ear, a suggestion or bawdy request. She'd respond.

Jacki sauntered through the competition. Boot quietly matched her steps. She smiled at the next competitor. Her lips parted, and he squeezed the camera trigger. He made a note to find this image later in the developing trays, but you never knew how things were going to turn out.

Boot checked his watch. Almost an hour remained before the scheduled rendezvous. He circled onto the path, hearing the stones beneath his heels again. Jacki sampled another rib, the juice streaking the fold of her mouth. The crowd opened up, and he bent to one knee to get the shot.

A young girl tugged Jacki's sleeve.

Boot got to his feet and stepped toward them, thinking of his first words.

The girl looked to be about ten years old. Boot judged the aloof demeanor of a child edging into womanhood. He studied her face, finding something familiar about her nose and mouth.

Jacki put aside the plate of ribs and adjusted the clasp in the girl's straight brown hair.

Boot paused. Jacki knew her. She was related.

He stepped closer, watching their lips move, picking up words and phrases.

The girl said 'mommy' several times, and he stopped short.

The crowd screened his view, as people darted across the trail to patronize the booths. Boot stepped backward, nearly bumping into several people. He felt too near to Jacki, the proximity stifling. He ducked beside a hundred year oak among a cluster of trees. His camera fell to his side. He'd been the one stalking. The game belonged to him, but he felt altogether spun around, as if the game was stalking him.

The girl left Jacki, pushing through a group of boys in line for the ring toss booth. She stuffed an empty soda can into a green oil drum. A woman giggled in the background. The girl looked around, setting her sights on the open lawn.

Boot watched her run. Her tan legs cut like scissors. The white soles of her sneakers flashed beneath her paces. She raced across the lawn to where the Barbados sheep roamed on display for competition.

Onlookers lined the temporary pens, listening to the judge talk over the babble of sheep. The people seemed engrossed, all except one man and the tallish teen-aged boy beside him. They kept their backs to the fence. They were tracking the girl—Jacki's girl—across the lawn.

Boot knew before he needed to be told. He felt numb. She can't be. Jacki never mentioned it. He wanted to disappear inside the tight stand of trees. He hated spying like this but felt compelled to finish. A dozen questions shot through his brain, forcing him to watch.

Up on a slight incline, along the slated-fence of the sheep corral, Boot saw a small family assembling. The girl fell into her father's arms, laughing. The parent and child looked up and waved their hands at the crowd milling below.

Boot studied Jacki's reaction, calculating her moves: the tilt of her head, her arm rising in the air. She waved back at the family, her family.

He turned away and cut a path for the sidewalk. *Get out of here. Don't be caught with that look on your face.* A rotten feeling swept through him like the cusp of a bad dream. He'd certainly awakened from a dream. Why didn't he see this coming? A quality woman like her didn't stay available for long. How could he believe she was unattached? He recalled snippets of past conversations. Had she told him? Had she dropped clues?

The crowd thinned on the street. Boot kept walking, breaking into the open spaces beyond the park. Sometimes he was so stupid. He didn't want her to see him surprised. He had to be wiser than that, but a single feeling that haunted him. How dare he ask for more? Everything he'd ever lay claim to was already in his pockets.

CHAPTER 13
CAPTURING THE SUNSET

Boot sat on a bench across from Jacki's studio apartment. There were smarter places for him to be in the city, but he needed to hear her speak. He wanted an incredible excuse to blot out his anger.

The sun slipped behind a single cloud in the sky. Jacki brought her Lexus to the curb. Boot saw no one else in the car. She rose from the driver's seat and stood in the street, expecting Boot to join her.

He watched her tan legs fidget on the pavement. He raised his Nikon by instinct, capturing her perplexed look.

Jacki crossed the street. "We were supposed to meet in the park."

"I didn't want to cause a scene." He drew a tight close-up through his lens. The sadness returned to her face. Her eyes shifted downward, as if she expected trouble, a far cry from the confidant woman he'd seen in the park.

"I told you I'd be finished by three."

"I know."

"I'm sorry. Everyone at LeMaxxe is expected to volunteer for the festival."

"I'm not talking about that." He dropped his camera in his lap. "I'm talking about your family."

She slid her hands in the rear pockets of her jeans. Her big collar flipped in the breeze.

"Why didn't you warn me?" he asked, not really a question.

"I didn't expect them to come. They never come."

"That's not much of an excuse."

"There wasn't any time to phone you."

"What would you have said?" Boot heard the umbrage rising in his voice. Damn her. She wasn't offering any reasons. She seemed downright cavalier about it. Was it over now? Was he just a fling to her? He didn't know her as well as he thought.

"Do you want me to say they don't exist?"

"I've never been in this position."

"Never?"

"You sound surprised." He wondered if he would have slept with her anyway. She seemed to sense that about him. He'd spent his whole life breaking rules to keep his head above water, always picturing a moment where he no longer had to cheat. Now he understood his anger. She held a mirror to him. He was angry with himself.

"You're annoyed with me." She checked the sidewalk to see who approached. A woman with a dog trotted past, and Jacki waited for the noise of the leash and paws to trail away. "This isn't my habit either."

"That's your excuse?"

"You want explanations?"

"I just wished I knew ahead of time."

"I assumed you knew something."

"I forgot to check your ID, and you don't wear a wedding ring."

"I made a point of not talking about my personal life. I assumed that tipped you off. You seemed so on the ball."

The conversation stalled. Jacki scanned the windows of the apartment buildings along the street. Boot studied her angular face and the curve of her hips and legs. Painted toenails poked from new saddle leather sandals. She was beautiful but not his. That's the feeling that gripped him in the park. She was everything but his. He realized how much she'd gotten under his skin.

"Let's go inside," she said. "We'll talk."

"We can do it here."

"I thought you didn't want to make a scene?" She offered a hand, which he refused to accept. "Come. I'll try to explain."

Boot stood up and walked. It was further than he wanted to go, but he followed her inside.

When they reached the second floor studio, Jacki left the lamp off, drawing the curtain from the window instead. The afternoon sun filled the room with a warm orange glow, and she stepped near an easel with a half-finished painting. Moist black and red oils swarmed over a gessoed canvas.

"Your hair is blonde," Boot said.

She curled a lock in her fingers, conjuring a smirk. She glanced into Boot's eyes, admitting she'd dyed it for him. That's what he hoped. That's what he read on her mind, but whatever she thought, she kept to herself. She wandered into the kitchen and poured two glasses of scotch.

Boot waited in the kitchen doorway, watching her bang ice cubes from the tray. She tossed the empty tray in the sink harder than he expected.

Jacki handed Boot a glass and then took a belt. "I knew we'd have this conversation one day."

"Why not up front and let me decide?"

"It's not the kind of thing I've done before."

"Do I look like a pro?"

"I apologize for what I said in the street. You're different than I'd first guessed."

Boot thought she'd pegged him pretty well. His bad attitude and failing integrity made him ripe to become a rich woman's toy. He'd never noticed it before. No, they'd sized up each other just right. "Did you expect me not to care?"

"I thought you were more spur of the moment. You're younger than I supposed."

"How old did you think I was?"

"Low thirties, maybe. It doesn't matter. You carry yourself like an older man. You're hard to figure."

"I'm twenty-six, and you're ... ?"

"Thirty-six." She swigged from her glass and sat down. "I'm an old broad."

"Hardly," Boot said. She was smart. She was enough to handle in bed. When they were together, she poured a ton of attention on him. He felt like her legitimate partner, which turned out to be an illusion. Most of the lies that went down between them were told to him by himself.

He glanced at the couch where they first made love. They'd done it on the floor and the old mattress in the bedroom too. Geez, they really went at it sometimes. He took a seat beside her, allowing more distance between them than he might have hours ago. "This is weird for me, being with a woman like you."

"What's that supposed to mean?!"

"I've known guys who did this sort of thing, constantly searching for a good time. I just never saw myself as one of them."

"You're not."

"Look at me. I'm fooling around with someone's wife. I'm on her payroll. What does that make me?"

"What does that make me?"

"It's just the facts."

She shot a look as if forged by the ice cubes in her glass. "Don't judge me."

"I'm not judging you."

"Sounds like you're judging everyone. I didn't want a relationship, alright?"

"What do you call this?"

"I didn't want to get involved."

He wanted an admission from her, something to salvage the day. If he was only a fling, he'd button down his feelings and disappear. "We're involved, I think."

"What do you expect from me?"

She went to the kitchen and refreshed her drink. He watched her move. She looked the same, but he felt torn between two separate paths: the place where they once thrived and the opening void in which they tumbled.

When she sat down, she looked calmer. Scotch can do that for some people.

"Tell me about your family," Boot asked.

"You want to know everything?"

"Yes."

"Is this necessary?"

"Then keep talking in circles."

She swirled her glass and sniffed the scotch. "Remind me to never pick up a journalist again. They ask too many questions."

She leaned forward and grabbed his knee, inviting him to take her in his arms and scrap the confessions.

"I want to hear about your family," he said. "I want to know where you come from."

"Where I come from?" She withdrew her arm, closing down with the request.

He knew what he was doing: dissecting her like a fresh news story. He was going to destroy everything. He'd pull her apart and look at the pieces.

Jacki curled her legs onto the couch and leaned into the corner by the sofa arm. "Alright, you're going to hear it."

Between sips of scotch, she told him that her husband Jim owned a garden and landscaping outfit. Jim worked long hours, like she had as a fledgling professional. Hunter was seventeen and learning to drive, and Tammy was eleven, going on twenty. She released the details like a true mother. A father tended to boast. A mother defended her family members at all costs.

"I saw your daughter at the cook-off," Boot said. "She reminded me of you."

"Hunter looks like me."

"I wasn't that close to him."

"I'd gotten pregnant with Hunter in college. That's where Jim and I met."

"When were you married?"

"Sophomore year. We moved into a place near campus."

"How did you swing that?"

"Jim dropped out and started working for a landscaper, and I left the art program. Art suddenly became a luxury. One day I was discussing Jackson Pollack and Picasso, and the next, I had a screaming baby and loads of statistics homework."

"It's a big change."

"My friends drifted away, and my art dreams went down the tubes."

"That's how life got in the way."

"What's that?" She peered at him over the edge of her glass.

"That's what you said when we first met."

"Your memory's like a sponge, and here, I don't know anything about you."

"You know enough."

"I know you're younger than I thought, and you have a father you hardly speak to. That's about it."

"What else do you need to know?"

"You're the one who started this inquiry. Tell me all about Boot Means."

"I'm a photojournalist. I worked for a couple of papers."

"No, what's a baby from the east coast doing in Concho?"

He didn't approve of her thumbnail assessment, but her sassy, forward attitude was what first attracted him. "I'm asked that question a lot lately."

"Then you should know the answer."

"I'm here because I'm broke."

"Come on," she said. "No one in their right mind comes to Concho to seek their fortune."

"I have family outside San Angelo."

"And ..."

"I don't know who they are." He felt stupid saying it aloud.

"I thought you knew your father."

"I barely know him. I know my brothers even less. They're half brothers actually. We don't speak."

"Why not?"

"We only met last year."

"That's bizarre. I don't believe it."

He saw that he needed to explain it all. "My mother left my father and abandoned me in New York City when I was a baby. I grew up in foster care. That's why we're strangers."

"What's your mother say?"

"She's dead. I never met her."

She studied him as if another person had just showed up in his place. "That explains a lot."

Boot wondered if he'd provided another excuse for her to disregard him. He didn't want to make it easy. He'd thought of saying he was the son of a congressman or doctor. He'd told that lie plenty of times to gain access to places that refused him.

"Why don't you speak with your family?" Jacki asked.

"I can't say."

"Why not?"

"We're from different worlds."

"What's that have to do with it?" She drained her second scotch. "Do you know what I think?"

"You're going to tell me, aren't you."

"I think it's your fault. I think you're stubborn."

"Thanks for the advice." A nerve twinged between his shoulders. She made a lot of sense. The way she read him, they could've made a neat couple.

"Your situation makes my problems sound simple." She looked at his glass. "You hardly touched your drink."

"I didn't come here to get buzzed."

"Why did you come?"

He allowed himself to gaze into her eyes—soft brown ovals beneath blonde bangs. His desire for her remained, tainted with the facts. "I wanted you to say you weren't married."

"That's honest." She raised her glass to her mouth, noticing it empty. "But that's not the way it is."

"I know." He concealed his most important reason for coming. He wanted to ask if she could love him, if she'd considered it already, but their dialogue appeared permanently severed from those questions.

"Jim and I were thrown together by circumstance."

"What about now?"

"Time passed with Hunter and Tammy. I spent a lot of the early years getting my career off the ground. I was making more money, and with children, that's important."

"You look like you did well."

"But I botched the mother part. Jim practically raised them. He's better anyhow."

"That can't be true."

"Hunter hates me, and Tammy tolerates me. I spend as much time away as I can. They're better off."

"It's really none of my business." He watched the sadness assume her face, like a shade being drawn. He finally understood it. Most people envisioned their lives as a straight line to a specific destination, while they navigated through their lives by random acts, suddenly awaking to view the crooked trail that led them astray.

She gingerly held his bandaged hands. "This happened at the last fire?"

"Yes," he said, glad to change the subject.

"I read about it in the paper. You never called me?"

"I wish I had." He appreciated the things he didn't know then.

"You can always call."

"Not like this."

"I can't afford to break up my marriage, not with the children. I can't do that."

"Did I ask that?"

"No, but I don't want to stop. Jim and I are miles apart."

"It's not my business."

"We don't talk, and the sex, well, it was never like us, not even at the start. I had my art until I met you."

"I bet you wished we hadn't met."

"I don't. Do you?"

"I can't pretend where this is headed."

"Now you sound like a twenty-six year old."

"I mean it."

Jacki retreated into the corner of the couch. "Life's not black and white, Boot Means."

"I know. I report on it every day."

"In black and white newsprint. I think your job has hardened your perception."

He struggled to redefine their relationship on the spot, but he had no ambition to make it different. He wanted things back to the way they were, before he realized they operated on different playing fields.

"Is there any way we can talk?" she asked. "Can we still do that?"

"I have your slides to finish, unless you want to cut that short."

"My slides? It's business only then?"

"For now."

"Have it your way." She shrugged, but a false note rang in her voice. "You need to do this."

He watched her compose herself. She left the couch and moved about the studio, stopping to flip through a stack of canvases by the window. That's another trait he'd learned about her. Like him, she knew what she wanted and went after it. Was she simply counting time until he came back around? He already found her irresistible. He hoped his lust for her cooled over time.

"How about this one?" She turned toward him, holding a modern landscape in yellow and blue. The two colors blended in a multitude of shades, like the badlands at sundown.

He took a closer look. She'd captured the moment that the limestone escarpments came alive, a feat he'd never accomplish with black and white film.

"It's the Balcones," he said.

"Have you been there?"

"Once." He'd taken a footpath to the bottom of the canyon, and for a time, he got lost among the crenulated rock formations. He wandered through the fragrant huisache, worried about the hidden rattlesnake lairs. The wonderful, dangerous terrain resembled no place that he'd seen before. It was similar to getting to know Jacki. He hoped that he walked clear of this maze too.

She rested the painting by her feet. "It's for your father's birthday."

"I can't afford it."

"It's a gift."

"I can't take it."

"I figure you haven't found a present yet."

"No."

"I'm guessing you can't afford much either."

He wanted to laugh. She was right on the money again. He let her keep talking. It felt good to think about something else.

CHAPTER 14
WORKING THE TRAYS

S ome people meditated. Others took long jogs. Boot Means disappeared inside his makeshift darkroom and worked the trays. Black curtains blocked the kitchen door, and the smell of warm developing chemicals teased his nose. He felt invulnerable in this dark cocoon. Time stopped. Night and day no longer existed.

Boot soaked the film of Jacki's artwork in developing solution. The timer softly ticked on the counter. With color slides, he worked in total darkness, struggling with the exact position of the trays. He preferred not to process color positives, but the only lab in town had ruined prints from the first batch. He feared another mistake, followed by the inevitable trip to Jacki's studio to reshoot. He needed to wrap up this assignment and place her in his rearview mirror, even though it was the last thing he wanted to do.

In the dark, his thoughts returned to the smothered kids on Harp Street. Since the start, their images haunted him. Now the boy on Armada joined the pair. A screaming boy fixed in his memory, not a child at rest like the brothers on Harp.

Boot forced his memory past the final moment on the fire escape. He recalled lying in the ambulance, watching the boy's mother at a distance. She clung to a police officer. Her robe hung open, her knees bloodied from repeated falls on the asphalt. The loss of her son sapped the strength from her legs. Boot shut his eyes. He begged the ambulance driver to leave before she spotted him.

He reached for the kitchen light switch. He wanted to scatter his thoughts but knew the light would ruin his film. He grabbed the edge of the counter. The timer ticked in the dark. He felt paralyzed until the bell rang.

The film waited for the wash and rinse. Boot transferred the film, bumping his wrist on the counter. The simple touch of the bone reminded him of Jacki. As he left her, she'd grabbed his wrist to kiss him goodbye. He wanted all of her, not one part, not some token from a friend. He turned away, and she let go. It felt clumsy and strained. She got the message.

He let his thoughts linger on Jacki for a while, relieved to abandon the dead boys in another part of his mind. Jacki afforded him that option. She was candy for the brain. She'd arrived at an intense crossroads in his life, creating a beautiful distraction. Now, he felt sorry for her. She was trapped in an empty marriage. He didn't have cash or much of a career, but he expected to move on. He had options. Her choices seemed more difficult.

The air conditioner in the living room hummed louder than usual. Boot flicked up the kitchen switch, able to finish the film by normal light. He let his eyes adjust to the neon tubes on the ceiling. He needed to transfer the film to the color developing solution. More rinsing. More chemicals. The real tedium of the process lay ahead.

He shook the tray. A copy of Saturday's *Democrat* sat on the counter to his left. He studied his edited words in print. Newell kept on top of him, toning down his prose. Boot didn't mind. He'd adopted a sensationalist style in Trenton. His words in the

Democrat read more pure, the kind of writing he'd learned in college.

His article for Sunday created another issue. He'd milked the facts dry, and it showed in his submission. Even though Newell front-paged it for the fat Sunday edition, Boot needed to scramble. He'd let his investigation stall. Messages from Gally piled up on the answering machine. A couple of leads languished in his notes. For days, he'd chased Jacki instead of his story. Perhaps what transpired today was all for the better.

He eyeballed one of her art slides—a body form sculpture of clay and bits of iridescent desert stone. She had a knack for the absurd. She'd shrugged when he said it was over between them. She was audacious, and it irked him. Her claws were sunk in deep, and she knew it.

Putting down the film, Boot glanced up and shook his head. That's when he saw it. A gray haze blanketed the ceiling, although it only made sense when he smelled the smoke.

A jarring sense of panic gripped him. He tore the curtain from the doorway. An acrid cloud billowed into the room. He stepped backward, thinking he might retreat from it, but it followed him, consuming the narrow space in his kitchen. His back thumped the wall.

Boot crouched to the kitchen floor. A strange mechanical groan emanated from the living room. The phone was ringing too. He squinted his eyes, peering through the doorway. He saw no flame or bright reflections on the walls. He coughed, inhaling the smog with metered breaths.

The lights dimmed. His escape routes—the front door, the window above the air conditioner—dissolved into an ebony shroud of darkness.

He crawled through the kitchen doorway, slamming his head on the clunky wooden end table. The sharp edge nicked his scalp, and he started to bleed. He coddled his head, cursing.

The floor felt warm and dusty. He tried not to breath. Bits of ash gathered on his lips. They caught in his throat. He heard a pop, as the mechanical groan sputtered and ceased. It left behind the eerie crackle of fire consuming plaster, wood, and paint. He felt nauseous and ready to choke. He needed to find the door.

He pulled his T-shirt over his face and slid forward, clawing the carpet like a dog. The phone started to ring again. He dragged his hand along the wall, feeling for the corner leading toward the entrance. The smoke was incredible, and he shut his eyes against the burn. His tiny apartment never seemed so large.

When he reached the door, he tested the metal with his fingertips. It was cool to the touch. He collected a single breath and rose to his knees, gambling on the hallway outside. He threw the deadbolt, turned the knob, and fell through.

The hallway looked clear, at least what he saw through the uneven emergency floodlights and his slits for eyes. He doubled-over and vomited in the corner. Black smoke rolled over the doorframe, setting off the smoke alarms down the hall. His neighbor stuck his head outside the door and quickly ducked back inside.

Boot heaved some more. The retching took hold, an involuntary reaction whipping through his core. His palms throbbed as he braced himself above the floor. He couldn't stop from getting sick. He crawled a few feet and heaved again.

Startled residents evacuated the building. He saw the woman and kid next door. The couple across the hall skipped past. No one except the kid paused. He dropped a toy elephant, but his mother yanked him by the arm and into the parking lot.

Boot watched the door swing open and closed. Stars hung above the nearby homes. Gusts of fresh air bathed his face. It was now or never. He found his feet and staggered outside.

Sirens and flashing lights jammed into the parking lot. He escaped the barrier of smoke, gasping for air. He coughed and spit.

His knees went weak, and he collapsed in a small patch of grass by the parking lot.

When the smoke cleared, Boot sat on the bumper of a fire truck with a plastic oxygen mask strapped over his face. He breathed steadily. The nausea subsided, but he thought he'd never purge the smoke from his lungs. It was the second time in a few weeks and all he ever wanted in one lifetime.

Black soot stained the building above his apartment window. He saw the air conditioner. It looked charred and melted, the metal housing imploded around the machine's heavier components. He'd made the lucky choice by finding the front door instead of the window.

Gally stood on a step stool and peered inside the wasted air conditioner with a flashlight. He'd already pried off the back. Boot watched him jump down and approach the fire truck.

"Got some air in your lungs?" Gally asked.

Boot nodded. Anything felt better than dry heaving on the lawn.

"That shit runs right through you," Gally said.

Boot pulled the mask down and tested the air. He coughed.

"Take it easy." Gally patted his back. "It's going to take a couple of days.

"I never want to do that again."

"If you start liking it, I'll get you a fire coat and helmet."

"My smoke alarm didn't go off."

"The battery was disconnected."

"I put a fresh one ..." Boot looked at Gally, not wanting to finish the thought.

"The A/C was rigged, a nice job too. It's gonna smoke when it's hot-wired like that. Carries a lot of amps."

"Geez Gally, he didn't get into my place, did he?"

"Looks that way."

Boot searched for any excuse to deny the facts. "I keep the door locked."

"I suppose that would stop him." Gally mustered sarcasm in any situation, a flaw really. Boot imagined Gally standing over his own mother's grave uttering something acerbic.

"How do you know it was our torch?" Boot contended, but he remembered the phone ringing and shuddered.

"You're upset." Gally combed his hair with his hand, even though it didn't need it. "Let's piece this together."

Boot pushed the mask over his face. The pure oxygen sated his lungs.

"You're in the phone book," Gally said. "You're findable."

Boot nodded. Most journalists preferred it, not wanting to hide behind their words. In practice, Boot had garnered more than one decent story lead by standing in the open. Now, he questioned the sense of it.

"There's a bright side to this," Gally said. "He didn't want to kill you."

Boot failed to see the consolation in getting smoked-out in the middle of the night. What if he'd been asleep? He knew the answer to that.

"That's my theory," Gally said. "I think he wanted to scare the bejesus out of you, and by the look of you, he did."

Boot slipped the mask off. "So he's made his point."

"Are you certain he didn't contact you?"

"My phone rang."

"He's called you before. We'll check the phone records."

"Don't expect much."

"He's angry at you."

"Does your theory have a reason for that?"

"He didn't like you publishing his sketch. Maybe he didn't expect it. For shit's sake, he thinks he's smarter than God."

Boot didn't know what to say to that.

"He still needs you," Gally said. "There's no logic here, only a pattern to his methods. This fire has his signature all over it."

"You can't be wrong?"

"He's a clever son of a bitch, and for whatever screwed up reason, he's chosen you to be his voice."

"So as far as he's concerned, I've misbehaved."

"I bet that sketch looks too close to the real thing."

"I was thinking that too."

"I can't imagine a better reason."

Boot paused on that point. He remembered telling Gally how he planned to shake things up. He'd asked for this, and in a way, he was exactly where he needed to be—a little too close perhaps.

Gally grinned. "Maybe he thinks he looks better than the picture you drew. Maybe that's the reason."

"This is no time to joke."

"I wish I had something more."

Boot removed the mask and slid off the back of the fire truck. He coughed several times, but he knew he'd be fine. A thickness pervaded his chest, like jogging in the cold. If he got to work, he'd get passed it.

"He's stalking me," Boot finally said.

"In a way, and I'm not comfortable with that."

"I don't know what to do about it," Boot said but was already thinking that he might use it to his advantage. If the arsonist was able to find him, he might backtrack that path. It was the oldest trick in the book. He just didn't like serving as the bait.

"You can't stay in your apartment."

"That's a given."

"You can return in a few days. Your clothes and furniture are going to smell like beef jerky forever. That's for sure."

Boot glanced at the camera bag sitting by his feet. Gally had retrieved it as soon as the smoke dissipated. Beyond his trade tools, he needed little else. "I'll be okay."

"You need to get away."

He hesitated to admit that this story was the best thing he had going, perhaps the only thing.

"Didn't you say your father lived on a ranch somewhere?" Gally asked.

"That's one hundred miles from here."

"That's far enough."

"Too far."

"No, it's a good idea."

Boot never saw this side to Gally. It caught him off guard. "You and I are the only ones who know what they're doing on this case."

"That's true."

"And you asked for my help."

"I did."

Boot realized he'd gotten too tight with Gally. The marshal was a public source, someone Boot might use to gain an edge. Boot needed to keep that relationship straight.

"I'm staying," Boot said. Running to daddy's ranch was not an option. "I can't turn my back."

"I expected you'd say that." Gally combed back his hair. "Where are you going to stay?"

"Tonight, I don't know." Boot saw the pink sky forming at dawn. "Tonight's done with anyway."

"How about my place?"

"Is that the best idea?"

"Probably not. I suppose we can take it day by day."

"I'll think of something."

"You sure? It's an open invitation."

"I can take care of myself." Boot considered his options: the youth hostile, Jacki's studio by the park. She'd let him in.

"Well then, let's get some eats and a drink. I know a place that serves all hours."

"I was thinking about coffee and maybe some eggs."

"I'm buying."

"Sounds even better."

"We can canvas the neighborhood this morning."

Boot agreed. He was exhausted and scared but didn't know what else to do. He determined to keep his feet moving. When all else failed, he knew to do that. It made for a harder target to hit.

CHAPTER 15
THE BARRIO

After a few beers and a plate of eggs and grits, Boot walked down Harp Street in an old Mets cap and leather jacket with the collar yanked up to his neck. The rain poured down. A surprise storm arrived like a sneak punch, marking the start of the rainy season. Boot's eyes were bloodshot, and the scent of ash lingered on his clothes. He let the water wash over him and drench his soul.

Gally walked along side in a rubber coat, boots, and a chipped yellow helmet. He was not only fireproof but waterproof too. "It's hard to believe what's happened to this place."

Boot squinted his eyes, trying to picture the neighborhood in a better light. The old palatial homes were neglected. A few had barbed wire fences. People called this The Barrio, because of the crime and high number of Mexican boarder jumpers. Boot rarely mentioned that he lived around the corner.

"This used to be the place to live," Gally said. "There were doctors and bankers, not to mention the high brass from Fort Stead."

"How long ago was that?"

"Before your time."

122

"It looks like it."

"The illegals trashed the neighborhood."

"You mean the Mexicans."

Gally gave Boot a funny look. "That's right."

"There's not much you can do about it." Boot coughed into his freshly bandaged fist. His lungs felt like he'd inhaled photographic chemicals for days.

"They hate us here," Gally said. "They hate a man in a uniform."

Boot understood Mexican Law. He'd learned a few words of the language and chained every moveable part of his motorcycle down at night. The Barrio recycled everything. Nothing went to waste.

"Deport them," Gally said, "and they'll be back again next week."

"And in between, nobody gets their lawn cut or house cleaned."

Gally only stared back, like the thought hadn't occurred to him.

Boot wanted to change the subject. The marshal's logic confounded him. Everyone wanted a chance to step up the ladder, rich and poor alike. The Barrio residents guarded the bottom rung of society. Without them, Concho's disapproving eyes shifted to Boot's kind—the easterner without firm attachments.

"Where do we start?" Boot asked.

"Here." The rain dripped off Gally's helmet.

"On your list, which house do we visit first?"

Gally pulled the tip sheet from inside his jacket. It was a list of people who claimed to spot the arsonist but more than likely wanted a claim of the five thousand dollar reward. Most of it was garbage, but no one complained. Before Boot's articles in the *Democrat*, the list was empty.

"Number Seventy-two," Gally said.

"Have any of the sightings panned out?"

"Not yet, unless Homicide's holding out on me," Gally joked, but Boot wasn't so sure. Ojeda and Ancrum worried him. They possessed a clear set of rules, while Boot often found himself on the sharp edge of the law. What would the cops think of him tagging along with Gally?

"So they're checking the other leads?" Boot asked.

"They have the east side, and I took the Barrio. I thought you'd know your way around."

"I do, but do they know that?"

"You mean, did I tell them you were coming?"

"Yes."

"Not actually."

Boot eyed a series of homes behind a rusted cyclone fence. He imagined the Bario as a great place to hide. "Most of the homes are divided into cheap rental units. There might be hundreds."

"You mean hundreds of firetraps."

"It's not a bad place for the torch to get lost."

"No."

"I think you got the better half of the list."

"I'm not as stupid as I look." Gally swung open the metal gate to a pink stuccoed house. "This is the first one."

Boot tailed Gally to the front door. Roses bloomed in bright flower boxes, and the porch looked swept clean. Boot checked the homes on either side. One was boarded up and abandoned. The other had a mangy ankle-high excuse for a lawn.

A petite woman answered the door. She wore a white cotton robe with roses embroidered around the neckline. She was old, and the skin on her neck and wrists sagged over her bones.

Gally showed his badge, hardly necessary in his fire getup. He presented the arsonist's sketch and spoke a few words in Mexican.

"I've seen him," the woman replied in English. Her accent sounded refined, the odd combination of two dialects, north and south of the border. She talked quickly, letting them know she'd lived north for many years. "You have the eyes wrong."

Boot removed his camera from his jacket and joined Gally on the porch. "What's wrong with the eyes?"

She waited for Boot to flip a badge or ID.

"What about the eyes?" Boot asked again.

"They're more round and shifty."

"It's hard to show shifty eyes in a sketch."

"He's looking right at you. The man you want never looks you in the eye."

"He looks past you?"

"Never at you."

"We'll take it up with the art department." Gally tucked the sketch in his jacket. "Ma'am, where did you see him?"

She pointed a bony finger to the home across the street. "He comes in and out of there."

Gally tipped his helmet. "Have a nice day."

As they crossed to the opposite sidewalk, the rain slowed. Boot watched Gally stop mid-stride. The marshal put his nose in the air, turning toward the house beside their last interview. A thin screen of smoke rose from the backyard.

"Crap!" Like a bloodhound, Gally sniffed out a fire, even in the rain.

Gally retrieved the fire extinguisher from the Caprice. Boot had watched Gally do this so many times that he came alongside the marshal and pulled the ax from the trunk without saying a word.

They jogged through the tall grass surrounding the unkempt house. Boot's pants grew damp and sticky. Grasshoppers clung to his jeans. "What do you think it is?"

"A fire," Gally barked.

"I know that. How bad is it?"

"You never know."

Boot stepped into a clearing in the backyard and leaned the ax upon a whitewashed statue of the Madonna. He brushed the bugs from his pants and sleeves.

Smoke seeped from a tiny window on the first floor, and a fat green garden hose twisted through the back door. Gally unclipped the two-way radio from his hip and called Second Union.

Alarms kicked in across the city. Boot listened to the station siren wind up from a dead silence. It set the morning quiet on its side, and all along the connected properties, dark heads of hair poked from nearby windows.

"I'm going in." Gally scooped up the ax and headed for the door. The marshal's helmet disappeared inside the smoke.

Boot froze. Logic said that common fires occurred every day in each city of the country, but not when Boot was present. No fire appeared like an accident any longer. The torch probably tailed him, setting aflame the buildings around him. He glanced around, almost expecting to see the man from the sketch. The tricky bastard might even be in the house, waiting to spring yet another surprise.

"What do you want?" Boot yelled to the open air.

A few dark heads along the alley retreated in their windows.

Gally called outside. "You joining me?"

Boot clenched his fists, psyching himself up. He took a deep breath and plunged inside, half-crazed with fear.

In the doorway, he covered his face with his hat. The fumes smelled unusually sweet, but the smoke shot through him. He bunched his fist, coughing into his hat.

Two men cursed in Mexican. Boot recognized the worst words. He'd learned the insults before any other part of the language.

The argument grew louder, as he followed the hose on the floor. It snaked into the bathroom, where the drizzle of running water became evident.

Boot knelt down, letting the smoke pass overhead. A sliver of daylight crept down the hall. He kept the light within view, marking his path to safety.

Gally managed the garden hose, showering the ceiling above the tub. Water dripped down the walls and over the filthy tiles. A muddy stream flowed into the hall, and grasshoppers bounced atop the soggy carpet.

The marshal was laughing. "Look at this, will you?"

Boot only stared but then shook it off and reached for his camera. If Gally was joking, things were fine. Boot felt his pulse slow. He aimed his camera and spun the lens. The click of his shutter release soothed his nerves.

The Mexicans crowded the room, brothers perhaps. They traded rapid-fire insults, ignoring the other's reply. Boot imagined them going on, while the house burned around them. Their pace didn't slow, until their mother appeared in the hallway.

Mama wore a thin polyester nightgown and woven leather sandals. She was wider than both her sons but nary chest high, inches taller than Boot kneeling down. She waddled beside him, her feet squishing upon the carpet.

"You stupid boys," she said.

Boot didn't catch every turn of phrase, but he got the gist. It was the same speech in any language, where a mother reduced two grown men to cowering fools.

When the smoke subsided, Boot got to his feet. His knees were soaked from the runoff. The brothers leaned against the wall and stared at the floor. Gally sprayed the tub.

Mama turned toward Boot, as if noticing him for the first time. "What do you want?"

He translated her question in a snap. "I'm with him." He stuck his thumb toward the marshal.

"Take a look at this," Gally said.

Boot peered inside the bathtub. "It looks like meat."

"Get closer." The marshal sprayed the smoking contents. It sizzled beneath the water. "It's exactly what it looks like."

Boot stepped to the edge, seeing a half-cooked pig inside the basin. It sat in a charcoal pit made from a split metal drum. The enticing aroma of mesquite and roasted pork lifted with the steam.

Gally tossed his head toward the brothers. "I gather we interrupted their barbecue."

"They're cooking indoors?"

"They started outside, but when it rained, they brought it in."

Boot laughed, but he caught Mama's nasty expression and sobered up. Her glaring eyes might re-ignite the room.

Captain Benjamin Sheerssen barged into the bathroom, toting a flashlight and another extinguisher. "Got it under control, Gally?"

"Affirmative." The marshal soaked the tub. "I believe we're medium to well done."

Sheerssen popped up his helmet visor. "Now, I've seen it all."

"Grab a plate. We're having a luau."

In an hour, Second Union wrapped up the fire. Forms were filled out, the squad cars left, and Sheerssen lectured the brothers while keeping the straightest face possible. As a precaution, the half-cooked pig ended up in the cabin of the fire truck. Boot imagined roast pork for Sunday dinner at the station.

Boot stood with Gally and Detectives Ojeda and Ancrum. The homicide cops looked as spiffy as ever. Ojeda wore a red silk tie and onyx cuff links. Ancrum donned a silver iguana pin on her lapel.

A pair of fighter jets from Fort Stead thundered above the clouds. Boot stepped away from the group, but Ojeda kept staring.

"Morning, Mr. Means." Ojeda's disdain simmered beneath the rumbling jet engines. "I see you survived last night's ordeal."

"Just call me lucky," Boot said.

"I've noticed your luck of late. Wherever you show your face, there's a fire."

Boot sloughed off the implication. "It's my job to be where things happen."

"Ours too."

Gally twisted the heel of his patent leather shoe in the asphalt, crushing a plump spider in the road. "I asked Boot to join me."

Ojeda fished for a reaction from Boot. "I was just noticing the coincidence."

"Then notice this," Gally said. "We've got a legitimate sighting across the street. A woman ID'ed the man in the sketch."

"No kidding."

"Means is coming with us."

"You think that's wise?"

"Nobody's wise here. If somebody was, we'd have more than bit clues."

"Yes, but ..."

"He knows this case as well as anyone."

"I'll leave," Boot said. Things were shaky enough between him and the Concho PD. Later on, he'd pump Gally for information.

Gally latched onto Boot's sleeve. "Hold on. If these two don't want to look at you, they can leave."

Boot watched the men square off in the street. No doubt, he needed to leave. He'd be the only loser in this match, but Gally flashed his angry dog look, and Ojeda folded his arms, clutching his own elbows.

Detective Ancrum was watching too. Her glance darted between the men. She threw her hands from her sides, like a basketball referee fed up with men scuffling on her court. "I don't care."

Ojeda stared at her

"I have no problem with him staying," she said. "We need to pool our resources."

"I don't trust him."

"You don't have to trust him, as long as he keeps out of the way." She stepped in the direction of the house across the street.

Boot almost forgot why he followed Gally to Harp Street in the first place. He saw Ancrum move, seizing his chance to join her. She was the friendliest member of the bunch.

Ancrum led them across the street. Ojeda muttered beneath his breath, and Gally relished the victory. Boot kept a smart distance from everyone, waiting to see how things panned out.

Their destination was a boxy three-story home with an ornate roofline like an old railroad flophouse. The lawn was patchy and weak, and the shrubs grew wild around the foundation, blocking many of the windows on the ground floor.

Ancrum found the superintendent's apartment. The super peered through the slit in the door, until Ancrum flashed her badge.

He was a heavyset Chicano with crescent-shaped eyes that looked unnaturally weepy. He jiggled a souvenir coffee mug with a silver imprint of the Alamo. "I don't know nothing about the fire."

Ancrum displayed her copy of the arsonist sketch. "Does he live here?"

The super appeared irritated by the intrusion. "Not anymore."

"Where did he go?"

"If I knew, I'd collect last month's rent."

"He skipped on the rent?"

"He was real smart about it. He moved in three months ago, gave me the first and second up front; then skipped the last."

"Didn't you see his picture in the paper?"

"So?"

"Why didn't you call the police?"

He sipped his coffee. "You gonna collect the rent for me?"

Ancrum glanced at Ojeda. "Lovely."

It was comical to Boot how unhelpful people were until you appeared in their doorway, and then they gave up almost any information to get rid of you.

"When did he leave?" Ancrum asked.

"Three days ago. I don't know. A week maybe." The man scratched his thigh. "I don't keep tabs on the tenants."

Gally stuck his chin above Ancrum. "Can we see the apartment?"

"Whatever you like." The super removed a key from a series of pegs by the door and tossed it to Gally. In another neighborhood, people phoned lawyers and asked for search warrants. In the Barrio, people knew the cops were coming in anyway. "Don't break anything."

"I'd like to see the rental application," Ancrum said.

"What?" the super replied.

"You're supposed to have one on file."

"I've got it."

They checked the records first. The rental agreement was signed by Johnny Smithenson. The information looked about as useful as Boot's overdrawn credit cards, except the banks knew where to find Boot. The torch remained an enigma.

Boot saw the super's dispassionate expression. The super lost a month's rent and looked to fill the space with the next Johnny Smithenson who knocked on the door. As far as Boot knew, half the people in the house went by Johnny.

"At least he didn't use John Doe," Gally said.

Boot laughed but only a little. The cops, with their expensive clothes and rarely used handguns, failed to see the humor. Boot buttoned his lip, not wanting to rub the defeat in their faces. He'd picked up a bad habit from Gally. The marshal rubbed everyone's face in it.

They gathered outside the suspect's apartment. They didn't expect to find Mr. Smithenson at home. Ojeda unlocked it and threw open the door.

They entered a three-room apartment with more space than Boot's. He cautioned behind the others, stalling inside the doorway. His heart raced like it did outside the previous house fire. Was this a booby-trap? He glanced around the doorframe, searching for wires or suspicious devices. Before the Concho fires, he took every light switch and appliance for granted.

"What's with him?" Ojeda asked.

Gally recognized that Boot was spooked. "Leave him alone."

The marshal took a step toward the door. "Boot?"

"I'm going to leave the door open," Boot said.

"That's a good idea," Gally replied without sarcasm. "You want to wait here in the hall?"

"Give me a second."

"Take what you need."

Ojeda flicked on the light with a pencil. A drab collection of mismatched furniture filled the room. A tattered futon with a floral print, a yellow armchair, and an imitation wood coffee table appeared strategically pushed against the walls. They sat equal distances from each other like a display in a thrift shop.

Ancrum ran her index finger over the armchair. "He's very neat."

"Either that or cautious." Ojeda disappeared into the bedroom.

"I bet he's anal about being clean," Gally said.

"We'll try to lift prints anyway. Don't handle anything." Ancrum headed into the kitchen.

Boot followed her. He wanted to fish around too, a habit since his early reporting days. During interviews, he sometimes snuck into kitchens on the pretext of a drink of water and sifted through the cabinets and refrigerator. He discovered a lot about people by the food on the shelves or the stuff jammed into the junk drawers. Once another journalist questioned this habit, and he replied, 'take a look in your own place and see.'

Ancrum pried open the refrigerator without touching the handle. She stuck her head inside.

Boot glimpsed a partial sack of potatoes and a near empty ketchup bottle. "What's the date on the milk?"

She spun the carton around. "It expires on Tuesday."

He noticed Ancrum wore a hair comb with a Gila monster etched on the broad metallic spine. "We published his sketch on Thursday. He may have been here until then."

"I was thinking the same thing."

"I guess the newspaper scared him."

"But it led us here."

"I hope there are fingerprints." Boot wondered if it mattered. He was starting to believe that the torch had no police record, nothing beyond his compulsion to burn that created distinction. His sketch proved it—no scars, no funny nose or eyes, nothing for people to latch onto. "I hope we get a name."

"Galloway doesn't think we will."

"I've heard him say that."

"No one's been able to locate a history on this guy."

"It's like he's just getting started."

"That's an awful thought." Ancrum opened the cabinet. Assorted papers piled atop the shelf. She hoisted herself on the counter, a delicate procedure in a suit skirt, but she brought her knees together and swung her legs around.

With her back turned, Boot spotted the electrical service panel embedded in the tile work. He thought to look inside and see if the torch had rigged the circuits.

Ancrum knelt on the counter, unloading the papers from the cabinet. "Look at all this stuff."

He stepped around the detective and eased open the metal door to the panel. He used his left hand just in case a nasty surprise waited.

A picture postcard fell out, descending to the floor like a falling leaf. It landed by his feet, face down. He immediately recognized the arsonist's handwriting.

"Looks like magazines and newspapers. He's a pack rat." Ancrum held her back to Boot. The cabinet door screened her view. She hadn't even seen Boot open the service panel. "There are brochures from the commerce department too."

Boot squinted to make out the script on the card. It was addressed to him. He imagined the cops mumbling about yet another personal letter. Was the arsonist trying to make him look bad?

He glanced at Ancrum. She still hadn't noticed it on the floor.

"Is there something in the very back?" Boot said. "Some food or supplies? Old mail or anything?"

As Ancrum buried her head in the cupboard, Boot snatched the postcard off the floor. He stood up, seeing Ancrum's skirt and the gritty soles of her shoes. He tucked the postcard in his jacket. He didn't trust the cops to decipher it, much less tell him what it said, especially if Ojeda got his hands on it.

Ancrum pulled back from the shelf and knelt over the pile on the counter. She flipped through a bimonthly magazine covering the state. Copies of *The Concho Democrat* sat beside her.

Boot heard Gally and Ojeda ransacking the next room. He felt self-conscious about the postcard, but if it spoke about the future—his future—he needed to know.

Ancrum held open the magazine for Boot to see. The article showed an aerial view of Concho. "Research."

"He's got a thing for this town."

She slid off the counter. The lines around her eyes went smooth. "I keep wanting to think this isn't real."

"I know what you mean."

"We had to cover all possibilities. We were looking for other explanations."

"This is what it is." Boot coughed into his fist. He recalled his apartment full of smoke and the dead boys on Harp and Armada. Like a sheet of photo proofs, he harbored a gallery of terrifying images. Capturing the torch might erase them all? He needed to read the torch's latest set of instructions.

"I know this is real," Ancrum said. "We wanted to be certain."

"I don't blame you."

She folded the magazine in her lap. "You seem like you've been through this before."

"Nothing like this."

"I know this isn't your fault."

He barely listened. He was so busy guessing what the postcard said that her statement caught him off guard. "Excuse me?"

"I don't think you asked to be caught up in this."

"Well, I hung around the fires. I was on assignment."

"You don't have to explain."

"Some people believe I ask for trouble."

"Not everyone at the precinct thinks you're a troublemaker."

"You guys give me more credit than I deserve, either way." Boot noticed the electrical service panel wide open. Police evidence was stashed in his jacket. He nervously tugged up his zipper an inch or two. *Be reasonable. Don't give it to her now. She'd never understand.*

"I just wanted you to know," she said.

"Right." He let his hand drop to his side, trying to act natural.

"Are you alright?"

Boot glanced at his watch, but a second later, he couldn't say what time it was. "Maybe Gally's right. It's been a long twenty-four hours for me."

Ancrum scanned his face. "What are you looking at?"

She turned and noticed the opened panel. "You don't think the arsonist would do something here?"

"I don't trust him for a minute," Boot said, building a case for his jitters. "If you don't mind, I want to get out of here."

"I thought you wanted to stay?"

"It looks like he swept this place clean." He pointed at the papers. "Other than that stuff, and what is that stuff really? We know he hates this town."

"There might be a surprise in the stack."

The surprise was in Boot's jacket. He already pictured himself leaving the building. He needed to get someplace alone. He headed for the door.

Boot rode in the back seat of the No. 19 bus. For a dollar and a half, he toured the desolate business district on Sunday afternoon. Some locals hopped on and off, most not bothering to take a seat. From time to time, the bus driver eyeballed Boot in the convex mirror.

Three blocks from the Democrat's building, Boot pulled the postcard from his jacket. It was a print of Salvador Dali's 'Persistence of Memory'. Boot recognized the painting from the Metropolitan Art Museum. The surreal image of floppy watches had amused him, but it didn't make much sense. Was it supposed to now?

He ran his finger over the raised gold lettering at the bottom. THE CONCHO ART MUSEUM. He'd visited the CAM at the start of the summer, disappointed by the mundane collection of regional artists and minor works, nothing on par with Dali.

The bus discharged the last passenger, and when Boot was sure he was alone, he flipped the card over.

BOOT MEANS:

IF YOU ARE CLEVER, YOU WILL DISCOVER THIS NOTE IN TIME. START APPRECIATING THE INCREDIBLE GIFT I HAVE GIVEN YOU.

EARTH RANGER

Boot flicked the postcard in his fingers. It was another cryptic message. The arsonist operated on a level Boot didn't understand. Gally called the torch downright nuts—a compulsive freak, wrapped inside himself, concocting outrageous theories about the outside world.

The Concho Democrat building rolled past Boot's window. The bus driver studied him in the mirror. Boot yanked the overhead cord, signaling the next stop.

The brakes started to engage. Boot stood, waiting for the door to retract. He considered how he'd been manipulated. He promised himself a year ago to never be played again, but here he was, pawned off by a radical stranger and lied to by a woman that he almost loved. He cringed. People looked past him, as though they recognized his orphan background and discounted his potential.

When Boot hopped outside, he landed firmly on the sidewalk. He pictured only one solution. When no one expects much, you must deliver the knockout punch—not a bloody nick or a sting to the jaw but a knockdown blow, straight up the middle. It required defense and patience for the momentary opening that no one else saw. He was glad he'd stolen the postcard. It belonged to him anyway.

He started walking. He needed to create an advantage, although he hadn't a clue how. He touched the postcard in his vest pocket. No rules. The torch had set the tone.

CHAPTER 16
THE PERSISTENCE OF MEMORY

n a Dallas tavern, Oscar Van Hise sat in the last booth and finished his lunch. He'd picked the furthest seat from the windows, facing away from the other people and their incessant banter. His notebook lay open on the table. French fries twisted on a plate dotted with ketchup.

Oscar closed his eyes and pictured the Concho Art Museum. The CAM rose three stories from a concrete plaza. It was an art deco design with skewed floors like a stack of white shoeboxes. That was the thing that drew him to Concho—all those clean buildings and sunlight. He'd turn every one black as coal.

When he lived in Concho, he visited the CAM every day. He liked to sneak into unlocked offices and sift through the paperwork of strangers. He crept into the musty basement and studied the floor plan and equipment. He committed the building to memory, inside and out. The CAM was a blueprint of his imagination, the one thing left undone.

He felt a visceral attraction to the CAM's harsh lines and sheer glass windows. He'd walk the plaza after closing time, spreading seed for the pigeons and chipmunks near the fountain. On cooler evenings, he sat beside the trickling water and stared at the intriguing structure, unraveling the CAM's potential. Always he imagined the dark and incalculable stain of fire against the lucent geometry. It was a blank canvas that needed to be filled. The CAM was to be his masterpiece.

The open notebook on the lunch table was full of ideas and drawings. Oscar jotted down the schematic for one of his special electrical devices. Boot Means needed to understand the process. Not many people viewed the path to genius. He might be repulsed at first, but when his emotions cleared, he'd want to know. Journalists formed a relentless breed, and Oscar had experienced the worst of them. The press had dogged his family for years.

Oscar envisioned his triumphant return to Concho. He intended to arrive unsuspected at the CAM, navigating past the water fountain and stone benches. He pictured the maintenance man opening the front doors with keys on a retractable chain. The round-shouldered man wore an olive green jumper with the name 'Pete' embroidered above the breast pocket. Pete had short brown hair and a full wiry mustache that seemed to block his nose. He stepped into the CAM's shaded interior and disappeared into a stairwell.

Sunlight shined from all sides, but the interior columns and walls loomed like gray shapes through the tinted glass. Oscar watched the ceiling spotlights illuminate. He heard the circuit breakers trip in the basement. One by one, the switches clicked in his head.

He felt a rush of adrenaline. The building was armed. He had spliced his devices to the overhead light circuits. That way he'd know if a short occurred and foiled his plan. For months, he'd tested his design, perfecting the timers and remaking the heat coils, but not until he saw each floor going bright did he know for certain. His trap became a living thing. Electricity pumped through its tiny parts like blood through his veins.

The first visitors appeared at noon. Oscar saw a woman pushing a toddler in a stroller. An older couple walked hand-in-hand like a pair of teenagers. A college girl carried a red sketchbook beneath her arm. Oscar expected many more by the 1:10 P.M. deadline, yet he took special interest in the early arrivals. He'd waited a long time for each of his guests. His snare encircled them as they entered.

In tenth grade, Oscar raised white mice for the science fair. He demonstrated Darwin's theories of natural selection by gradually reducing the food and water. He used to press his nose to the glass tank, awaiting the instant when the starving mice turned and ate one of their own. They huddled in the corner: emaciated, panting, confused.

In his mind, Oscar tailed the early arrivals into the CAM's ground floor. The room smelled like astringent cleaner and cured oil paint. Pete tinkered with the broken lid of a trash can. The mother paused to hand her daughter a bottle of water. More people wandered through the doors. No one suspected a problem.

The doors swung gently open and closed. They still worked but not once fire overtook the ceilings and walls. People would claw the doors with their bare hands. A few might reach the third floor balcony, debating whether to jump to the concrete plaza. He left that decision to fate. The indeterminate path of fire would summon the predictable course of panic and refine his plans.

He toured the floors, gathering energy, sometimes hovering above the crowd. He spotted the college girl. She knelt by a Greek urn, duplicating the image in a drawing tablet. She had thin brown bangs that cupped her eyebrows. A handful of pencils poked from her back pocket. Graphite smudges stained her fingertips.

She resembled a girl that he knew in high school. He never spent more time preparing for a woman. They shared a drafting table in class. Elaine Franks displayed a knack for oblique drawings in freehand. He tried to convince her to use the straight edges, even though she got it right without the tools. They argued. He demonstrated the methods for bringing lines to an exact vanishing point, while she swept uncanny perspectives across the page. They had reached an understanding, but when he invited her to the Spring Festival Dance, she laughed in his face.

Oscar placed Elaine on the floor of the CAM. He left her undisturbed. He no longer wanted her apology. If she saw his potential—recognized his ability to draw far outside the lines—she might come around. She might adore him.

By 12:45 P.M., the CAM bustled with locals for the art show. Oscar returned to the ground floor, passing the refreshment table for the opening festivities. He saw the Levenberg's. He'd summoned them to perish inside the CAM with the others. They were still holding hands. They did everything together. They probably shared a toilet at the same time. As a child, Oscar never suspected that when he spoke to one Levenberg, he really spoke to both. Psychologists weren't supposed to behave that way, even if they were married.

After his sister Heather succumbed to smoke and flame, Oscar's parents sent him to see the Levenbergs. It was his fault. He understood that from the start. He felt vulnerable to their probes, stripped naked by their unflinching stares. Rich and Marsha shuttled him between their offices, trying to release a confession. He hated those sessions. Some weeks, he went every day—all those questions. Oscar discovered long ago that you learned the most by holding silent and listening.

The Levenbergs occupied the wine and cheese table. Rich handled a clear plastic glass, sniffing the freebie wine like an expert. Marsha nibbled on a carrot stick that matched the color of her hair. Oscar heard their snooty voices offering uneducated opinions about the art. Years ago, he'd sat on their beige corduroy couch, listening to them in the adjacent room. He brushed his hands in rhythm over the upholstery, muffling their conversation.

He refused to hear their assessment of him. The words *fetish* and *neurosis* stuck in his craw.

Today, Oscar prepared his confession—a memorial to Heather. The Levenbergs would see it in the walls burning around them and smell it in the blackened air. They'd breathe it in. It'd fill their lungs, leaving a permanent blotch on their thoughts as it followed them to their graves.

By 1:10, Oscar took position on the plaza. He tossed a handful of peanut shells to the cement, watching the chipmunks assemble near his feet. He heard the security locks engage. Electric dead bolt cylinders slipped into the doorframes, striking a cold seal.

Thirty seconds later, the security system lost power. He saw a woman trying to open the door from the outside. The party circulated within his prison of plaster, glass, and steel. The woman tapped the window and giggled.

At 1:15, the heat coils on the light circuit grew hot enough to ignite the ceiling tiles. The materials were rated for two-hour fire protection, but Oscar had sprayed the tiles with chlorine bleach and glycerin to promote the burn. He felt guilty about using an accelerant. It was akin to cheating. He convinced himself that he no longer needed to hide the facts. He'd become a celebrity in Concho, and with Boot Means on his side, they'd be searching for the details of arson. Oscar made it easy for them, scribbling his materials list inside his notebook.

Flames crawled across the inside of the walls with a life of their own, unseen by the visitors on each floor. A few sniffed the air, sensing smoke and shrugging it off. The maintenance man noticed the woman outside and rattled the door handle. He pulled the manual override near the upper right corner. The lever fell loosely down, defunct and useless. The door remained sealed like the others.

Elaine Franks descended from the second floor. Her hair and shoulders were damp from the fire sprinklers. She yelled. Heads began to turn. 'Fire' was the word they recognized, just as the first floor sprinklers engaged.

The party cowered beneath the hard burst of water, but just as suddenly, the water stopped.

Oscar clenched his jaw. He suspected that residual water remained in the sprinkler lines and gambled it didn't retard his fire. He tensed every muscle, wavering in place, until a familiar amber glow emerged from the ceiling. Beautiful flames caressed the off-white tiles, edging onto the top of the wall. He breathed easier. The transformation progressed, each floor set to burn like a candle. The occupants owned enough time to consider their brief future.

The woman on the plaza rushed to Oscar, pleading for a reaction. He stared at her—a frightened bird of a girl. Her little nostrils flared. Her hands trembled. He slapped her across the face. She ran, screaming across the concrete, her voice trailing away in flight.

Smoke assumed the better air inside, a gray mist that wafted down from the ceiling. Without windows to open, people gathered at the doors. They pressed their hands to the reinforced glass. The pinkness of flesh—palms, forearms, and knees—assembled like bugs on a light bulb. A man threw a chair, and it bounced harmlessly to the floor.

When the fire hit the kerosene pouches, they burst and sprinkled the crowd with dripping tongues of fire. Oscar heard the cries of women and children. Men screamed just the same.

He strolled closer to the windows, spotting Mrs. Tamayo huddled in the corner. She clutched her child, coughing into the toddler's disheveled hair. He was glad to see her. She deserved this. She'd accused Oscar of killing the neighborhood cats. She hadn't seen him harm a single animal, but she planted her witchy face on his family's doorstep, asserting her suspicions. She got the neighborhood behind her. It had happened before. His family was forced to move again, followed by more torturous sessions with moronic doctors.

Pete fought his way to the basement. The phones were dead, the fire alarms stood silent, and none of the sprinkler systems operated. He knew the CAM like the back of his hand, unable to believe that every system failed at once. He entered the dark stairwell, setting off after the controls.

The Levenbergs held each other, finally overcome by logic and incident. A wall with a collection of water paintings—portraits of someone's grandparents—enveloped in flames and toppled on the hopeless doctors. Marsha reached out for her husband's charred hand and burned alongside him.

People continued to stream downstairs, piling into the main hall. Smoke lifted through the stairwell like a chimney. They jammed onto the lower level, holding their breath, pushing for the foyer.

Elaine Franks was being trampled by the latecomers to the door. They clawed for the exit—the door she'd reached ahead of them. Unsatisfied at her attempt to survive, they brought her underfoot. She braced against the stone floor. The people nearby were still alive. A faint pulse showed in their eyes. A woman gasped, as men mounted her back to pound the door in vain. Elaine felt the thick heel of a boot upon her neck. An incredible weight bore down on many points of her body. Others were layering atop her. She stared at the wire spiral on her sketchbook. It pressed into her neck and cheek, perforating the skin. She hoped someone smashed the glass open soon, and then everything went black.

Below the hysteria, Pete groped the cinderblock walls, searching for the sprinkler system's main cutoff valve. He recalled the odd looking arrangement of pipes. It reminded him of a menorah, branching up into several arms. He found the vertical pipes and reached for the large knob that controlled the flow. His palm scuffed across the square metal shaft of a bolt head. He followed the pipes again, discovering the same rough bolt. It couldn't be. The knob was missing.

Pete flailed, blind and desperate in the dark. Oscar gleaned pleasure from the struggle. Oh, if he was only able to reside in a man's head as he discovered his mortality.

The trial had come full circle. In college, Pete had spotted Oscar roaming around the Materials Lab at night, and after the wiring mysteriously overloaded and caught fire, the Dean turned to Oscar with questions. Again, the world chose to persecute him. The disciplinary board amassed circumstantial evidence and outrageous claims. They quoted testimony from Pete. It was a conspiracy, designed to expel him from school.

Pete clutched his chest in the CAM's basement. It felt as if someone knotted a heavy rope around his rib cage, squeezing it tighter by the second. Before his knees hit the floor, he recognized a face emerging in the dark. He saw a young man from college. This man was someone he'd underestimated and then forgotten, a kid by the name of Oscar Van Hise.

When Oscar's coffee arrived, he shook free from his daydream. He hoped that the real fire in Concho promised the rewards of his imagination.

The waitress tapped the table to get his attention. "Sir?"

Oscar rubbed his eyes, one foot in the present and another in the future. His plans for the CAM felt so alive that he almost smelled the place burning. Fire was a strong persuader. It changed solids into gas. It wrought dreams from reality and plummeted them into nightmares.

"Sir?" The waitress tapped again.

Oscar saw his notebook exposed. He slammed it closed, shielding his words from view. In a few days, he'd return to Concho and implement his masterpiece. Then everyone will know.

"Refill?" She stood over him, holding a sludgy pot of coffee. She was young, what he sought in a woman. She had wavy long hair like Heather and smooth eyebrows. This was the woman he'd slapped outside the CAM. Her cheeks were round. Her ears were small and flush, like embossed shells upon the sides of her head.

"Th–thanks," Oscar said, daunted by her beauty.

"Would you like anything else?"

"N–no." His eyes shied away. He fumbled with the pen in his fingers. His thumb clicked the tip open and closed.

"Another piece of crumb cake?"

"No thanks, ju–just a check."

He let her leave before daring to look again. She bent over another table and filled the mugs. He tried to think loud enough so that she might hear. His perfect woman already understood his genius, without having to ask. After Sunday, he expected that woman to appear.

CHAPTER 17
SLEAZE YOU CAN TRUST

Boot sat on the couch in Jacki's studio, checking his voice mail at the *Democrat*. Newell reserved a desk for Boot at the office, but in two weeks, Boot rarely showed his face, other than to deliver fresh copy. If he closed the arsonist story, his attitude might change. He'd walk through the newsroom and take his place among the other reporters.

The first six messages echoed in the receiver. Boot skimmed through the ploys for reward money and attention. After weeks of this, he quickly differentiated between the real and phony calls. People who didn't dial the police hotline directly generated a lot of suspicion. He pressed the phone buttons, transferring the calls to the special mailbox for the Concho PD.

One woman left a message late at night. "I think I know who you're looking for. I'll call back."

Boot skipped ahead, until he recognized her voice.

"It's me again," she said. "Do you check this thing? I'm sure I can help you. Call me. Ask for Deena."

He dialed Deena at her east Texas area code. A receptionist at the Yancy Institute answered the phone. Boot waited for Deena to come on the line. He heard the sound of children singing in the distance.

"Mr. Means," she said, "I wasn't sure if you got my message."

"How can I help you?"

"I read about the fires in Concho."

Boot's stories were being picked up by other papers in the state. This might explain why he hadn't heard from the arsonist in a while. Gally and he searched the newswire, waiting for the torch to resurface.

"What do you have?" Boot asked.

"I know who you're looking for. I mean, I know who knows."

"Could I have a name, please?"

"Come see me in person."

"Where are you?"

"Austin."

"That's a long haul for me."

"Not for me."

He took down her information, and as soon as he hung up, Jacki entered the apartment. She carried a white bag and paper cups. She stopped by with breakfast, each morning on her way to the LeMaxxe building.

He watched her open the bags, smelling the fresh sugar twists and coffee. "You don't have to keep doing this."

"Do what?" She wore a smart peach suit with a short skirt and a scarf with a Roman print. She hadn't finished putting on her makeup and jewelry, not that she needed them.

"You don't have to keep bringing breakfast," he said.

"We both have to eat."

"I guess." He went to the kitchen counter and grabbed a twist from the bag.

She came beside him. "Try my scent. Come on, smell."

He barely heard her. He bit into the twist, thinking about Deena in Austin. He expected the long drive on his motorcycle to punish his injured hands. He'd have to take a lot of breaks. Too many painkillers was risky with only two wheels on the road.

"Hello?" She nudged him. "Indulge me."

"Huh?"

"It's brand new, just out of the lab."

He noticed that she'd arched her neck. He bent over to sniff the small depression where she dabbed her perfume. "What's it called?"

"Purple Sunrise."

"The name's stupid."

"It's a working name. It won't last, if I have anything to say about it."

He gobbled down the twist and walked to the window, not wanting to stand so close to her. A lot of issues needed to be sorted out: his feelings for her, the lack of material for his arsonist story, and a nameless torch lurking in the shadows. His brain gridlocked for a minute.

Jacki followed him, clutching her coffee. "What's going on?"

"Nothing."

"You're miles away."

He wanted to tell her to stop acting so casual, but he told her about the phone call from Austin instead.

"Austin?" She sipped her cup. "Are you going?"

"I have to. I've got nothing else."

"Austin's nice this time of year. I can recommend a good restaurant."

Jacki retreated to the bathroom to put on her makeup. Her reflection shifted in the mirror.

Boot sat on the couch and unwrapped his hands. He pulled the gauze pads from his palms. The second-degree burns looked red and puffy. The worst parts started to bleed. He gazed at the parallel lines of blood beading on the surface. They matched the spots where his skin touched the searing hot bars on Armada Road. So he'd always be reminded.

Jacki hovered over him. "They don't look so good."

He quickly brought his palms together, conscious he might drip on the floor. "They're better than yesterday."

"They have to hurt."

"Only when I use them."

She watched him mop up the blood and press on sterile gauze pads. "You're not thinking about riding your motorcycle to Austin?"

"How did you know?"

"You can rent a car."

"What's the difference," he said, but the cost was another factor. His slim paycheck from the *Democrat* barely kept him afloat. He appreciated Jacki letting him use her studio to sleep, and it was hard to beat the rent.

He started wrapping his hands, careful not to bind them and start them throbbing again.

"I can't stop you?" she said, fishing.

"Why should you?" He stared at her. She needed him out of her life. Why didn't she see that?

"I was thinking."

Boot looked away. Those words from a woman aroused his concern.

"I was thinking." She laughed out loud, as if knowing he'd step on any idea. "I have a lot of vacation time saved up."

"I know what you're offering. You think that's smart?"

"Is riding your cycle with those hands smart?"

Boot saw that she'd already made up her mind. Besides, she wasn't bad company in any respect. "I'm out of smart ideas."

"Then it's settled."

They drove southeast, away from the city to where the western plains end. Boot sat in the passenger's seat, watching the scrub swell into topaz heads of maturing corn and then rising into lush clusters of trees. The cabin of the car filled with Jacki's experimental perfume and the swagger of B.B. King on the CD player. He let the cool ambiance cloud his worries, glad to gain distance from Concho.

The Austin skyline scaled the horizon. Boot knew the city by reputation: a bigger and smarter version of Concho, the capitol city that Trenton intended to be but never reached. He felt disconnected from this big stretch of earth called Texas. The more he saw of it, the more he knew he belonged somewhere else. The west boasted confidence and space, while the east wanted grit and elbowroom. He envisioned himself back in New Jersey, uncertain of how or when he'd get there.

When they reached downtown, Boot waited in a hotel lobby for Deena to show. He sat in the furthest corner, sipping sugary lemonade. He popped a painkiller to keep his mind off his hands.

A large-hipped woman in a peasant dress passed from the sun into the placid air conditioning. She wore a billowy shirt, attempting to mask her husky frame. In New England, they'd call her a sturdy woman. In Texas, they might say she possessed girth. Boot immediately sized her up as fat and dumpy.

Deena locked onto Boot right away. "Are you alone?"

"Yes." Boot glanced through the revolving door. Jacki disappeared inside the art gallery across the street.

"I don't want this to get out," Deena said.

"What don't you want to get out?"

"Us meeting like this."

"No one knows I'm here." Boot understood Deena's type. He'd dealt with sneaky people before. Most arrived with pockets full of trouble. "Why don't you have a drink and tell me your story?"

"I don't have a story. I have information."

"Please. I've come halfway across Texas to see you."

They sat on the lobby couch, making small talk about Austin and the sights to see. Boot ordered more lemonade—hers spiked with bourbon. Deena was a huge Willie Nelson fan, and the popular singer lived somewhere in town.

Boot studied her voice. He didn't rush his subject, mimicking her lingo and cadence. "Do you want another drink, Ma'am?"

Deena checked her watch. "It's almost dinner time. That might be nice."

Boot signaled the waiter to refresh the glasses.

"You're so nice," she said. "I'd never guess you weren't from Texas." She pronounced Texas like an easterner said taxes.

"It's easy to see why." Boot focused on Deena, not even smiling when he spoke. He found himself able to lie with sincerity, a skill he'd acquired with practice. "I've taken to this part of the country."

"You have."

"I don't mean to head you off, but perhaps we can discuss why we're here today?"

"I've let my tongue wag, haven't I."

"The conversation's been interesting."

"I couldn't believe the terrible things that man did in Concho."

"We've had a spell of bad luck."

"And those boys. My sister sent me your articles." She shook her head, glancing at Boot's hands. "I read you were at the fires."

"I try to put it behind me."

"I can imagine." She stopped herself. "No, I can't."

"Can you help us find the arsonist?"

"I saw something interesting at the Yancy."

"That's the institute where you work."

"Yes."

"What kind of things do you do there?"

"I work with special kids."

Boot figured she meant the mentally retarded or deaf—something like that. Teachers in her line of work tended to get snippy when asked to classify handicaps. "What did you find at the institute?"

"There's a woman there. She's had a history with your firebug."

"Did the arsonist spend time at the Yancy?"

"I doubt that."

"What makes you think she knows him?"

"I can tell by the look on her face."

Boot studied Deena's mannerisms: the steady bead to her eyes, the clear focus of her words. She sounded honest, seemingly convinced of herself, but that didn't always add up to a reliable testimony. "What did you see?"

"I was talking about the fires with a friend at lunch, and this one woman in the speech department started asking questions."

"What kind of questions?"

"What happened? Who did it? Did they catch him?"

"Did she seem curious or nervous?"

"Real curious, but once she got a look at the picture in the paper ..."

"The sketch of the arsonist?"

"Once she saw him, she clamed up. I never saw such a scared look before, and I've seen a few things. I've seen kids at Yancy who come in terrified."

"Anything else?"

"Later on, I caught her bawling in the ladies room. I tried to ask her about it, but she clamed up even more."

"What do you think it means?"

Deena leaned back against the sofa, propping her arm on a pillow. "Have you ever seen a ghost?"

"No, Ma'am."

"This woman saw a ghost. I asked her about the fires, but she didn't want a hair of the conversation."

"She shut you out again."

"This woman's sweet as this drink." She turned the glass. Pieces of lemon twirled in the mix. "She was burned real bad as a kid. I think your firebug had something to do with it."

"That's a mighty big assumption," Boot said, although he considered a similar possibility. He sipped his lemonade, keeping his hopes from flying high. If he uncovered the torch's background, it might lead in a hundred new directions. It certainly filled pages of newsprint down the road.

"What makes you so certain?" Boot asked. "Maybe she's just scared of fire."

"When she got up from the table that first time, she whispered, 'it's him.' I didn't get it right off. I looked at the door and thought somebody was coming in, but there wasn't anybody."

"She meant the sketch in the newspaper."

"Had to be it. She had a far off look about her, a far off scared look."

Deena piqued Boot's interest. For weeks, he'd poked and prodded the story, waiting for someone like her to drop out of the tangled mess. He remembered his training. He needed to discover her motivation. His first editor had taught him that: find an informer's reason for talking, and you know everything you need to know about them, both good and bad.

Boot finished his drink. "I have only one thing to do."

"Talk to her."

"But she's not going to like that."

"No."

"You might pave the way for me?"

"Mister, I don't even want her to know that I told you. I have to work there. It's a good job."

"I appreciate your phone call. What's her name?"

"Before I tell you, let's make something certain."

"Ma'am?"

"She never learns it was me who told you."

"That's why you called me instead of the police."

"You have me right, Mr. Means. That's part of it."

"Tell me how and when I can find her."

"I said that was part of it."

"What else then?"

"Yancy is a great place to work, but I could use a little more."

Boot read her right away, partly relieved by her new tone. Her aspirations for cash were as honest as any he'd known. "You mean the reward money."

"Yes."

"I don't give it out."

"But you can lead me to who does. You can make certain I get credit."

"Okay, Ma'am. You have a deal."

CHAPTER 18
BLINDFOLD

Boot and Jacki drove to the Yancy Institute and parked outside. A Gothic brownstone structure sat amid a sprawling lawn. The huge building had a slate roof with red and white inlays and elaborate details along the ridge. It looked like a lord's manor in the medieval countryside.

"Who are we looking for?" Jacki wore a sleeveless shirt. Her bra showed beneath the scooped opening as she reached to yank the keys from the ignition. A collection of silver and turquoise bracelets jangled around her wrist.

"Kate Womack," Boot answered. "She's supposed to work here."

"What is this place?"

"It's for special kids." Boot watched a group of preteens in blindfolds. They fumbled about the grass, picking up sticks and rubbing them in their hands.

"They look like they're on a scavenger hunt."

"I suppose."

"But it looks weird. Maybe they're geniuses."

"Maybe."

"Do you want me to come?"

"No, thanks." He noticed the sun heading for the hills outside Austin. He wondered how Jacki planned to explain her late arrival at home. "I'll move faster without you."

"What time is she expecting you?"

"Any minute." Boot feigned a look at his watch. He'd tried to arrange an interview by phone, but as soon as Miss Womack discovered his purpose, she hung up.

"So there's no exact time?"

"Now is good." Boot reached into his camera bag and removed two pages of photographic proofs. He folded them once to hide the images.

"Are you sure you don't need me?"

He opened the car door and placed his foot outside. "You better wait here."

Inside the grand foyer of the Yancy Institute, Boot was stopped at the security guard post. "I'm here to see Kate Womack."

The guard had razor burns along his chin. He scratched his face, as he flipped through a black binder. "She's not expecting you."

"No?"

"If you're not in my book, she's not expecting you."

"There must be a mistake." Boot leaned over the binder, trying to look perplexed. "I've come all the way from Concho."

The man glanced at the paper in Boot's hand. "Do you want to leave something for her?"

"I must do it in person."

The guard shut the binder and walked to the office. Boot watched from the mission bench near the door. A glass window separated the receptionist from the foyer. She handled the phone, eyeing Boot behind the glass, but as soon as all eyes shifted away, Boot slipped out the front door and jogged to the back lawn.

The kids were taking off their blindfolds, standing in a rough circle. A shapely woman with sandy blonde hair held her back to Boot. He ducked behind a hickory tree, before the children noticed.

The Yancy towered above Boot like an old-fashioned prison. If Kate Womack was deep inside, he'd never reach her. He thought about phoning Deena and putting on the pressure, dangling the promise of the cash reward. He might squeeze some cash out of Jacki as a down payment.

The guard marched around the building. Boot turned nonchalantly, walking as fast as possible without breaking into a run. He heard the guard calling after him.

Boot wove through a brief stand of trees, discovering another group of kids. They stood in a creek at the bottom of a gully, milling aimlessly in the ankle-high water.

He crept behind a tree by the creek. A girl stood close enough for him to whisper. She wore black shorts and a yellow T-shirt. She faced the sky, swallowing mouthfuls of air like a bird at feeding time. A teacher mumbled orders in the background.

"Hey kid," Boot whispered.

She didn't speak, staring up at the sun. The water rippled over her bare toes. A collection of shoes lay on the mossy stones beside the creek.

"Hey kid," Boot said louder. He began to think the kids were slow, although they held none of the visible distinctions.

"I can hear you," she said, without looking. "I'm not deaf."

"I need some help."

"No kidding. You don't belong here."

"Do you know where Ms. Womack is?"

"Lurch is going to get you."

"Who's Lurch?"

"The security guard. He's coming over the hill."

Only after she mentioned it did Boot hear the guard approaching. The man's change rattled in his pocket as he mounted the top of the slope. He swung his head, searching for Boot.

"Where is Womack?" Boot asked.

"Over there." The girl pointed her arm back up the slope. She still hadn't turned her head away from the sun.

Boot saw the head of the sandy blonde woman on the lawn. "The blonde lady?"

"I guess so."

"With long hair?"

"Yes."

"Thanks, kid." He stepped away, splashing his foot in the creek. A handful of kids flinched, but none of them looked, although the teacher locked onto Boot.

"Excuse me, sir," the woman said. She wore jeans rolled up to the calf, wading in the creek like the others.

"Sorry," Boot replied.

A few children put their arms down, as Boot splashed the water again. He suddenly realized that none of them could see. They were blind. It was his noise that alerted them.

The girl in the yellow T-shirt stared past him. "You're screwed now."

The guard was coming down the hill.

Boot ran, sprinting for the blonde woman on the lawn. His photo proofs flapped in his hand.

He saw the blonde rise from the circle of children. "Ms. Womack? Kate Womack?"

She twisted around, alarmed by Boot's rapid approach. The kids in the circle, blind as the others, perked their ears. They heard Boot, and they recognized the guard rattling behind him. They appeared ready for an exciting conflict to begin.

Boot closed within ten steps of Kate Womack. He wanted to get to the point, before the guard caught up and shut him down. He saw her watching and uttered his first words; then he noticed her face and stopped cold. Deena hadn't warned him. She'd mentioned burns, but this was much worse.

"What do you want?" Kate's face was scarred, especially the right side. Old burn damage marred her eyelid, cheek, and nose. Her right ear was partly screened by hair. The lobe appeared melted to the side of her head. Smooth white patches of skin swept over these spots, denying her intended form. She posed as an incomplete sculpture, as if the artist began to work the clay and abandoned the project.

She glared. Boot felt ashamed of his cold curiosity.

"Alright, wiseguy." The guard grabbed Boot's arm.

Boot focused on her eyes—her most normal feature. "You have to speak to me."

"She doesn't want to." The guard tugged Boot backward.

"My name's Boot Means."

"You," she said. "I told you to leave me alone."

As the guard bent Boot's arm, the photo proofs fell from his hand. A series of shots from the Harp Street and Armada Road fires settled on the lawn.

Kate stared down at the images of the dead boys and gutted buildings. There wasn't anything pretty about those either.

The guard twisted harder. "Come on, pal."

The pain resonated in Boot's hands. He kicked the pages closer to her feet. "Look at them."

She bent down, retrieving a proof page in each hand. Her gaze never left the ugly little snapshots.

"Keep them," Boot said. "I know them by heart. I carry those images in my head."

"That's enough." The guard struggled to lead Boot away, but he caught a glance of the pictures too and stopped.

"It's his doing," Boot said. "It's what the arsonist does."

When Kate looked up, the anger was erased from her face. A more complicated emotion infused her expression. "Why are you doing this to me?"

"We don't even know his name."

"Oscar." Her tone resided between a declaration and a confession. "Oscar Van Hise."

They sat in a side room off the lobby. The guard rambled in the hallway about a television show. On the walk over, Boot had tried to make the guard comfortable. He passed his business card and talked about the *Democrat*. Sometimes his entire job involved getting people to feel at ease.

The tiny room held cartons of copier paper and printed Yancy Institute brochures. Boot smelled the new paper and dust.

"Oscar did this to me." Kate Womack lifted her hand near her face. Even at this late stage, it seemed too much for her to touch.

It took most of Boot's willpower not to stare. He opened his note pad, concentrating on the woman behind the scar tissue. He knew what it was like to be judged for reasons beyond your control. "How do you know Oscar?"

"I used to be the family baby sitter."

"When was this?"

"Thirteen years ago."

"What happened?"

"He lit the house on fire."

"Do you know why?"

"He wanted a new bike."

"A bike?"

"It was called an Earth Ranger."

Boot looked up from his pad. He pictured the arsonist's signature and those chunky block letters. He wished Gally were here. "Earth Ranger?"

"That's correct," Kate said.

"Can you speak about the circumstance?"

"I'll try."

He watched her tensing up. Her arms and shoulders pulled together. This woman knew more than anyone. He decided to draw her into his confidence. "I'll tell you something important. The Concho police made me swear not to reveal it."

"What is it?"

"He's been signing his notes with the name, Earth Ranger."

Her chin dropped. "So it's finally happened."

"What do you mean?"

"I knew it was that boy all grown up. I saw his face in the paper."

He thought about faces and how hers matured beneath the scars. "He's retained a boyish look."

"But nothing's further from the truth."

"Yes."

"My father had the right idea. They should've put him down like a dog. It's what you do with wild things."

He listened to her merciless tone, surprised that a woman of her profession manifested such spite, but in the same sense, he understood it. Oscar Van Hise drove people beyond their limits.

"Daddy tried it, you know."

"To get even with Oscar?"

"Daddy was arrested for assault. He went after Oscar with a baseball bat, broke his collarbone, missed his head by inches. It wasn't assault, Mr. Means. I know my father. He was trying to kill him."

"Naturally."

"We didn't even suspect Oscar at first."

"Why not?"

"Why should we have?"

He saw her anger flare. Her fingers gathered in her lap, kneading the hem of her flowery dress. He sensed a moment of strength and decided to jump into the details. "How did it happen?"

"We were living in Dallas. I was asleep in the Van Hise house, downstairs on the couch. Oscar's parents were at dinner."

"And the fire started."

"I woke up in the dark. There was smoke everywhere. I ran upstairs to get the kids."

"Who else was there?"

"His younger sister Heather."

He scribbled this down. "Was Heather hurt too?"

She let go of her dress. "You don't know anything about him, do you?"

"No," he said plainly. "Any detail will help."

Kate closed her eyes. Her strange eyelid folded in place like a crinkled sheet of foil. "The fire spread through the back of the house. When I reached Heather, her room was in flames, and I wrapped her in a blanket."

"How old was she?"

"Four or five. I couldn't find Oscar. I started to panic. It was dark. Heather wasn't even conscious. She was already limp in my arms."

"Did she make it?"

"I tried to get her out. I bumped into the walls. I don't remember how we caught fire. It was everywhere, on my clothes. It felt like a warm hand on my neck. It's funny. You don't feel it right away."

"And Heather succumbed to the smoke and fire."

"Yes, while I only wished I had." She showed a remarkable balance of fear and contempt, and when she opened her eyes, she noticed the bandages on Boot's hands. "What happened to you?"

He hesitated to tell her. "I had an accident."

"Burns?"

"Yes."

"I can smell the silver cream."

"It has a unique odor."

"Was it him?"

"It's just my palms." He regretted phrasing it that way, although she seemed to draw courage from his response. He wanted to keep the dialogue on her.

She twisted her neck, revealing the blotchy skin that disappeared into her mock turtleneck. "The scars go all the way down. I spent months in the burn unit. They didn't think I would survive."

He scanned her face like a bad photo proof. Most photographers developed the skill to compensate for mistakes. From another angle, with her head and body turned, Kate Womack was beautiful.

She dared him to look closer, seeming to enjoy his keen attention. She scooped her hair behind her right ear. "You see this?"

He viewed the curvy blob on the side of her head, defying its natural form.

"The doctors built me a new ear," she said. "It feels like rubber to me."

"But it works."

"It does what an ear's suppose to, like my eyelid does what it's suppose to, like my mouth and face."

Boot put the brakes on this lurid discussion. He saw no use. To fix a bad image, a photographer needed to take another picture, but in Kate's case, he might shoot one hundred rolls of film, never finding one that hid the errors. "Where was Oscar during the fire?"

She let her hair fall beside her cheek. "He got scared and ran outside."

"Did he call the fire department?"

"Yes, but his story didn't add up. Children make lousy liars."

"He's gotten better at it, I'm sure."

"My father hired an investigator after the fire department and police stopped the case."

"Why did they stop?"

A smooth fold of skin collected near her cheek. "He was a minor. His parents kept the police away from him."

Boot shook his head. Oscar went scot-free, while Kate remained with her wounds, and she dealt with the worst parts every day, in the eyes of each person who shied away from her.

"That was insane." He became a lightning rod for her contempt. He wanted to avenge her scars. She represented the victims on Harp and Armada in all but one essential way. She was still alive.

"They protected him," she said. "He got away with it."

"It's hard to believe he did this for a bike?"

"The month before, the neighbor's house caught fire, and Oscar alerted the fire department. The people inside were saved. The fire department gave him a plaque. It made all the papers."

"He was a hero."

"That's why he lit his house on fire."

"He wanted the attention."

"He believed if he saved his family, he'd get the bike he wanted, the Earth Ranger."

"How did you learn this?"

"The police figured it out. Oscar piled paper scraps and sawdust on the tool bench in the garage and rigged up a toy—one of those sparking guns."

"Clever kid."

"He didn't expect it to get out of control. That's what the police believed, and it took Daddy a long time to discover the facts. The police sealed the files."

"To protect the minor."

"My father hired an investigator—an ex-cop. He found his way into the files, and once Daddy knew, he wanted to kill the animal."

Boot listened to the details fall into place. Oscar Van Hise fit the arsonist's profile: early trauma, followed by a vicious cycle of shame, paranoia, and rage. If Boot dug into Oscar's past, he expected to uncover a pattern of drinking, gambling, or even animal torture. Gally had laid it all out for him. Ultimately, a pyromaniac returned to fire, which was where they found Oscar, the young adult with a very bad habit to fill.

"How old would you say he is today?" Boot asked.

"Twenty-two? Twenty-three? I don't really want to think about him in those terms. If he were a dog, he'd be dead of old age. I'll feel better when that happens."

"Where do you suppose I might find him?"

"His family moved to Fort Worth. After that, we lost track. It was better for Daddy. Daddy never fully got past the fire. He saw it every time he looked at me."

Boot stood up to leave. He'd garnered enough information from Kate—Oscar's story, his name—but moving forward, she appeared as lost as everyone else.

"If I need more information," Boot asked, "can I call you?"

"You know, Daddy's investigator predicted this."

"What exactly?"

"Oscar would burn again."

"It makes perfect sense."

"I've tried to forgive him, but I live in a house without mirrors."

He noticed that she donned several rings on her fingers but lacked an engagement or wedding ring. He guessed that she hadn't done so well in that department. "You don't have to forgive everyone."

She got up and shook his hand. It was the first time they'd touched since meeting. She glanced at the guard in the hall and brought her sights back to Boot. She refused to let go of him. "If you find him, I want you to call me."

"I promise."

"I want to face him."

"You do?" You don't, Boot actually thought to say, but he let her make her stand in this quiet place away from the trouble in Concho.

"He needs to see me." Her grip surprised him, pinching his wounds.

He pulled back. He didn't have the heart to tell her the truth. She was a woman who understood her tormentor as a misguided child. The grownup version of Oscar Van Hise didn't care what she thought about him. He might even revel in her pain. "I'll do my best."

"That's all I ask."

CHAPTER 19
FREETAIL

Boot and Jacki sat on the terrace of a Tex-Mex joint within sight of the Congress Avenue Bridge. They sipped frozen margaritas, recounting their day. Mariachi music and the smell of freshly grilled tortillas teased their senses.

After the waitress refreshed their drinks, Boot told Jacki about Kate Womack.

"That's awful," Jacki said.

He'd spared no detail, confiding in Jacki for the first time. He marked the arsonist's trail back to the first fire. He felt relieved to share the story with someone not in the business of catching Oscar Van Hise.

"The man is utterly horrible." She scrunched up her lips and lifted her icy glass. Moist rings stained the glass tabletop. "That's it. I'm not letting my children downtown until this is over.

He looked away from her when she said that. A dark cloud emerged from beneath the Congress Bridge. Hundreds of Mexican freetail bats swarmed over the river at dusk. They moved in organized confusion, culling the air for mosquitoes.

"I need to find the trigger," Boot thought aloud.

"A trigger?"

He found her beautiful face. "I need to find the specific things that make Oscar want to burn. Otherwise, I'll be chasing one fire after another."

"You think he'll set another? It's been almost three weeks."

"It's only a matter of time." He watched her shudder. He'd told her too much.

"I don't know why you're doing this. Let someone else find him."

"You follow a story. You get involved."

"I admire your dedication. If I'd stuck with my artwork since the beginning, who knows where I'd be today."

"You'll get there."

"Not like you. It's clear you know how to work any situation. You have that confidence."

When it came to her, he wasn't sure about anything except his attraction. A woman like her could have any man—the pick of the country club circuit. A line might form around the clubhouse to kiss and not tell. He admired her even more for not choosing those men over him.

She dug in her purse for her cell phone. "I have to make a call." She gave him a funny look, before Boot got the point. They weren't making it back to Concho tonight. She needed to call home.

"I can take a walk." He took his glass and wandered through the bar. He assumed she made excuses about prolonged business in Austin. He'd known Jacki for two intense months. She'd made calls like this before and now he understood why.

When he returned, their food sat on the table. A blackened metal plate held searing hot strips of steak and peppers. The waitress set down a covered basket with warm tortillas, along with another round of drinks.

Boot felt a tad drunk. He knew he was mixing pills with booze and didn't care. "Everything Okay?"

"Sorry about that," Jacki said. The mention of her family often strained their conversation. They managed the rough parts with vague words like them, him, and her. "They're Okay."

"Are you sure?" Boot asked.

"Yes." She stopped rolling a tortilla and gathered her fingers around the stem of her glass. She held her drink at a slight tilt, just gripping the edge of sobriety. "What is it you want to ask me?"

"I was just wondering."

"I feel guilty enough, lying like this."

He was willing to let the subject drop, until she said that, like he'd forced her to lie. "You didn't have to bring me to Austin."

"You needed help."

"But ..."

"But what?"

"Nothing."

"What is it with you? Can't you just say thank you and leave it be?"

"Thank you."

She smacked her glass on the tabletop.

He chuckled. They resembled a married couple, except for the sex, which Boot desired more than ever. He needed that connection. He wanted to know what it felt like to be her husband, to understand that after everything she was coming home to him.

"What's so funny?" Jacki bristled.

"Nothing."

"Stop saying that."

"I was thinking how screwed up everything is."

"Oh, you're talking about work again."

"I mean us."

"Us?"

Boot egged her on. He liked it when she got fired up. Her eyebrows twitched. Her back went rigid. She was ready to fight.

"You can't say this is normal," he said.

"What do you know about normal?" Her reply sizzled like the meat on the tray before them.

He laughed, which steamed her more.

"You're the only orphan I know with a family," she said.

"Good one."

"That's screwed up. You're the one who's abnormal. You can't even ask for help when you need it."

"Jacqueline, look who's talking."

"What does this have to do with me?" She grabbed her drink and took a swig.

"Okay, sneaking around on your husband is normal."

Her hands shook for a moment. She pursed her lips and tossed the contents of her glass at Boot's face.

He shifted aside, getting the balance of it on his sleeve. If anything, he knew how to duck a direct hit. "You're going to have to do better than that, sweetheart."

Jacki pushed away from the table and stomped from the terrace. A minute later, Boot heard her Lexus burning rubber in the street.

Boot felt ridiculous. He was walking on the dark interstate outside Austin, attempting to hitch a ride. A town of prairie dogs jutted from their holes, tracking his steps. The day's heat lingered on the blacktop, yet the air grew chilly. He debated returning to Concho instead of the motel, but his coat and camera bag remained in Jacki's trunk. He'd have to retrieve his camera at least. He couldn't survive without it.

A semi truck took Boot the rest of the way. He sat in the cab, spotting the motel up ahead. A blue neon sign of a cowboy hat glowed from a distance. Boot had selected it from Jacki's travel guide to Austin. He liked the tacky sign. It was a decidedly cheaper standard, a place Jacki glanced past on the page. Boot's eyes went straight to it. She'd have to do business again in Austin. She might even take her family on one of those trips. She didn't need awkward explanations on his account. He knew she'd never choose a budget motel with hourly rates. He'd also convinced her to pay in cash.

As the semi paused outside the motel, it began to rain. Boot jumped from the cab and thanked the driver.

He saw Jacki's Lexus in front of their room and felt the hood. He hoped she was as cool as the engine. He regretted riding her so hard. His anger stemmed not from what they were but what they weren't. As long as they stayed together, they'd cover that same ground.

Jacki answered the door as if Boot was a traveling salesman. "What do you want?"

"We need to speak."

She scanned his shirt for the margarita stain, unable to spot it in the dull light. "Have a nice walk?"

"It's the perfect time of year for a midnight stroll."

"No coyotes or anything?"

"No such luck." He saw she was dressed in just an oversized orange T-shirt. He stared at her bare feet and ankles.

"Don't say those things to me. It hurts."

"I was out of line."

"It's easy for you to take the high road, you being so squeaky clean."

He felt the rain at his back. Even angry, her opinion elevated his status. He read her face, seeing the pain he caused by discounting her faith in him. It wasn't a fluke. She viewed him as the person that he wanted to become. The rightness of it astounded him. "Will my apology make a difference?"

"I was beginning to think you weren't going to. I wasn't even sure you were coming back."

"It isn't as easy for me as you think."

"Why?"

"I can't say." Boot smelled her perfume. He didn't want her so close. His mouth went dry.

"I don't know where you've been before me, but I know you've come a long way."

"And most of it on foot."

"You know what I'm saying. You're a strong person."

He didn't feel very strong. He wanted to take her in his arms. He recalled the times she offered herself and he refused.

"You've gotten under my skin," she said.

"I can see that."

"I don't believe I can shake you either."

Her words struck him hard, a direct hit to the soul. Just when he thought he'd built enough walls between him and her, she broke them down.

"You think you're so different than everyone else," she said, "but you're not."

"How is that?"

"I've fallen in love with you. Now how screwed up is that?"

"Very. It's probably the worst thing you could say." He grabbed her waist and kissed her. She followed him, erasing the distance between their last embrace.

She pulled her head back. "You love me?"

He found her eyes. *Do you really want me to close that link? Do we need to do this?* "It's my best secret."

"I want you to say it."

"I love you."

"I know."

Boot stepped inside the room, kicking the door shut with his foot.

"Nice move, Means."

"I've got a few more."

"This is crazy." Jacki edged toward the bed, hesitating that he might reject her again. He sensed that the pacing belonged to him. She'd respond in any fashion he liked.

He took hold of her, tearing at her shirt. She undid his belt and tossed it aside. He indulged his lust, laying claim to her affection. He blocked out her family, building his own attachments to suit the moment.

They tumbled on the bed, moving quickly, starving for the long awaited reunion.

"Don't try to hurt me again." She grabbed his back and forced him deep inside her, pleading through her breath. "Promise."

"I promise." He accepted her terms, regardless of the complications. He wanted everything she gave. He wanted to destroy the obstacles between them.

He focused on her intoxicating mouth. Her lip quivered at the height of her pleasure. They finished and fell back on the sheets, as if touching the bed for the first time.

Thunder cracked in the hills, as the neon sign bathed the walls with cyan reflections. They curled next to each other, not speaking, listening to the sound of each other up close.

When the storm relaxed, Jacki fell into a steady sleep beside Boot. He held her tight, letting time stretch. He wanted her to dream forever. If not for the coming of day, who they really were might dissolve into the pattering of rain against the windows.

CHAPTER 20
LOOSE SNAKE

At 4:00 A.M., Boot sat in front of Jacki's laptop computer. He waited on e-mail from PeopleSeeker. It was a web site he'd used before. After midnight, the twenty-four hour staff uncovered personal records faster than a financial institution.

Jacki's leg shifted beneath the sheets. The smell of their love-making mixed with her exotic perfume. Boot slid her LeMaxxe credit card back in her wallet, before she awoke and noticed it missing. PeopleSeeker required one hundred dollars per search, not to mention a valid credit card. Boot planned to pay Jacki back. Besides, she might have an easier time explaining the expense to her boss than her husband.

Boot culled the Internet for answers, searching the Dallas newspaper archives for articles about the Van Hise fire thirteen years ago. The press had tracked the story for months, badgering the families, day and night. From a distance of years, it read like cold facts, but that's what Boot did for a living. He cracked people open like oysters sometimes and told readers what he found inside.

An e-mail signal blinked in the corner of the screen. Boot hovered near the green glow of the laptop and scanned the reply from PeopleSeeker. Not a lot appeared for Oscar Van Hise in the past ten years. It seemed like PeopleSeeker failed their job, but Boot saw a deliberate attempt to drop off the radar: no credit cards, driver's licenses, or tax returns. Van Hise knew how to travel light and unseen. He did a better job than Boot.

Boot finished the e-mail. Oscar's father died four years ago, although his mother, Rita, filed last year's tax return from an address outside of Fort Worth. *There you go. Nobody's invisible.*

Before sunrise, Boot and Jacki drove north, looking for Rita Van Hise. They reached Loose Snake, Texas—a low plateau like a stretch of rocky desert, two hours in the wrong direction from Fort Worth. The tough land looked unsuitable for crops or cattle. Cactus and tumbleweeds spread out along every path. With one glance, Boot knew why they gave so much of it to the nearby Indians.

The address from PeopleSeeker led them to the Loose Snake Driving Range. Boot spotted a rusty metal sign and an orange clapboard shack. Big, cheesy-looking decals of golf balls were pasted upon the warped siding.

Jacki pulled the Lexus off the dusty road. "Who plays golf around here?"

"The armadillos." Boot saw a beige and white trailer. A German shepherd was chained to the axle. It jumped to its hind legs and barked at the car, although Boot barely heard it. Mozart's "Jupiter Symphony" blasted from a cassette player on the trailer stoop.

They left the car and headed toward the driving range. A woman plodded through the patchy scrub. She wore green camp shorts, black army boots, and a red bandanna over her grayed hair. She toted two large steel pails, harvesting golf balls from the black dirt.

"Mrs. Van Hise?" Boot yelled over the music.

The woman hunched near the 150 YARD maker. She set down her buckets and cupped her hands over her eyes to block the sun.

"Good Morning," Boot said. Jacki bumped his elbow, as she spread lotion over her bare arms. It was 9:00 A.M., and the sun cooked the ground like a skillet of fried peppers.

"The range opens at ten," the woman said.

"We don't want to golf."

"The reservation is six miles west."

"Are you Mrs. Van Hise?"

She put down the buckets and stared for a while, squinting at the two of them. Her gaze fell to the camera around Boot's neck. "What do you want?"

Boot swept his Nikon behind his back. He'd been taking random shots of the landscape and forgotten to stow it away. He stepped off the driving platform and onto the gritty fairway. "Can we talk?"

"Stay there." She retrieved her pails and walked forward, stopping to pick up stray balls.

Jacki whispered in his ear. "Is it her?"

"I think so." He examined the woman's repellent expression. He recalled some of her old quotes in the newspaper archives. Rita Van Hise despised the press and for good reason. He'd made a mistake not leaving his camera on the car seat.

"Better stay on the platform," Rita said. "I saw a few scorpions this morning."

Boot glanced around his shoes, unnerved by the thought of killer bugs. He held it together in front of Jacki, but he was definitely a city boy. The possibility of stray bullets and car wrecks never fazed him.

Rita pulled a rag from her rear pocket and cleaned her hands. She walked to the trailer stoop and turned down the music. The black and tan dog worked its snout against Rita's leg, ferreting for attention.

"Are you Mrs. Van Hise?" Boot asked.

She stepped up to the platform. "It's Darrow now."

Boot knew that she'd reverted back to her maiden name. It was in the e-mail report from PeopleSeeker.

"I read about Mr. Van Hise's death. I'm sorry."

"You are?" Rita said incredulously.

"Was it sudden?"

"He'd had heart trouble, not that any of you cared."

"Excuse me?"

"I haven't seen your type around since Daniel died. I don't miss it."

Boot noticed Jacki out of the corner of his eye. She watched him work the interview. He pretended to understand Rita, letting her draw points and conclusions until he struck useful material.

"I didn't realize you got that many visitors," Boot said.

"Every year," Rita said, "the reporters came around on the anniversary, trying to revive the story."

"That was a terrible accident. I'd read about the fire."

"It's a wonder my boy grew up at all."

"Let me assure you, I'm not interested in the past."

"You're late anyway. It was two months ago."

He nodded.

"I don't see the point of bringing it up again," she added.

"I won't."

"Then what's your business?"

Boot wanted to find her son, at least garner a clue to where Oscar lived. He fought to keep the conversation rolling, scanning the pitiful property for a tidbit of interest. He saw an old bike beside the trailer and a few vases in the side windows. The spiny arms of orchids twisted behind the glass.

"Do you live here year round?" Boot asked.

Her ankles looked swollen, possibly from arthritis. Her fingers were bent and callused. "No, I fly to Pebble Beach on the weekends."

"Is business good?"

"You're poking fun at me, right?"

"Just making conversation, ma'am."

"Daniel bought this place on speculation. The reservation was supposed to build a casino."

"I didn't know the Indians had a resort."

"They voted it down. They decided to stick with the rugs and beaded dolls, I guess."

"It'll come back around."

"It's people like you that drove us here. I can say this: it's quiet."

He let her acerbic remarks fly past. "At least you get to practice your stroke."

"I hate golf. Daniel was the golfer."

"I see."

She brushed her foot in the stony earth, kicking one of her pails. "You didn't come out here to buy the place."

"I'd like to discuss Oscar."

"I knew it as soon as I saw your pale face in my parking lot. I should've let you walk out among the scorps."

"I appreciate the warning."

"Don't thank me yet."

Boot heard the dog snarl. The animal paced, and the chain links scraped the bumper.

"Have you seen Oscar?" he asked.

"You're asking if I know where he is."

"Yes."

"He drops in whenever he feels like, and he doesn't stay long."

"Does he contact you? Does he let you know he's coming?"

"What business do you have with him? He was a child when that incident happened. I'd be surprised if he remembers it."

"He's not a child anymore."

"They never proved it was him."

Boot took the sketch from his pocket and held it up for her to see. "Does this man look familiar?"

Rita never blinked.

"Your son might be involved with a situation in Concho." Boot was careful not to use the word fire. "Have you heard about it?"

"I have no use for the news."

"I didn't think so."

"I don't even watch television."

"I'm sorry about what happened. It must've been difficult."

"You don't know anything."

"I know about Heather."

"That was a long time back."

"Still, it must've been hard."

She stared, squinting against the sun. Her face hardened, resistant to grief and compassion. "You have to protect your children anyway possible."

Boot had heard enough. He didn't expect her to give up Oscar. He only hoped to find a clue, see if she slipped. As it stood, Rita offered little for anyone beyond a sandy plot of earth and a bucket of balls to strike, and there didn't appear to be many takers for those.

From his rear pocket, Boot produced the same photo proofs that he'd shown to Kate Womack.

"Don't," Jacki said. She held strange sympathy for Rita, which Boot didn't care to decipher.

He stuck the proofs in Rita's hands. "I know what you mean about children. There are three dead kids in Concho."

Rita dropped the pictures in the sand and headed toward the trailer. Her steps were deliberate as she plodded away.

Boot bent down, collecting his proof pages. He noticed Rita unleashing the shepherd from the bumper. The animal leapt forward, testing the lack of resistance on its collar. It barked and snarled, and then it started to charge.

They ran for the Lexus. Boot reached the car first and jumped in the passenger's seat.

He saw Jacki fumble with the handle, glancing back at the dog. He leaned over and flipped open the latch.

The dog sprinted closer, just ten yards shy. Boot kicked open the door and yanked Jacki inside. The force of his pull slammed the door shut.

When the dog jumped for the car, Jacki covered her head and screamed. The shepherd smacked the window, slobbering on the glass.

Boot leaned over and punched his fist on the door. The dog jumped down on all fours.

Rita watched from the trailer stoop, stone-faced and sober.

Jacki glanced up at Boot, breathing hard. "Do you run from every interview?"

"A few."

"I can't believe she did that."

"And you wanted me to show mercy." Boot saw her keys dangling from the ignition. "Take off."

"Gladly." She switched on the motor and peeled onto the blacktop.

Boot fixed his eyes on the side view mirror. The shepherd straddled the white line on the highway, growing smaller with each turn of their car wheels. The sign for the driving range fell back behind the first hill, as the last trace of Loose Snake sunk into the barren wasteland. He never wanted to see it again. It looked like hell, and he was pretty sure Rita thought so too.

By midday, Boot wandered through a Dallas cemetery, searching for Heather Van Hise's grave. He studied the map given to him by the groundskeeper, checking the names on the older headstones. In the distance, a funeral service commenced on a treeless ridge, and black-clad mourners gathered beneath a green and white tent.

Jacki lagged behind Boot, doodling in her sketchbook. She harbored a fascination with headstones. The theme repeated in a number of her paintings.

"I have an idea," Jacki said.

Boot looked up from the cemetery map. He saw Jacki stick her pencil behind her ear. "What's on your mind?"

"Let's take a trip to New Orleans."

He hesitated. "Why?"

"The mausoleums are phenomenal."

"I've heard."

"We could get a room in the French Quarter."

He let her describe her dream vacation. The Crescent City was a romantic haven for outcasts and lovers, perfect for them. He'd fantasized about similar getaways, never daring to voice them. He wondered how lovers shared the same thought.

"When do we do this?" he asked.

"In the fall."

"Why?"

"New Orleans is better in the fall."

The fall seemed like a long time away. He tried to picture their future that far ahead. Would she fold him into the world she loved, or would he tear her away from it? It didn't seem likely that they'd create a world together and keep it hidden for long. He feared that the best place for her might be wherever he was not.

"New Orleans sounds like a wonderful place," he said.

"It is."

Boot came upon Heather Van Hise's grave. The headstone balanced a small angel on top. It was the kind of marker given to a five year old, when no one conceived an evil thought about a life so young and untouched. Oscar Van Hise was once five years old too.

Bending down, he read the inscription: OUR HEARTS REST WITH YOU. It seemed more than ironic for the Van Hise family.

Boot immediately recognized Heather's date of death: July 13th. He'd seen it last night on the Internet, but it didn't make sense until he viewed it etched in stone. Oscar chose the anniversary of Heather's death to start burning Concho.

He stood up. The clues fell in line, each one interlocking with the previous. A nervous twinge started between his shoulder blades. The coincidences were no longer odd or funny. They told the rest of the story.

"Jacki, come here."

She closed her sketchbook and moved beside him. "Did you find the grave?"

"More than that. I found Oscar's pattern. I have the trigger."

She stared with a blank expression.

"Check her date of death?" He stabbed his finger at Heather's stone. "It's the first fire in Concho, the Harp Street fire."

"Oh my God, and she was born on August 28th."

"Yes. Sunday is her birthday."

"Do you think he'll ...?"

"Yes."

"Oh God." She grabbed his hand. "That's only four days away."

"Every fire's been worse than the next," he said without thinking.

He gazed at the freshly cut cemetery lawn. A line of graves marched over the grassy hills, and the relentless sun beat down over everything. It wasn't always best to know the future.

"We better go home," Boot said.

CHAPTER 21
HEADQUARTERS

By nightfall, Boot reached Concho. He'd called Detective Ancrum from the road, and she asked him to come straight to police headquarters. She sounded urgent. He hung up the phone, distracted.

Jacki stopped the car, a block shy of the PD building. The engine pinged and crackled from the long drive through the open plains. "Is this good?"

"Close enough." Boot peered down the block, spotting the quaint brick facade of the Concho Police Headquarters. It was planned as a cozy addition to the city's oldest neighborhood, with stone steps and glass ball lamps, but the immense complex stuck out like the big dumb kid on the block.

Jacki turned off the ignition. "Will I see you on Sunday?"

"I suppose."

"What's your schedule look like?"

"I'm not sure." He heard the lift in her voice. They'd bounced around different plans in the car, revising their weekend with each passing mile. Jacki spoke as if she no longer had a husband or children. Boot let her ramble, not knowing what to make of her shift in attitude. Was she changing her mind or simply dreaming out loud?

"Is there a problem?" She leaned toward him on the seat.

The PD building loomed overhead. He felt the gravity of Concho upon him. It drained away the joy he'd captured beyond the city limits. "I'll be busy."

"With work?"

"Newell will want new pieces on Oscar Van Hise."

"That won't take all weekend."

"Do we have to discuss this now?"

"Are you joining me on Sunday?"

"At your art show opening? I feel like I have an investment in it."

"You do."

"Will you be alone?" He hated to mention her family. It shaved away little bits of his fantasy.

"You'll be there."

"Am I going to run into Jim?"

An odd looked pass over her face. "I don't think so. We'll discuss that on Saturday."

"Why Saturday?"

"We'll be together." She smirked. "Remember your father's birthday party?"

"Right. It slipped my mind."

"I'm your date, or did you forget that too?"

"I didn't."

"You can't disappoint your father."

"I guess not."

She grabbed hold of him and kissed him. He strapped his arm across her waist. He liked that she wrought passion on sudden notice. She might be telling the truth. She wanted him above everything else. He felt like turning the car around, abandoning whatever business lay ahead, but the same feeling deflated his ego. He was tired of running. He needed to finish with Concho first.

He grabbed the car door, focused on the emerging reality. Oscar Van Hise wasn't finished with Concho either. "I'll see you later."

"Knock them dead, Boot."

"Right."

An officer escorted Boot to the PD's top floor. Boot came to an open conference room with a wood veneer table and cushioned chairs. A metal sculpture hung from the wall. It looked like twisted and welded bits of a car exhaust system.

Boot stutter-stepped inside the door. He expected to see Ojeda and Ancrum but not both the police and fire chiefs. The top brass sat side by side at the furthest end of the table, eyeing Boot like a member of the current lineup downstairs.

He tried to act unsurprised. Damn it. Newell and Gally were there too. No one looked particularly friendly.

A chair was drawn from the table, awaiting Boot's appearance. He plunked his camera bag on the tabletop and took a seat.

"Thanks for showing up on time." Ojeda appeared reserved and in control of his temper. "Where have you been?"

"Finding your arsonist." Boot reached into his camera bag and tossed an old Dallas newspaper article on the table. He'd printed it from the Internet archives. He enjoyed seizing the reins of the investigation. "His name is Oscar Van Hise. He burned his sister to death when he was a child."

Ojeda slid the article closer. Ancrum and Gally leapt from their seats to read over Ojeda's back. No one spoke for a moment.

"I found out what Earth Ranger meant." Boot explained about Kate Womack and the bicycle Oscar wanted. The story sounded so sad and pathetic that it created an irrefutable argument.

"Of course," Gally said. "I thought I recognized it."

"It seemed obvious once I saw it. It's one of those things."

"Good work." Gally shot a glance at the chiefs.

Boot felt relieved. On the highway, he'd pictured the scene when he revealed the arsonist's identity. He anticipated shock and jealousy, but in the end, Gally's approval was the only worthwhile result. The marshal worked the case without a personal agenda.

"How did you get this?" Ojeda asked.

"I followed a tip to Austin."

"We didn't hear about it," Ancrum said.

"I needed to check it out first," Boot replied.

"That's not the procedure."

"It seemed vague, and she refused to talk on the phone. She wanted to meet someplace discrete."

"Did she give a reason?"

"She's not interested in catching Van Hise. She's interested in the reward money."

"Why didn't she call us?"

"She didn't want to talk to you, not directly. Some people don't like cops."

Ojeda folded the article in half. He seemed to be folding up his emotions too. It gave Boot the creeps. "What does she know about Van Hise?"

"She knows someone from his past. I can lay it all out for you."

"I'm listening."

As Boot filled in the details, the detectives scribbled more notes. They stopped him to clarify and repeat certain points. Boot didn't flinch. He had no reason to worry. For the first time since wandering into Concho, he formed a vital cog in the machinery that drove this town.

"This is very good." Ancrum wore earrings with miniature gecko lizards cut from mica. "Thanks for sharing it."

The police and fire chiefs sat with folded hands. Boot thought they might never speak, until one finally stirred.

The police chief stood and placed his knuckles on the table. "I'm satisfied."

The fire chief quickly rose. "Galloway, can you handle it from here?"

"If you want." Gally didn't turn his head to face the chiefs this time. He rubbed his temples instead. "Do you still think this is necessary?"

"We'll speak later."

"Yes, sir."

The chiefs left the conference room, without acknowledging or thanking Boot. A salesman presenting a new type of photocopier might have garnered more approval. They strutted down the hall, talking to one another. Their voices muffled in the carpet.

Boot heard them laugh by the elevators. "What's going on?"

The question sat unanswered long enough to ice Boot's confidence.

"We were concerned where you were," Newell said.

"Concerned?"

"You didn't leave word at the office."

"I was researching the fires."

"We couldn't find you."

"I work. I investigate. That's what I do."

"I understand, but you're somewhat of a wildcard."

"If you want status reports, I'll start filing them."

"Don't bother."

Boot studied their faces, except for Gally's. The marshal refused to meet Boot's eyes, staring at the metal wall sculpture instead.

"Did something happen while I was gone?" Boot asked.

"We received another letter from Earth Ranger," Ojeda said.

"Was there a fire?"

"No."

"Was the letter addressed to me?"

"It was sent to the paper."

"But to me."

"Correct."

"What did it say?"

"More of the same."

"The same?"

"His usual talk. How he's smarter than everyone else."

"Can I see it?"

"The more times we review it, the more times we think there are other letters we haven't received."

"Did you lose something?"

"I was going to ask you that."

"You think I'm holding back?" Boot recalled the postcard he'd stolen from Oscar's apartment. It was tucked in his pocket, rolled up with the last of his cash. He was hiding evidence, and somehow they knew that. "I've given you his name and ..."

Newell held up his hands, pitching forward in his wheelchair. "I think the problem is ..."

"What problem?"

"You prefer to work alone."

"So?"

"We had a long discussion about this."

"We?"

"We discussed your style." Newell checked the others in the room. "Then there's the issue of your past. I've spoken to your previous employer. I see things more clearly."

"Damn it, Shep."

"I can see why you'd rather not discuss your reasons for leaving Trenton."

"I can't believe this. That was a year ago."

"Barely."

"What about today?"

"I stand on procedures at the *Democrat*."

"Procedures?"

"Like I said, you're a wildcard."

Boot imagined how the details of his dismissal unnerved Newell. He'd used unreliable sources to break a big story. "That piece turned out to be right."

"Turned out to be right? I wish you hadn't said that."

"You never made a mistake?"

"But you still wouldn't come clean about it when I asked."

"Would you hire me if I had?"

Newell didn't answer.

Boot wanted to grab his wheelchair and shake it. "You're stuck in your procedures."

"We don't make the news. We report it."

"How have I damaged the reputation of the *Democrat*? How have I hurt Concho?"

"Don't get defensive."

"Defensive?"

"You're the type that prefers to work alone. You should probably keep it that way."

"You're firing me?"

"Not in that manner."

"But I won't be working for the *Democrat*."

"No."

Boot looked to Gally, who wasn't helping. Ancrum appeared uncomfortable with the discussion, while Ojeda's reserve now resembled a serene state of spite.

"This is beautiful," Boot said. "I nail the best story the paper's seen in years, and you're telling me to walk."

"I am," Newell said. "I think it's for the best."

Boot considered whipping out Oscar's postcard, just to expose their trite suspicions, but that only played into their fears, another excuse to edge him out. "Then I'm done."

Ojeda cracked a smile. It was a flat, forced expression, befitting his weak features. "I suppose we'll have to double-check everything you've told us."

"Go ahead." Boot stood. *Let the city burn to the ground.* "You need help from everyone. You're still no closer to stopping Van Hise. You might be sitting in the next building that catches fire."

"We can take over the investigation from here," Ojeda said.

"Good luck."

"I don't expect to see you poking around on your own either."

"Yeah, yeah, I get it." Boot walked to the door, turning around to take the marshal in his sights. "Thanks for standing up for me, Gally."

The irascible marshal let the comment roll off his back. He had a hangdog look about him. Dark circles hung beneath his eyes. "It's out of my hands. I can only walk so far with you."

"I expected more, I guess." He stomped to the elevators and pressed the button, but waiting a few more seconds in the Concho PD seemed like an eternity. He scanned the hall, spotting the gray metal door to the stairwell. He went for it.

Ancrum slid beside Boot.

"What do you want?" he asked.

"We need to talk." She entered the stairwell ahead of him.

Boot took to the steps, Ancrum by his side. "Come to say I told you so?"

"I wouldn't do that."

"What do you want then?"

"We've been watching you."

"I'm not surprised."

"We haven't been following you as much as keeping track of you."

"What's the difference?"

"After the fire at your apartment, I had the idea that the arsonist might be tailing you. Do you understand?"

He pushed past her. Would anyone in Concho hold up to this level of scrutiny? "I hope you stopped it."

"We have."

"Why tell me now?"

"I knew you were out of town." Ancrum looked concerned. She glanced down, as if she didn't fully believe the story he told in the conference room.

"Why didn't you tell the others where I went? It might've spared me some embarrassment."

"I think I saved you embarrassment."

He stopped on the ground floor landing. "What are you saying?"

"I know who you were with?"

He didn't speak. His pulse jumped up a notch. Jacki was home with her family. Their affair might already be blown wide open. It wasn't right, the worst possible scenario.

"Don't worry." Ancrum's voice hushed. "I haven't told anyone, not even Ojeda. He thinks it's business."

"Business?"

"He doesn't understand why she'd do business with you, but he believes it for now."

With only his own reputation at stake, he'd tackle the subject head on, never letting a police officer hold the facts over his head. "I don't know what you're talking about."

"You don't have to be that way with me. At first, I didn't understand what was going on."

"What makes you think you do now?"

Ancrum paused, letting a uniformed officer pass in the stairwell. She spoke differently, not as a detective but as a woman, partly ashamed for knowing the truth. "You were working for her, but you started spending a lot of time. It seemed strange, until it all made sense."

"She's a big girl. She can handle herself."

"Her husband owns quite a large business in town. People know him. He works with charities."

"What's your point?"

"If you think you're on the outs today, try after this leaks out."

"Has it happened already?"

"That's up to you. You better watch your back."

"What does that mean?"

"I won't tell anyone, but if I were you, I'd clean it up fast."

He watched her ascend the stairs. She looked back, fingering the handrail. She knew the dangerous details of his life, while revealing nothing about herself. Her parting words struck him as hard as any statement she'd made. "You're pretty clever, Means. You almost fit in around here. It's not all true what Ojeda says. We like upstarts. It's what built this city, but what you're doing is the kind of thing that gets you beat up or worse."

"I understand."

"I didn't know much about arson before, and I thank you for what you've taught me. But I'm familiar with the results when you mess with another man's wife. I've worked those cases."

CHAPTER 22
REMAKING THE CAM

O scar Van Hise plodded through the sewers below the CAM. He followed the phone lines underground and into the tunnels below the plaza. His boots shifted in the calf-high water, and the air smelled dank. He focused his flashlight on a section of exposed phone wires. He wrapped them with red electrical tape and labeled them according to plan. For him, tracing wires through conduit was an art form.

After midnight, no one noticed a man roaming the sewers but the rats. They gathered near his boots, sniffing for wire cuttings and scraps to chew. Oscar spotted a bent piece of iron protruding from the water. He whipped it toward the rats, scattering them into the tunnel. Their scaly feet pattered the water, until only the noise of his breathing remained.

Oscar cut and splayed the phone lines. When he'd snuck into the CAM's basement, he noticed stubs for a cellular backup to the security system. With that in place, he'd never get this far, but the CAM's limited artwork didn't demand the extra cost. Oscar snorted through his nose. The geniuses in charge never saw the value in protecting people until too late. After the CAM burned, they'd think differently. They'd rewrite the manuals in his honor.

He spliced the phone lines, bridging the wires with a remote control switch. He kept his design simple—the hallmark of brilliance. He stood back and tested his device. With the push of a button, he enabled and disabled the security system.

Up on the plaza, Oscar navigated past the water fountain and stone benches. The air was dry, and the sky burst with stars. On a dozen nights like this, he cased the CAM, envisioning his masterpiece in action. He didn't expect the city to understand at first. They'd be distracted by the horror. He recalled a fire in New York City where the bodies piled up by the doors. The coroners needed to pry the melted limbs and torsos apart. Oscar regretted not plotting this result sooner.

He paused outside the CAM, clutching his tool kit and supplies in opposite hands. He viewed the clean white building one last time in its nubile state. Everything was going to change. His crotch felt warm and stiff just thinking about it. The inside of the CAM waited to receive him.

Oscar disabled the alarm and picked the door lock in seconds. The CAM's simple security system never challenged him. He pushed open the glass door. He'd gotten so good at foiling alarms, locks, and electric sensors. No system deterred him.

The CAM's doors locked from a master switch near the front door. He'd seen a similar system on a yacht in Corpus Christi. That night, he fried the electrical system from a service panel near the stern. He overloaded the circuits with a car battery until the wires smoldered and caught fire. He sat in a nearby café and witnessed the entire event. The huge craft threw up a puff of smoke and disappeared below the water. In the early days, just a tickle of flame satisfied him. The recollection and newspaper clippings carried him for months.

Oscar dragged a chair into the center of the room and climbed up to push aside the fiberglass ceiling tiles. With a spray bottle, he applied a glycerin and kerosene mixture to the back of the tiles. He felt the least proud of this aspect and wanted to be done with it. He squeezed the trigger, and a noxious mist rose to his face. He squinted his eyes.

Car headlights spun through the plaza, reflecting off the glass windows that surrounded the building. The intense light shocked him, jarring him from his work. He jumped off the chair and crouched to the floor.

A dark blue sedan joined the curb. Oscar read his watch. Security wasn't due for thirty minutes. His heart beat faster. *Don't panic. They don't suspect.*

He scooped his supplies into the canvas bag and zipped it shut. Not one but two guards strolled toward the door. He crawled to the office, sliding his bag ahead of him. The blood rushed to his ears. Idiots! The check time was 1:45 A.M. He'd clocked it a dozen times. Why didn't anyone on this planet operate with consistency?

When he reached the office, he huddled beside the doorjamb. He saw his tool kit near the chair in the center of the room. A pair of ceiling tiles teetered on the edge of falling. Any disturbance—a bump in the room, the breeze of someone walking past—might send them crashing to the floor and expose his activity.

The guards stood several feet from the front door. One was clearly heavier than the other. His chin gathered above his collar like a full bladder of wine. He reached for the door, just as Oscar clicked on the alarm system by remote control.

Chubby entered first. The alarm emitted a shrill warning blast. Oscar cringed, covering his ears. He spent so much time in solitude that he found the noise excruciating. He jammed his fingers in close until the alarm ceased.

Flashlight beams roamed over the floor and works of art. Oscar ducked behind the door, listening to the sound of the guard's shoes on the stone floor. A beam of light rolled through the office, reflecting off the plaques and posters. A bolt of light illuminated a gold medallion.

"You see, it's a chair." Chubby's voice sounded more mature than the other guard's.

"It looked like a guy bending over," the younger man said.

"Maintenance must've left it."

"Ya think?"

"Ron, see the toolbox?"

"I swear I saw somebody."

"It happens all the time. It's just shadows in the dark. Don't let it bother you."

"I swear."

"Go move it, Ron, before the next shift makes the same mistake."

Oscar heard the fuzz of a two-way radio. Chubby spoke to the central office. "It's only a chair. ... That's right. ... We'll take a look around."

"Where do ya want this?" Ron asked.

"Put it in the side room."

The sound of footsteps drew closer. Oscar heard the grit of the stone floor beneath Ron's feet. He withdrew the razor knife from his pocket and pushed the blade forward. *This can't be happening.*

A quick plan came to mind. Oscar knew what to do. He needed to be precise and make a determined cut. The artery on the side of a man's neck, when sliced open, drained blood like an open faucet and killed him in seconds.

Oscar held the blade like an extension of his hand. He prepared to cup his palm over the guard's mouth. Cover and slice. He'd never done this before, and his mind flooded with details: clean up the blood, dump the body in the sewer, complications he didn't need. Then there was Chubby. Like the other, he'd walk into the office, concerned. Oscar would have to kill him too. It might be harder. One of them might put up a fight.

Ron drew closer, humming a tune from the radio. Oscar sensed the anticipation on his own breath. Why was this happening to him? Would these minimum wage flunkies ruin his masterpiece? Brilliant devices sat in his bag. He'd created special switches and igniters just for the CAM. How dare they destroy his work!

Oscar spotted the desk against the wall and shimmied beneath it. He gathered the knife to his chest. Disaster lurked a step away. If the guard spotted him, there'd be a moment of surprise, precious seconds to slice him cleanly and in relative silence.

Ron flicked on the light and rested the chair against the wall. He plopped onto the cushion, bending over to tie his shoe.

Oscar watched the guard's face from beneath the desk. He looked young and stupid, like a million kids his age. If he didn't get curious, if he left the room without poking around, if he didn't as much as turn his head in the wrong direction, he'd live to say he survived the great CAM fire.

"Where are you?" Chubby called from the next room.

"Hold on." Ron finished his laces and walked to the door.

"Get the light."

"Sorry." Ron stopped walking. "Hey, what's that smell?"

"Oil paint."

"Ya think?"

"Let's get moving. We're behind schedule."

Oscar watched the overheard light fade to black. A moment later, he heard the alarm beep as it engaged. He became so angry that he saw nothing but red—the bright hot glow of molten metal, the crucible of fire. He shook for a while beneath the desk. He wished he could set the world aflame just by laying his hands upon the ground. He felt his fingertips approaching the flashpoint.

The car drove away from the curb. Oscar heard the engine retreat, as his anger cooled. Primary elements defined him: blood in his veins, perspiration on his wrists, thoughts racing through his brain. His plans began to reshape, as he emerged from the desk. He recalled the motion detectors on the first floor. He disengaged the alarm and caught his breath.

His ears rang a little. There were men in isolation that construct-
ed entire houses in their minds. Oscar understood their labor. He
remade the CAM in this fashion, honing the details over and over.
His version of the CAM, his masterpiece, stood half complete.

Oscar went after his tools.

CHAPTER 23
THE GRATEFUL WED

"**T**he bride wants a few bong shots." The best man wore a tie-dye T-shirt with a print of a tuxedo on his chest. His jeans were ripped at the knees.

Boot gripped his Nikon in the center of Lee River Park. He was back in the freelance game, and the Concho Libertarians were desperate and willing to pay in cash. Fifty people milled beneath the statue of Robert E. Lee on Saturday morning. They drank cans of beer and got stoned. The Grateful Dead blared from a boom box at the hooves of Lee's horse.

"I have to be out of here by one o'clock." Boot made a list in his head: get back to the studio, shower, change, and arrive at his father's party before dark. He hoped Jacki was ready and waiting.

"No problem." The best man toked on a joint. "Thanks for coming on short notice."

A nasty cloud of smoke blew past Boot's face. Any minute, he expected the Concho police to bust up the wedding. Wouldn't Ojeda love to take Boot down another peg? He glanced at his surroundings. He didn't need Jacki bailing him out of prison. She didn't even know he'd lost his job.

"Make sure we wrap this up by lunch," Boot said.

"No problem-o." The best man turned the joint on Boot. It smelled like burning trash. "Want a hit?"

"No thanks."

"Acid? I've got good blotter."

"I'll pass."

"It's your loss."

Boot circled the statue. The bride leaned over a three-foot bong. She had spiky hair and so many freckles that she nearly looked tan.

"There he is." She wrapped her lips around the bong's wide tubular end and sucked hard, as if siphoning gasoline through the tailpipe of a car.

Boot focused the camera lens and pressed the shutter release. "Alright, let's get one of the groom."

The groom toked the bong, until his ears turned red.

"I want one of us together." The bride wedged her lips beside the groom's. The newlyweds worked like a machine, puffing and grunting smoke, a candid wedding shot for *High Times* magazine.

Boot aimed his lens at the spectacle, but in the edge of the viewfinder, he noticed a man with fine hair and thin lips. It was a common face that only Boot might pull from a crowd, an ordinary man resembling Oscar Van Hise. Boot lowered his camera, seeing the man fold into a group of revelers.

"Ready?" The bride asked.

Boot stepped forward, his eyes locked onto the shifting periphery. Flashes of Oscar's face sliced between the profiles of others. He let his camera fall to his waist.

The bride coughed. Boot glanced at her and then back to the crowd. In a blink, he'd lost his target. He twisted his neck to locate Oscar on the lawn, unable to find a trace.

"Hello?" The bride dangled off the groom's arm in exaggeration. She raised her dainty wrist, hacking into a lace handkerchief.

Boot studied the park grounds. He was jammed, cut off from the search for Oscar. No one at the *Democrat* spoke to him. Gally refused his phone calls. He never felt more out of touch, yet the stories of fire and death festered inside his brain. Last night, he lay in bed with Jacki, keeping one eye open and an ear peeled to his police scanner. Static-filled fire calls rose in the dark, and each one resembled Oscar's next strike on the defenseless city.

"Hey camera man," the bride said with a hoarse voice, "how about some action?"

Boot snapped the picture and looked around. Several people passed a bag of potato chips. The groom's brother swigged a bottle of Jim Beam. Sweat formed on Boot's brow. He'd imagined Oscar among them. That was the problem. He knew too much. He'd gotten too close to the inside. He wiped his forehead with his sleeve. His anxiety swelled like the August heat.

"Take the damned picture," the bride yelled.

"Sorry." Boot bracketed more portraits by the statue. It wasn't his best work. His mind wandered as he composed the shots. He hoped the happy couple was just as stoned when he presented the proof pages.

Two rolls of film later, Boot scrambled for a drink. The wedding party hid six-packs of beer in the fountain. He plunged his hands into the tepid water and retrieved a can.

Boot sat on the cement lip of the fountain, calming his nerves.

Oscar's face wandered among the trees at the edge of the lawn. Boot dropped his beer and ran after the torch that tormented his days and nights.

The man ducked behind a large oak with a split trunk. Boot saw the knob of his shoulder protruding from the rough bark. The man peeked around the edge. Dark oval eyes scanned the lawn.

Boot circled the trees, locking onto his target. He dug in his camera bag for an old can of mace. If Oscar wanted a fight, Boot was ready. He knew a couple of moves—an arm pinch to bring a man down, a knee kick to tear the ligaments. He'd envisioned this showdown for weeks. The arrogant son of a bitch needed to learn a lesson, and Boot planned to teach him the terms of getting even.

When he hit the cluster of hickory and oak, the shade blinded him. He let his eyes adjust, creeping up behind Oscar. The torch was shorter than he imagined. His hair was thinning. He looked a little out of shape. He wore a ratty suit jacket with the sleeves rolled up, blending into the bohemian party scene. It amazed Boot that Oscar knew to find him here.

Boot set his camera bag softly beside a tree. The mace canister felt wet in his palm. His footfalls matted the grass. A dry twig snapped beneath his heel. He paused, less than a full pause. His breath caught in his throat.

Everything became distinct: the rumble of the party, the feel of the grass and peat black soil, the stink of himself about to strike. Boot summoned the images of the dead boys on Harp and Armada. If he must, he'd go all the way.

A few paces shy, he picked up a pointed rock and focused on the back of Oscar's head. The torch reached up and cricked his neck.

Boot cued the mace. He grasped Oscar's shoulder and spun him around, but the sight of the man's face stunned him.

"Shit!" the man yelled. "Oh shit!"

Boot lowered the canister. Not Oscar Van Hise. No, not him. His nose was too thick, the chin all wrong, pudgy cheeks. The veins in his eyes were red and thick like the others at the party. Boot wondered if he'd recognize Oscar Van Hise at all.

"Please don't hurt me." The man's eyes darted between Boot's face and the loaded can of mace. He raised his palms to his full cheeks, shaking. A damp spot stained the side of the tree. His penis hung from his trousers like the head of a dead snake. "Take what you want."

"What?"

"I've got forty dollars and a Seiko."

Boot dropped the rock, hearing it thud against a tree root. He stuffed the mace canister in his pocket.

"I won't fight you," the man pleaded. "Take it all."

"I thought you were someone else."

They sized each other up. Fear met rage, equalizing in the short space between them. A queer collection of seconds stacked up like a derailed freight train.

"Sorry." Boot smelled fresh urine and stepped back.

The stranger zipped himself up and ran.

Boot stood beside the split oak, watching the man hoof back toward the celebration. His anger subsided, replaced by paralyzing anxiety. It resurfaced without hesitation, as if a gear shifted in his head.

For a while, he stared at the wedding party. People smoked joints and clinked foaming cans of beer. The bride and groom laughed out loud. That was how things ought to be: blithe, fearless. He knew this deep down. He used to operate by those pretexts.

As his energy channeled away, his back collapsed against the tree. Concho formed a prison sentence, a dreadful set of days to end the summer. Whenever he hit a bad rut, he envisioned his plans ahead. He might build upon the smallest success, but this town offered nothing but barriers, and each one pressed against his nose like a locked window. He needed to leave Concho, maybe for good.

CHAPTER 24
IRON CREEK

"Take a look at this." Boot led Jacki to the corral behind the main house. Three appaloosas strutted inside the split wood rails. He recalled his first days at Iron Creek, after he lost everything in Trenton. He didn't work. He hardly ate. He felt empty down to his soul. He thought the wind that blew through his father's wide-open ranch might carry him away. He used to walk to the corral and watch the odd-looking horses with blotches on their rumps. They made him laugh. They hopped like children, nudging heads, digging in the dirt, and all of a sudden, he had images to fill his viewfinder. He reached for his camera and quit worrying about being absolutely nothing in the world.

"Charles collects appaloosas." Boot used his father's first name. 'Dad' seemed moot at this point. "He's got a thing for spotted ponies."

Jacki's eyes were wide open from touring the outside of his father's mansion. Boot knew what she was thinking. She wanted a peek at the sprawling mahogany floors and eight-foot high windows from the inside.

"You're surprised, aren't you?" he said.

"My God, you're rich."

"No, Charles is."

"He won't share it with you?"

"I owe him a few hundred already."

"Owe him?"

"I don't want charity." He didn't look her in the eye, not wanting to debate old decisions. There were things about him that she thought she knew but didn't. When he'd arrived in the west, he came on the worst terms that a man can manage—homeless and broke.

"You're a head case," Jacki said.

"See over there." Boot pointed where the steely prairie grass swept down to the creek for which the ranch was named. The muddy waters twisted away like a bronze road into the rangelands. More than a hundred head of cattle dotted its banks.

"What are those?"

"Texas Longhorns."

"I thought they were extinct."

"Charles raises them to keep the breed going. He's part of the preservation program."

"Does he sell them?"

"I doubt it. Trucking is his deal. It's what paid for all of this."

"He must have a lot of trucks."

"More than cattle, and they're spread out further too."

She looped her arm around his. It felt good to have a woman by his side, especially one with more style and class than he ever thought obtainable. She fit right in with his father's ranch. She wore riding boots, a knee-high skirt, and a peach cotton blouse, as if expecting to mount one of the horses sidesaddle. With Jacki at his side, the place felt more agreeable.

"Wow," she said.

"That's what I used to say."

"You don't visit?"

"Not since the first week."

"You're incorrigible."

"I don't stick around where I'm not much use."

The breeze shifted, and the smell of horse manure wafted from the corral. They pulled away to see the back of the main house. Four dozen family members and close friends mixed beneath a white tent on the great lawn. Boot watched a plume of smoke rising from the gray earth. Three Mexicans from the stables opened the barbecue pit, working the coals with long-handled shovels.

Boot held her close, pinching her arm to his side. His bandaged hands barely hurt. The scabs were healing. "I meant what I said."

"About what?"

"Not sticking around."

"I get your point."

"No, I'm leaving Concho."

"Why?" The hurt reflected in her eyes, a stain in something perfect. She was letting him see her thoughts more than ever.

"I'm done. There's nothing for me in Concho." He felt the muscles in her arm contract. He wanted it to sound better than that. She was a good reason to stay, but without his job at the *Democrat*, he became another camera jockey, hawking weddings and birthday parties for pitiful pay. She'd lose respect for him and grow to resent it.

"You have a job," she remarked.

"I lost it."

"Lost it?"

"They didn't say I was fired, but that's what happened."

She pried away from him. "What did you do?"

He thought she asked that question a tad too quickly, although it was hard to blame her. He operated on the edge. She saw it up close.

"They didn't like my resume," he said.

"After they hired you?"

"I told you about my troubles in Trenton."

"What did you say?"

"Nothing they wanted to hear."

"Did you apologize?"

"I doubt that would've helped."

"How could you let this happen?"

"The damned town is caught up in appearances." He watched her purse her lips. She knew it. She'd told him how to act with certain people, warning him about this person and the next. She'd lived in Concho for most of her life. She knew the language. "You need to give it more time."

"I'm a journalist. If this paper doesn't want me, another will." He needed to redeem himself among his own kind. Back east, they only cared about results and deadlines. It's what you did that afternoon that defined you.

"There's no reconciliation?"

"It's not a question of that."

"Give it more time."

"For what?"

"I need more time."

He saw her point. She needed more time for herself. She was deep into an affair, weighing a rotten marriage, comparing it pound for pound against the good times with him. She'd put him up in her studio while she sorted it out, but he refused to live like that, waiting on someone else's decisions, even hers.

"I'm going east to patch up my career." He saw her bristle. "I'm not going to be a part of this place, probably never will."

"You'll ruin everything." Jacki cut a path for the bar. The sun poked through the clouds, and the limestone escarpments lit up on the horizon. All but Jacki's temper shrunk against the oversized landscape.

Boot watched her leave. Let her stew. She'll see his reasoning. She couldn't join him, not yet. She couldn't just pack up and leave her family without a word. He studied her shape from a distance and shook. It was a downward spiraling feeling. He'd remain in Concho and abandon his sanity to stay with her.

He sent his deepest wish into the wind. "Come east with me."

The Mexicans brought the side of beef up from the pit. Boot watched them carry the smoking hunk on a metal rail to the butcher table. The smell of barbecued meat drew him in that direction.

His father stood at the block. Charles dressed in a white apron and fancy chef's hat that piled to the sky like an exaggeration of the real thing. He sharpened a long carving blade with determined strokes. He liked to eat, and he liked to show off. It was his birthday, and no one dared to tease him.

Boot approached the table. Charles worked the fattest part of the steer, cutting thin slices for the buffet. Bloody juice ran into the wells around the table's edge.

Charles didn't raise his head. "That's a very nice lady. We spoke earlier."

"Thanks." Boot glanced at the bar. A glass of white wine dangled from Jacki's hands. It swirled in the ball of the glass as she spun her sights away from him.

"She's not put together too badly either."

Boot watched Charles pile the beef upon a metal tray. He felt weird discussing Jacki's looks. Was this how fathers and sons acted? "Have enough meat on there?"

"I don't want my guests to starve." Charles cracked a smile. "You can take some with you when you leave."

"I'll take it back to Trenton with me." Boot didn't know how to break the news, so he stuck it in the conversation like a fork to test the meat. He'd packed up and left places before but never with people to tell. It complicated everything.

Charles glanced up, waiting for Boot to fill in the blanks. Tan lines gathered about his eyes. "Is it a visit or more permanent?"

"Permanent, I think."

"What's your young lady say?"

"I just told her."

"I bet she had a word on the subject. Most women do."

"I don't think she likes it."

"Then she's not going with you?"

"She's sort of tied down."

Charles looked at him longer this time. Charles wanted to impart some advice. In the handful of times they'd met during the year, he was getting better at keeping it to himself. Boot started to miss the banter.

"I have something to show you." Charles turned over the knife and fork to the Mexican in the lavender shirt.

"Finish what you're doing," Boot said.

"You're going to like it." Charles pulled off his apron and hat. "Come with me."

They entered Charles' office from the lawn. This room was different than the others in the house, one of the few with a ceiling at normal height. A wall of French doors overlooked the range beyond. The windowpanes cast long rectangular shadows over the Navaho rugs.

Boot sank into one of the big leather chairs near the stone fireplace. The smell of oil from the rich cowhide mixed with ash from the hearth. He noticed two of his appaloosa photographs above the mantelpiece. They were framed and matted, replacing the family portrait.

Charles stood before the hearth, clasping his hands behind his back. "Do you approve of what I did with them?"

"You didn't have to hang them."

"The man at the gallery said black and white photography needs white matting and a simple frame."

"He was right." He studied his work like always, picking apart the perspective and cropping. "I could've burned in the corners a little longer on the left one."

"They look great to me. The framer wanted to buy them. He asked to put them up in his gallery."

"I don't think so." Boot had considered art photography prior to this, mostly in the portrait arena. In New York City, this was high art. He didn't see himself in that league.

"They get a nice penny around here for landscapes, especially someone with your eye. That last part's a quote from him, not me."

"Tell him I said thanks."

"It's something to consider."

Boot saw Jacki on the lawn. She spoke to Charles' wife. Sandy was a wisp of a woman in height and stature. Considering Charles' size, Boot thought Sandy and Charles made an odd match, but the elements that drew people together were still a mystery to Boot. No matter how strange the chemistry appeared on the surface, the end product always made sense. He was younger and more intense than Jacki, yet he felt a stronger attraction to her than any woman he'd known.

Charles walked to the closet and removed a tattered cardboard box. "I was rummaging in the cellar. I forgot I had this." He set the carton on a desk and plunged his chunky forearms inside the dog-eared flaps.

"Your mother left a lot of things behind when she bolted." Charles raised a porcelain box from the carton.

Boot rose to examine the box. Blue paintings scrolled along the edges. A landscape with trees and roses adorned the lid. "What is it?"

"A music box." Charles put it on the desk and opened the lid. The gears cranked for awhile, before Gershwin's "Summertime" began to chime.

They listened to the mechanism pluck out the tune. Outside, the Mexicans set fireworks into the air, and a roar from the party muffled behind the wall of glass.

Boot watched his father staring down at the music box. One hundred memories swept through the expression on his old man's face. He wanted to reach out and touch them, see what they were, discover how he fit into them.

"It meant a great deal to her," Charles said. "She had it since she was a little girl, but she was traveling light, and she had you with her. It wasn't practical, so she left it behind."

"And you kept it?"

"It was buried in the cellar. Sandy's not the kind who wants another woman's keepsakes around. She asked me to sell it years ago, but I couldn't. As soon as I saw it again, I wanted you to have it."

"What will I do with it?"

"Hold on to it for a while."

"Really?"

"It's all that's left of her. You'll know what to do with it."

"Don't you want it?"

"It's your mother's, a part of her."

"You would know that, not me."

"When you were a baby, she used to take you to the front porch every morning and hold you up to the sun."

"What was she doing?"

"It's an Indian ritual, something about showing you to the world."

Boot felt somber. His personal history was a combination of sparse fact and rich fantasy. He pictured his mother as a gutsy and strong woman, and he hesitated to hear his father's version. It might replace his ideal image of her with a lesser woman. "What did she want for me?"

"What every mother wants. Happiness. She thought I couldn't give that to you. I guess she thought she couldn't either."

Jacki had said the same thing. After making love, they'd lain in her single bed and discussed his past. She created her own version, deriving details about his mother and father from what she knew about Boot. She tried without success to get him to play along. She called him tight-lipped and hardheaded, but in truth, she knew as much as he.

Charles faced Boot in his office. The decor exuded the man's personality: dark leather and wood, cowboy and Indian relics, a crucifix made from twisted banyan vines. His place overlooked the ranch and everything he created from nothing. "Why are you leaving us?"

Boot realized that he admired his father, enough not to show his face around his house as a failure. "I need to start over."

"I thought that's why you came west."

"I appreciate your help, and I'll get that money back to you."

"I don't care about the money."

"I do."

"I assume your lady doesn't want you to leave."

"She'll get over it."

"I was pleased to see you with her. You make a nice couple."

"We do in some ways."

"I thought you were putting down roots. That's why your announcement surprised me."

"I'm sorry. I should've waited until another day to tell you."

"Pay no mind to me. I was thinking of her. What was her name?"

"Jacki."

"This is where I blame myself. You haven't had much of an example of family life."

"It's not that."

"If you keep burning women ..."

"This isn't going to be a belated birds and bees lecture, is it?"

Charles didn't laugh. "I'm concerned about your lifestyle. Putting down roots is what I hoped for you when you first came here."

"I'm telling you, it's not like that." Boot didn't want to get into it, but now he felt that he must. Charles was sort of like him. He saw that his father needed to unravel stories too. "She's not available."

"She's seeing someone else?"

"So to speak."

"She's engaged?"

"No."

"She's not ..."

"Her marriage is falling apart. I expect it to be over soon."

Charles sighed, a big sound that deflated his chest. It didn't seem to fill again. "But it's not yet."

"No."

"Children?" Charles groped for some solace.

"A teenage boy. A younger girl."

Darkness fell over Charles' face. His eyes seemed to recede. He put his hands behind his back and went to the doors to observe the party.

Boot heard more fireworks on the lawn. He eyed Charles' reflection in the glass. Charles looked disappointed, yet Boot felt oddly relieved by his confession.

"I didn't know at first," Boot said, "but now I want her to come with me. I want to ask her."

"You can't do that."

Boot resented hearing Charles speak so sternly, although it sounded like it came from the heart. "It's what I want, anyway."

"I can see."

"It hasn't been easy."

"You're not going to ask her, are you?"

"I don't know." He wanted to but already knew he couldn't. Jacki had to make her own choices. She needed to end her marriage by herself. She waited for Boot to prod her along, but

Boot knew one true thing. You were alone in every big decision in this world.

Charles turned away from the doors. "Take advice from someone who knows. You can't break up her family."

"It's going to happen anyway."

"Let it happen on its own."

Boot didn't answer him. This was what family did. They solidified your feelings. You either faced them or ran.

"Look into your past," Charles said. "You'll find everything you need to know."

"It's got nothing to do with that."

"Don't fool yourself."

"She loves me."

"Your mother loved me too."

"Then why did she leave?"

Charles looked flushed. He came to Boot and gathered Boot's shoulders in his meaty hands. "The worse thing your mother ever did was bust up the family. She believed she had no choice, because she couldn't count on me. I want you to know that. I'm to blame too. We both let you down."

CHAPTER 25
NO MAN'S LAND

A t sunset, Jacki's Lexus sped through desolate brush country. Boot felt boozy from the party but remained behind
the wheel. Hulking oilrigs churned in the distance, as
Jacki stewed in silence. Hardly a soul passed them on the highway.

Boot stared at the length of his high beams, searching the
blacktop for stray armadillos. The scaly critters had a curious habit
of defending themselves. They leapt about grille high, as your car
sailed into them.

Jacki kicked off her shoes and folded her legs in the seat. Her
voice rose out of the quiet. "You're going to leave, aren't you?"

He let the question sit for a while. The car tires skipped over
cracks in the asphalt. His answer wasn't black and white, something she'd accused him of doing before.

"I'm not enough for you?" Jacki asked.

He disliked hearing her confidence erode. She loved him. He'd
challenged her to do it, and now he was asking her to stop. "You're
not mine."

"My marriage is over. You know that."

"I'm the only one who does, besides you."

"You can't bully me into ending it."

"I don't want you to."

"What?"

"It's your decision." He bit his lip. Charles was right. If Boot drove a wedge into Jacki's family, he'd be a fool, plain and simple. The wreckage of her family would be strewn throughout their future together.

"You're talking gibberish," Jacki said.

"You say that to me a lot."

"I wish I knew what was going on inside your head. I thought we were doing great."

"We're pretending."

"I don't pretend that I love you." She grabbed his arm. The car swerved and righted again.

"We pretend."

"How?" Her anger dissipated. Worry pervaded the edges of her speech. Boot didn't often hear that tone with her. He wondered if she'd been scared all along, and he finally recognized it.

"We're pretending that your family doesn't exist," Boot said. "I pretend every time we're together, but if they didn't exist, I'd ask you to come east with me. You've said a million times you could work in New York."

"I can."

"You have ties in Concho."

"But what about us?"

"Is that enough?"

They drove for a spell without speaking. Boot chased his thoughts back to Charles' office at Iron Creek. Was there ever a good reason for breaking up a family? His mother did it because she was crazy. Dana had a lust for blowing things apart. He used to believe she was fearless, but whenever he debated a drastic move, he heard Dana daring him to pull the trigger. It wasn't a spoken word. He didn't see ghosts, but his drive to shake things up often made the difference. It came directly from her. Was he doomed to end up crazy too?

"I–I don't know." Jacki squeezed his arm.

It took all of his courage to turn her away. "You can't do that to your kids."

"Don't use that argument with me. It's not fair."

"I'm not leaving you. I'm leaving Concho. I've been black-balled."

She undid her seatbelt. She leaned over, placing a hand on his thigh. "You can work nearby."

"There's no decent opportunities."

"Dallas has a great newspaper. San Angelo does too."

"I know how things work in the east. It's my best shot." Boot studied the road. A second ago, he was leaving her, but with a touch, she made him forget. She nuzzled her head near his shoulder. He smelled strawberries in her hair. The nearer she came, the more she confused him.

She whispered in his ear. "We can kill time. It won't matter. You'll see."

"We've been killing time."

"You'll be alright. I make a ton of money."

"It's not only that."

She rubbed his crotch. She answered his questions as soon as he thought to ask. "You can stay at my place."

"I have to get on my feet again."

She unzipped his pants and made him erect. "You don't know what you need."

He thought to say the same thing. For the first time, he had what he wanted but needed to walk away.

"I can fix everything," she said.

As the Lexus rolled over seventy miles per hour, she began sucking his penis. He felt her lips upon him, electrifying his brain. He focused on the broken white line in the center of the road.

"Jacki," he said.

She wasn't going to stop, determined to alter his thinking. A lone passing car flashed light upon her blonde head of hair.

His knees grew weak, but he managed to keep the gas pedal down. This was all wrong but right too. In time, she'd convince him of anything. She'd put his career plans on hold and his life on hold too.

She stroked him harder, bringing him closer to the edge. The car hummed over the blacktop, a cocoon of invulnerability. Boot saw the road stretch out to infinity.

In Concho, Boot parked a block down from Jacki's studio. They strolled the sidewalk after midnight, locked in each other's arms. The night was unusually cold for August, and Boot felt goose bumps rise on Jacki's skin. He drew her to his hip.

He was spent from the long drive and their interlude at the outskirts of town. He wanted to lie beside her and sleep, ignoring the subject of his departure until morning. Today was a test, a chance for Jacki to sample the idea. Tomorrow he'd try again. He envisioned this as the typical end to an affair. It was a gradual pulling apart, regardless of what either person wanted.

On the stoop leading up to Jacki's apartment, Boot saw a teen-aged boy with dark curls. He wore a Dallas Cowboys T-shirt and cutoff bluejeans. He had lanky arms and bony knees. His age fell around seventeen years old.

The kid sprung up as they approached. Boot fought to recall the kid's face, until Jacki called him by name.

"Hunter?" Jacki dropped her arm and separated from Boot. "What are you doing here?"

"Mom?" Hunter dithered on the sidewalk, his arms moving, his hands grasping the air. "Is this him?"

Jacki didn't speak. Boot figured he better not.

"He was right." Hunter forced out the words. He'd worked himself up in advance. Tears welled in his eyes. "You are sleeping with him."

Jacki leaned forward, thrusting her hands upon her hips. "Who told you that?"

Boot knew the answer: Manuel Ojeda. It wasn't enough that Ojeda displaced Boot from his job and any decent career contacts in town. Ojeda tossed a monkey wrench into Boot's personal life too. Boot wanted to strangle the weasel.

"Are you going to tell Dad?" Hunter asked.

"You don't know what you're talking about."

"Does he already know?"

"You have it wrong."

Boot listened to her struggle with the lie. Of course, Hunter knew. The kid taunted her with the facts, forcing her to deny them and humiliate herself. Boot thought she barely kept her head above water.

"What about Tammy?" Hunter asked.

"Honey."

"Are you coming home?"

Boot saw that a child's questions were direct and brutal in the face of a parent. They weren't really questions at all. He heard some of himself in Hunter.

"Honey." Jacki suppressed her anger. If it'd been someone else, she'd ball up a fist of words and thrust it between his eyes. "Does your father know you're out this late?"

"Why do you care?"

"Go home."

"Why? You're never there."

"You will not talk to me like that."

"Save it, Mom." Hunter pushed between them, giving Boot an extra shove with his elbow as he passed. He was young and cocky, an inch or two taller than Boot. He probably believed that he could bring Boot down.

Boot half-expected Hunter to throw a punch. He stepped back. He'd give the kid one shot. That's it. He didn't want to have to embarrass the kid by taking his knees out from under him.

Hunter glared at Boot. "Who are you?"

"No one you need to know."

"I've never seen you around."

"Let's leave it that way." Boot poised on the sidewalk, keeping his cool. He saw the panicked look on Jacki's face.

"Screw you." Hunter charged off. He dropped into a silver Camaro and spun the wheels away from the curb.

They didn't speak, watching the kid burn up the street. The Camaro disappeared around the corner, and the noise tapered off. The smell of burning rubber lingered in the air. This was Jacki's kid for sure. He had her temper.

"He'll be alright." Boot felt relieved to see him go.

Jacki held her hand in front of her mouth, her lower lip quivering. "Are you sure?"

"He's young. He believes everything's supposed to go his way."

"Oh my God." Jacki started to cry. Her head collapsed in his shoulder.

He folded his arms around her, wracking his brain for the right reply. So good with words, his speech failed him. Jacki had lost something valuable, and he was to blame. The clean getaway—the one he'd planned for her benefit—vanished with Hunter's arrival.

"Why?" she asked. "Why did this happen?"

Boot burned inside, a seed of rage that he fought to squelch. He vowed to get even with Ojeda. And Ancrum too; she'd promised not to tell. Neither he nor Jacki deserved this.

Jacki looked up with wet eyes. "What am I doing next?"

"You already know." He loved her. That wasn't wrong, but staying was, especially after tonight. This mistake happened because he refused to take charge. He savored every moment with this beautiful lady. He'd let his ego get the better of him. "You're going to deal with this."

"How?"

"You're going to lie about me."

"I can't." She didn't sound convincing. He knew she saw the way out as well.

"You're going to tell Hunter he was mistaken." Boot erased himself from the picture. He never thought he'd care enough to do that, but Jacki changed him. It was a tricky business worrying about someone else beside yourself.

She sank in his arms. "He won't believe me."

"It'll be easier when I'm not around."

"Why are you doing this?" She seemed out of breath.

"It's better this way."

"What will you do?"

He looked past her, shading his thoughts from her eyes. He was disappearing, returning to a drifter's existence. He knew the routine as well as anyone. For a brief time, Jacki had made him believe those days were over. "We've been through this."

"Is that what you want?"

"No. You always treated me like I belonged here."

"Why can't you?"

"It's you that belongs here, not me. I can keep that safe for you by leaving."

Her glance fell to his chest. She seemed to search for a response and come up empty.

"You see," he said, "I can give you something too."

CHAPTER 26
CULVER'S BEND

At sunrise, Boot rode his motorcycle twenty miles past the Concho city limits. His camera bag and some clothing were strapped to the rear frame. He recalled Jacki on the stoop of her apartment. The sun hit her angular lines, and her lips were full and turned down. She agreed to ship the rest of his stuff when he found a place. She promised to keep in touch. She swore they weren't through. The sadness that lingered in the corners of her mouth resembled a hunger that consumed her face. She was unsatisfied with many things. They shared that trait since the start.

He pulled into a gas station. Three fighter planes raced overhead in formation. He popped the gas cap between his legs and jammed in the pump nozzle. The vapors stung his nose, but he refused to dismount and waste a single second leaving Concho.

The man at the pump wore a striped jumpsuit with a big red star. He didn't speak until the pump clicked off. "That'll be six dollars."

Boot dug in his jacket and pulled out a small wad of cash, along with the postcard from the CAM. He stared at Oscar Van Hise's meticulous block letters. For one evening, the deadly pyro had slipped his mind.

"Sir?" The man's hands were dirty. Dark rivers of grease stained the folds.

Boot stuck out a ten dollar bill.

The man counted out the change. "Take it light on the road."

"Thanks."

"Watch out for Culver's Bend."

"Right." Boot knew about the hairpin turn. During his early days in Concho, he rode through Culver's Bend and almost skidded out. It seemed fitting that he was about to ride through it, a lot wiser.

"The road's slick in the morning."

Boot flicked the postcard in his fingers. He thought about tearing it to shreds, scattering the pieces among the prickly pears and cinnamon sand, purging himself of Oscar Van Hise and Concho with one flick of the wrist.

"A nice girl was killed last week," the man said.

Boot looked up. "Really?"

"She flipped her VW Bug. You didn't hear about that?"

Boot noticed a gold crucifix around the man's neck. Today was Sunday, Heather Van Hise's birthday. He glanced at the postcard again. Oscar never did anything by random.

"Sir?"

Boot remained in thought. Ideas connected in succession. He ran his fingertips over the raised lettering: THE CONCHO ART MUSEUM. Boot knew the exact location of Oscar's next target.

Leaving the pump, Boot dropped some change into a pay phone near the stinking restrooms. Gally came on the line, hoarse and groggy. Boot almost sniffed the booze on his breath over the wire.

"Get your butt out of bed," Boot said.

"Boot Means." Gally coughed and cleared his throat. "I've been meaning to call you."

"It's Sunday. Are you ready to put out a fire?"

"All's quiet on my end."

"I know where it's going to happen."

"Where?"

"The Concho Art Museum." As soon as Boot said it aloud, he recalled Jacki's art show opening. She'd be inside the building with hundreds of others.

"What makes you think that?"

"There's going to be a show there."

"You must have something else to go on."

"I have a note from Oscar Van Hise."

Gally paused. "You're a lucky bastard, aren't you?"

"He wrote it on a postcard from the CAM."

"When?"

"That doesn't matter."

"For shit's sake," Gally grumbled. "We better get a look at the place."

"Do that. I've got to go."

"Where?"

"I need to warn someone."

"Wait for us ..."

Boot hung up the phone before Gally finished. He dialed Jacki at her studio. The phone rang a dozen times. He checked the number and dialed again. It rang without an answer.

The man at the pump watched Boot frantically punch in the phone numbers. Boot turned his back. Jacki might be showering, preparing for the show. She might've left already too.

"Come on," he whispered, "pick up the damn phone."

He slammed down the receiver. He refused to gamble on Gally and the Concho PD, not with Jacki's safety. He hopped on his bike and pointed it in the last direction he wanted to go: downtown Concho.

As Boot approached on his cycle, a dozen people gathered outside the art museum plaza. Gally's red Caprice, four police cars, and three engines from Second Union parked in frantic arrangement on the street. Their flashing lights and sirens wrecked the Sunday morning calm.

Boot throttled down and drove onto the cement. His knobby tires jumped the steps to the plaza, before he abandoned his cycle near the water fountain.

Uniformed men carried axes and strung police lines in front of the CAM. A herd of badges and patent leather shoes roamed outside.

Ducking beneath the yellow tape, Boot sprinted for the CAM.

"Excuse me," an officer said.

Boot ignored him, heading straight for the main entrance.

"This is a crime scene," the officer yelled.

Boot spotted Gally near the doors. The marshal spoke with Ancrum and Ojeda. Boot didn't even pause to glare at them.

Gally lurched, grabbing Boot's jacket as he tried to pass. "Hold on there." He waved off the officer in pursuit.

Boot looked at Ancrum. She wore a nylon tracksuit, and her hair was tied with a lizard clasp.

"Is she here?" Boot asked.

Ancrum thought for a moment.

Boot yanked away from Gally's grip. "Is Jacki Rush here?"

"No."

"I owe you big time for last night."

Ojeda perked his ears. He stopped taking notes and latched onto the thread of the conversation.

Boot's sights filled with Ojeda's pointed expression. He wanted to punch the weasel back to yesterday when things weren't such a mess. "Don't even start with me."

"I was going to thank you for tipping us off," Ojeda said.

"It wasn't a favor to you."

Gally looked at everyone. "Did I miss something?"

Boot balled his fists, but he didn't want to stay in Concho any longer than necessary. He bit down on the urge to start swinging.

"I'm not sure I want to know," Gally said.

Boot looked at the marshal, trying to eclipse the troublesome detectives from thought. "Was I right about this place?"

"Yes, it's a booby-trap in there."

Boot peered inside. Men with dogs walked the stone floor. Ceiling tiles lay scattered about the room. Firemen stood on ladders, gently lowering plastic pouches filled with bright fluid.

"We found kerosene in the ceiling," Gally said. "And some kind of device wired to the lights. There might be other things. I'm still not sure this place won't go sky-high."

"Don't bet against it. Did you cut the power?"

"You're thinking like me now. We did, and all nonessential personnel are outside."

"Did you check each floor?"

"She's not here." Ancrum was more confident this time.

Boot scanned the plaza. A collection of bystanders gathered at the base of the concrete steps. Jacki's Lexus wasn't parked in the lot or on the street. He noticed his watch. 10:00 A.M. Where in hell was she?

"I still can't believe you figured this out," Gally said.

Boot withdrew the postcard and slapped it in Gally's palm. "I put two and two together."

Gally flipped the card over, as Ojeda huddled close to see. "Very nice."

Boot marched toward his bike. The CAM was suddenly uninteresting to him. He needed to see Jacki safe. He wanted to view her gorgeous smile one more time unspoiled by these concerns.

His cycle leaned against the fountain. The handlebars dipped in the water. He heard footsteps behind him.

Ancrum was tailing him. She caught up with him by jogging. "What did you mean about last night?"

He yanked the bike upright and straddled the seat. "I don't have time for this."

"Time for what?"

"I know it was you. You had to do it."

"Do what?"

"You told Jacki's family."

She digested his reply. "It wasn't me."

"No?"

"I didn't tell anyone."

"I heard you the first time." He didn't want to entertain her lies. The fact that she sought his favor exasperated him. He kick-started the engine and throttled up. The tailpipe spewed oily smoke on the sun-bleached cement.

"I'm being honest," she said.

"Right." It bothered him that she denied it so flatly. He imagined Ojeda lying that well but not her. He'd never get satisfaction from those two.

"Ojeda still doesn't know."

"You might as well tell him."

"Someone else must've told on you."

"Who else knows me that well?" An awful thought socked him in the gut. Right then, he understood the depth of his stupidity. Oscar had picked him out of a crowd. Oscar had found his apartment. Oscar discovered his affair and tipped off Jacki's family. How far would Van Hise go?

"What's the matter?" Ancrum asked.

Boot rattled off Jacki's studio address. "You better get over there."

"Why?"

"Jacki's in trouble."

CHAPTER 27
OSCAR'S FINAL NOTE

Early Sunday morning, Oscar Van Hise began setting small fires around Concho. He tossed lit matches into garbage cans and dried up shrubbery, pausing for the first taste of smoke and flame. At this hour, he might torch an entire block before anyone noticed.

He strolled past the closed boutiques and genteel row homes near Lee River Park. He wore bluejeans, a hardhat, and sunglasses. He'd let his thin beard grow in, lending his face some edge.

In his tool belt, he kept his remote controls for the CAM and a can of lighter fluid. He doused pay phones, reducing them to melted blobs of plastic, wire, and exotic parts that he knew by name, number, and size. He saw a park bench and sprayed it with lighter fluid. The flames spread out like a burning cross. He longed to torch the entire city with a single glance.

By 9:00 A.M., he arrived at the street door to Jacki Rush's apartment. He considered lighting the building from the outside, enveloping it in a ring of fire, but he wanted this one to be specific. Let there be no doubt in Boot Mean's tiny brain that Oscar Van Hise was responsible.

He started picking the lock, working the bit and steel into the keyhole. The hard part was popping the lock without jamming it. He noticed some ants on the sidewalk and stopped to crush them with his heel.

The knob began turning on its own. Oscar withdrew his picks and straightened up. He stepped back as the door swung open.

Jacki Rush stood at the foot of the stairs in a black linen jacket and leather miniskirt. "Can I help you?"

Oscar glanced her over. She was blonde and well built. A citrus smell wafted from her body, orange or kiwi. He shivered, inhaling the wonderful scent. Boot Means didn't deserve her beauty.

"Ph–phone company," he said.

"I'm not having trouble."

"D–did you use it re–recently." He had seconds to absorb this change in plans. He didn't expect to see her, not after he'd exposed her affair. He wondered if that boy of hers had the guts to follow through on the information.

"I used it this morning," Jacki said.

"There's a problem on your line, lady." He feigned a look at the wires on the telephone pole. Means often chained his motorcycle to the base by the curb. The cycle was missing. They were alone.

"I'm just leaving. What do you need?"

"F–five minutes to test your line." Oscar forced himself to meet her eyes. She didn't recognize him. Women like her were trained to look past true genius.

"Are you sure?"

He studied her face, wondering why he'd been intimidated by hair and makeup. She didn't appear so dangerous. His chest started to swell. He was going to be attractive to her in the future. He felt close to the change. If he took one step forward, he might cross into it and become a different person.

"It's standard procedure," he said.

Jacki huffed, blowing her bangs away from her forehead. "Alright. Five minutes."

As she turned, Oscar pulled the steel flashlight from his belt. He saw a glimmer of surprise, as he smashed the fat end across her temple. She put her hand up, her eyes rolling backward. She collapsed without uttering a word.

He stood over her. She lay upon the stairs. Her hair was slightly mussed as if she'd fallen asleep awaiting his arrival. Sunlight illuminated her lower half. He saw dark stockings, the bones in her ankles, and black suede heels. He closed the door, covering her in darkness.

The upstairs apartment was quiet. Nothing moved. He heard no harmless thumping of feet. He sat on the stairs and cupped his hands beneath her arms, dragging her up the steps. He started to sweat and heaved his hardhat upstairs.

When he reached the foyer, he stopped to rest. Jacki's limbs sprawled at odd angles upon the floor. She lured him onward. He wanted to fuck her. He wasn't like those sick bastards he'd heard about in the morgue. She wasn't dead yet. She was going to enjoy it.

Jacki moaned. He snipped the electrical cords from the lamp and radio and bound her wrists and ankles. He laughed a little. Better than rope.

He noticed her coming to. He lifted her onto the mattress in the bedroom and lashed her to the frame. Her arms stretched above her head. Her feet pulled at the bed frame. She looked like an animal tethered to a chain at both ends.

"Who are you?" Her eyes crossed at times. A trail of blood seeped from the split in her left eyebrow, pooling in the well below the socket.

Oscar found a towel in the bathroom and ripped it to shreds. He listened to her mumble. Her voice gained volume and clarity. He gagged her mouth before she thought to scream.

Her eyes were wide open, as he unzipped her leather skirt.

"Now you understand." He tore the skirt from her waist. He watched her expression come alive. Women didn't wear clothes like this unless they wanted to be fucked. She'd invited him in.

He unbuttoned her shirt. She wriggled on the bed, as he cut the material from her sleeves. Her screams muffled beneath the towel. He sliced her underwear free with a razor knife.

Her skin glowed in the light. He'd nicked her a handful of times. He felt sorry about that, but she was gorgeous and struggling, and the blood rushed to his crotch. He smelled the fear—panic mixed with terror. She verged on a rebirth, ready to learn a new way of existing. She'd thank him later.

Oscar lingered at the edge of the bed, watching the madness grow. It roamed in her expression. Like a snake in her veins, it writhed in the twists of her wrists and ankles. He leered at the beauty of it, hardly coming this close before. *This must be what it feels like right before you burn.*

He ran his knuckles along her bare breasts and the tight lines in her face. She gasped and shimmied, suffocating on emotion. Chemical changes overtook her body. The brain was ready to assist in madness. Oscar drew witness. He wanted to make it perfect.

Leaving her for a minute, he took a hammer and clubbed the smoke detectors from the ceiling. He returned to the bedroom, seeing Jacki roll on her stomach. She fought to free herself with short jerking motions. He studied her bare ass, before unzipping his pants and completing his erection.

He sprayed a trail of lighter fluid around the bedroom walls and struck a match. A spiraling pattern burned on the flowered wallpaper, igniting the hanging pencil sketches. The places where he'd dribbled on the hardwood floor flared like tongues of fire. He squeezed his firm cock. The smell of smoke enlarged his senses. He was king.

Spreading her legs was more difficult than he'd imagined. He rolled her over and wedged a hand between the bones in her knees, but she pinned them together. He beat her hip with the heavy flashlight. The lens shattered, and the batteries flew against the wall.

Jacki held on. Oscar rammed the broken flashlight into her thigh. She was his to use as he pleased. She flinched in pain, as he stabbed her repeatedly. Her skin changed from strawberry red to a pulpy blue. She sighed, and her legs became weak.

He slid between her knees. She shook like a little girl. He prepared to thrust inside her, but she began to cry.

"Stop it!" He raised the flashlight, threatening to crack her across the head.

Tears smeared her makeup. They ran toward her ears, mixing with the caked trail of blood. She gasped beneath the towel. Her nose dripped.

"Stop it!" He grew limp, losing his momentum. He feigned a swing with the flashlight, and she winced. "S–stupid!"

He pulled away, disgusted. Fire overtook the wall at the back of the apartment. Smoke hugged the ceiling, ushering toward the open window. He stood by her head, inhaling the electric scent of sex, smoke, and fire. He stroked himself, rediscovering his desire.

Smoke billowed over the window sash. He bunched her hair in his fist. He needed her to watch. She ceased crying, glaring with a familiar hatred. He recognized it in the eyes of his detractors. He stroked harder and faster. He hated her, hated them all. He released himself in their faces.

CHAPTER 28
BOOT'S CHOICE

Boot skidded the motorcycle onto Jacki's street. Fingers of smoke curled between the rooftops. He throttled up his motorcycle, praying Jacki's place wasn't burning, but as he raced closer, he already knew.

The rear wheel spun in the air, as he dropped the cycle on the sidewalk. He fumbled for his keys and pushed inside the stairwell. His heart pounded. His tongue felt too fat for his throat. His brain split between the push of adrenaline and the reins of caution.

Each step upward, the heat increased. Boot's face flushed. Acrid fumes filled his nose. The trademark sounds of flame crackled and popped ahead of him. Steam hissed in his ears, as spent materials escaped the building.

Boot penetrated the foyer, awash in a wave of heat and ash. The air in the stairwell sucked into the room, fanning the flames higher. He gauged the shifting dynamics. The bedroom burned. Fire consumed a portion of the living room wall. Gray smoke fogged everything. He marked the positions of the windows and doors, as if viewing them for the first time.

Ducking below the haze, he charged the bedroom. He spotted Jacki's body laid out and naked upon the mattress. He thought she was sleeping, but he saw her move and the cord binding her hands and feet.

He lurched toward the bed. Someone closed behind him. Boot's senses were acute, as if the nerve endings poked through the skin. He heard a sound—a footstep, a sudden breath—or perhaps he expected to see Oscar Van Hise from the moment he arrived.

Boot dodged to the side, avoiding the main thrust of the lamp. It clipped his shoulder, the bulb shattering. Glass fragments pricked his cheek and neck. A dull pain vibrated down his arm.

Turning, he set his sights on the deadly pyro. He led with his right arm. A stone of rage gathered in his fist. He'd imagined this so many times that the real punch landed with the force of the others behind it.

Oscar reeled back, stunned. His lip was split. He brushed his fingers over his mouth, enraged by the sight of his own blood. 'How dare you,' his eyes seemed to say. He scowled and flashed a razor knife from his pocket.

Boot sprung back. The blade cut open his jacket at the chest, but he knew Oscar was aiming higher. He thrust for the hand with the knife.

Oscar returned low, slashing him above the knee. Boot went down, instinctively collapsing, preparing to recoil and fight. A crimson line seeped through the fine cut in his jeans.

The temperature inside the tiny apartment broiled. Boot felt trapped and lightheaded. Snippets of information from Gally raced through his mind. Panic kills. Collect your wits. Find the exits.

"You tried to use me." Oscar stepped closer. His tone complimented the noise of the fire, a high register born of flame. "I decide what happens."

Boot scanned Oscar's face: slight nose and mouth, dark eyes, a weak chin, but nothing divergent from the ordinary. He donned a thin beard and bright polo shirt, like a young professional, a go-getter barging through the public, sipping cocktails between deals.

Except he didn't smile, and beneath his gentle features roamed his real energy, an attribute stronger than his outward parts. His teeth ground. His slender fingers tensed around the knife. You needed to pause and look at him to sense the anger. His cold eyes held a mirror to hatred and rage. It appeared endless, like staring at the naked horizon. It made Boot shudder.

Oscar hovered, gaining confidence. "You underestimate me."

"You're insane."

Jacki screamed beneath her gag, as fire crept onto the bed sheets. Boot felt their last seconds draining away inside this tinderbox. He seized the shaft of the lamp from the floor and smacked Oscar's ankle.

Oscar cursed, slashing the blade again, but Boot rolled away and got to his knees. He batted the pyro another time. Oscar missed with the knife, stumbling from his own momentum.

Boot crawled to the mattress. The wallpaper peeled away, and glowing bits of paper floated through the air. They covered Jacki's skin, taking flight again as he untied her gag and wrists. The plastic cord felt hot to the touch.

She inhaled deeply and coughed. "Help me." Soot lined her nose and mouth.

Boot fought with the cord about her ankles. He saw Oscar in the corner of his eye. Oscar sprayed the doorway with lighter fluid, drawing their window of escape even tighter.

Oscar struck the match. The head of it flared, reflecting off his hateful expression. He stared at Boot, allowing a second for Boot to decide.

A shiver cut through Boot's spine. The bastard offered him a choice—a choice between saving himself or dying with his lover. He never hated anyone more.

Boot rushed for the doorway, abandoning Jacki on the bed. She sent out a scream that he'd never forget. Her fear fueled his anger, strengthening his stride. He piled into Oscar and brought him down.

The men tumbled onto the living room carpet. Lighter fluid sprayed Boot's right eye, a wash of burning chemicals. He clamped his eye shut and clubbed Oscar in the side of the head. His face burned. The blood pumped through his hands. He was not the man he was ten minutes earlier, even ten seconds ago.

"I'll kill you." Boot clasped his hands around Oscar's throat. He needed to squelch the life from this freak. He tried to crush his thumbs into Oscar's windpipe.

Oscar threw his fist, choking. Boot took a shot in the cheek and another in the jaw. He heard Jacki screaming in the next room. Her sound was different, shrill and piercing. He recognized it instantly. She was burning.

Boot let go and pushed away, but Oscar wrapped his arms around Boot's knees and tripped him. Boot's face slammed to the floor.

A trail of flames zipped across the carpet and toward the can of lighter fluid. Boot scooped the can up and aimed it at Oscar.

Oscar gripped Boot's hand, but Boot straddled Oscar's chest. He gazed into the black ocean of the pyro's eyes. He saw the dead boys on Harp and Armada drowning in there. He saw Kate Womack's scarred face. He heard his lover screaming. He bent Oscar's wrist, hoping to snap it in two. Lighter fluid arced through the air, dousing Oscar's shirt.

Boot smashed the can into Oscar's nose and wrestled free. Oscar frantically wiped his shirt with his palms.

"Die." Boot thrust a heel into the small of Oscar's back. He heard it crack, as the pyro rolled into the trail of fire.

Oscar's sleeve ignited, followed by his chest. A blue line of fire spanned his shirt, spreading like a crashed wave. Boot looked away, hearing the cries of a burning man. The hideous stranger flailed upon the carpet.

Boot limped into the bedroom. The mattress was aflame. Jacki had passed out. Her legs lay in the smoldering sheets.

His hands shook as he threw a blanket and smothered the fire. He reached for the cord. His eyes filled with tears. His beautiful woman. The cord melted to her skin. Her charred flesh pulled from her ankles as he tugged. His arms went weak, and he stopped.

Fire engulfed the walls. Stifling fumes expanded in the limited space. The heat drove Boot mad. He teetered on the edge of consciousness. Soon, it wouldn't matter if he cut Jacki free. He summoned his last bit of strength and yanked the cord, snapping the melted wire from the bed rail. Beads of melted plastic and wire whipped back at his face. His bandages tore loose. His old scabs bled anew.

He lifted her in his arms and took his last breath. He pushed forward. Smoke burned one eye. The other was swollen shut. He lugged Jacki to the foyer. Her body felt light, dead in his arms. It seemed like a dream. Oscar moaned and bounced off the walls, his upper torso charred and darkened. The stench of burning flesh permeated everything, grafting to his memory like the worst of all nightmares.

The stairwell appeared as yet untouched. Boot stepped toward it. *Fire burns up.* Go down, his brain repeated, go down, but his legs were failing.

He staggered into the space and blue sky ahead. Hulking shadows of men in fire coats and hats emerged on the steps. Boot fell forward, descending through clouds and open space. He might be dying. He might be dead already. He fell into the transition between the two, and the hands of angels caught him before he touched the ground.

CHAPTER 29
LEAVING CONCHO

The burn unit was on the third floor of Concho Memorial. The city council lobbied for years to build a trauma center, and its doors opened just two months ago. Boot was grateful for the luck. At the moment, there seemed little going around.

Ancrum and Ojeda kept Boot out of the Rush family sightlines. They tucked him in a doctor's office on the same floor. He sat among the black vinyl chairs, stacks of paperwork, and several diplomas for a Doctor Jacob Davids. The window peered into a stagnant airshaft.

Gally slumped in a chair across the room. His hair was combed and shirt looked pressed, but he appeared tired and shrunken, like a man dressed in someone else's clothes. He badly needed a drink to invigorate his spine. "I don't think it's a good idea."

"I want to see her," Boot said.

"Why don't you wait a few days?"

"I'll be gone by then." Boot touched the patch over his right eye. The emergency room staff had flushed it with neutralizer to counteract the lighter fluid. They coated his hands with silver cream and wrapped his palms. They stitched his knee too. He ought to be lying in a hospital bed, under observation for smoke inhalation and shock, but if he stood still, it might finish what Oscar started. Boot planned on riding his motorcycle out of town before morning. Nothing but a long stretch of earth between this place and the next promised to cure his ills.

"I'm sorry," Gally said.

"Me too." Boot stared at the marshal. A truckload of apologies floated around on this Sunday evening. Gally offered excuses. Ancrum and Ojeda respected Boot by uttering as few words as possible. Even Shep Newell jumped in on the act. The editor tracked Boot down at the hospital, reinstating Boot's position at the *Democrat*, but even Newell heard how hollow it sounded. Boot found no pleasure in telling him to go to hell.

"You know," Gally said, "if you stayed, you might reconsider that offer from the *Democrat*."

"What, and give you guys another chance to bust me down?"

Gally seemed disappointed that he was unable to change Boot's mind. A wretched look assumed his face, as if he'd failed Boot as a friend again. It was the worst sentence for a fireman. A member of that brotherhood tended to bet his life on those closest to him.

"I can call him for you?" the marshal asked.

"Let it go, Gally." Boot coughed into his fist. He recognized the burning feeling in his lungs. Except for thoughts of Jacki, his mind traveled a far distance from where he stood. "Tell me about Van Hise?"

"He might make it. He might not. There are burns over sixty percent of his body."

"Is he here?"

"People are coming down from Austin to keep an eye on him, as if he's going anywhere on his own."

"I hope he dies," Boot said without conviction, but Oscar Van Hise was a poisonous weed. If you yanked him from one spot, another popped up somewhere else.

"He'll suffer."

"It's not enough."

"It'll never be. At least he's finished burning."

Ancrum appeared in the doorway. Her hair was pulled from the clasp, and her smile was out of place. Boot waited for a month to glimpse her out of composure, and now he no longer cared.

"It's your turn," she said.

Boot waited for her to qualify the remark.

"The family's taking a break," she said, knowing what he wanted to hear. "You have a few minutes."

"How is she?"

"Delirious."

"Is it the pain?"

"Heavy does of morphine. It's not pretty."

"Then there's no use talking to her."

"You won't even get that close." She crooked her mouth even more. "Maybe you want to change your mind."

"I want to see her."

Ancrum seemed like she wanted to debate it further, but she glanced at Gally and fell silent.

Boot followed Ancrum down the hall to burn unit no. 3. Gally trailed close behind. No one spoke. Boot's steps were unfamiliar, as if his feet weren't his own. He was lightheaded, yet his senses remained sharp. He thought if someone touched his arm or bumped his elbow a wave of pain might resonate down his spine.

They reached the outer door, where Dr. Davids received them. He glanced at Boot's hands and decided not to shake. "You're the man who saved her?"

Boot shunned the question. This was his fault too, no matter how he shuffled the facts. If he hadn't pursued Jacki, she might be sitting in her big home outside of town, sipping a white wine with her husband.

"She's received second and third degree burns on both legs," Davids said. "We're concerned about infection. We want to save them."

"Save them?" Boot asked.

"There's a chance we might amputate one or both below the knee."

Boot felt woozy. He'd prepared for bad news, but this was tentative, lingering. There were worse things than dying.

"The next twenty-four hours are critical," Davids said.

"Are you doing everything?"

"Can you pray?"

Boot stepped to the glass that separated outsiders from Jacki's room. A nurse adjusted the i.v. line, while two others applied moist white wraps to the hideous black and red skin upon her legs. The burns didn't look real, as if a makeup artist had stepped in to frighten the wits from onlookers.

"At this stage, she's an open wound," Davids said. "Only specific staff goes in there. It's a sterile environment."

"Will she make it?"

"One way or another. If the legs pull through, there will be skin grafts. It's a long process. Recovery depends on her stamina."

Boot vaguely recalled the procedures from speaking to Kate Womack. He already saw the future of Jacki's legs—an unnatural ripple of flesh, an embarrassment she'd keep hidden. He believed she possessed the courage to survive the ordeal, but you never knew how rich that vein ran until you tapped it at full strength.

Jacki tossed her head from side to side. Her lips were moving.

"What's she saying?" Boot asked.

"She's rambling."

"Can you make it out?"

Davids stared into the glass. "Something about deserving this."

Boot flashed a look at Ancrum. She was thinking the same thing. Jacki spoke of her affair with Boot. What else could it be?

Ancrum's glance fell to the floor and her clean white track shoes.

Dr. Davids missed the exchange. "She's heavily sedated."

Boot closed his good eye for a moment. He wished that he could open it up and view Jacki without the pain and misery, but that was a long way off for her. His head and hands began throbbing again. He had to get out of here.

"Thank you." He pulled away from the window and walked down the hall. Gally took a few steps after him and stopped. Would he ever see Jacki or Gally again? He didn't know. By pushing the limits, he reduced them to ghosts and haunting images. He needed distance. Sticking around served no one.

The Rush family departed from the elevator. Boot saw Tammy clinging to her father's side. Hunter hunched over, hands in pockets. They'd come close to losing Jacki in a variety of ways, ignorant of half of them.

Boot ducked into the stairwell and hit the lobby alone. Media from statewide bureaus waited upon couches and huddled in corners. They poised for a glimpse of the mad torch Oscar Van Hise. Boot disappeared into the bowels of the building and found a quiet exit leading outside.

The air felt stifling hot. The temporary cool spell had passed during the day, and the Gulf served up a dose of arid winds and stinking heat. Air-conditioned cars sped down Mission Avenue, racing nowhere in particular.

Boot stood on the corner, not far from the cafe where Jacki and he first met for cocktails. He felt grateful that she remained with her family. He envisioned loads of healing ahead for her, every step without him in the picture. When the bottom falls out, your only hope is family and ultimately your capacity to accept change.

He considered the ride east but noticed himself facing the limestone escarpments to the west. He might reach his father's ranch beyond San Angelo in a few hours. He felt strong enough to go that far perhaps. If he retrieved his motorcycle from Jacki's place, he'd knock on his father's door before sunrise. He started in that direction. They had many things to discuss. It might take a while to clear the air.

THE END

Christopher Klim worked on observation and exploration satellites for the space program, until departing for the private sector to develop leading-edge communications technologies. He now teaches and mentors emerging writers. He is the senior editor of *Writers Notes Magazine* and primary architect of the website www.WritersNotes.com. In his lectures, writings, and workshops, this award-winning storyteller entertains with contemporary tales that extend the American experience while transcending the ordinary. His first novel *Jesus Lives in Trenton* was released to critical acclaim, followed by a popular manual on the writing craft, *Write to Publish: Essentials for the Modern Fiction & Memoir Market*. He currently lives in New Jersey.

Contact the author:
c/o Hopewell Publications
PO Box 11
Titusville, NJ 08560-0011
Author@ChristopherKlim.com

www.ChristopherKlim.com
www.Write-to-Publish.com
www.WritersNotes.com